THE MASTER LOVERS

Allen Kirby

"We that are true lovers run into strange capers...."

–William Shakespeare

1

Last week I was shot by a beautiful young woman in downtown Baltimore. The bullet struck my right side and lodged a few centimeters from my heart. According to my surgeon, a cheerful Nepalese gentleman, I'm a lucky man. I'm going to recover completely.

"Who knows," he said smiling, "you might even live forever."

I managed a weak grin, but he had just performed major surgery on me and I was still groggy from pain medication. I didn't feel lucky and I certainly wasn't thinking about immortality.

That was several days ago. I'm still in a great deal of discomfort, but I *am* alive and feeling better physically. It's the mental part of my recovery that I'm dealing with now. I have occasional nightmares and I'm saddened and depressed by the shooting. A psychologist dropped in one day, and though she was pleasant and kind, I was reluctant to open up to her. Maybe later I said. I needed time to work things out in my own way. So during my alone time that's what I've been doing – pondering the rollercoaster events that led me here.

A year ago, I could never have imagined I would one day be lying in an ICU trying to survive a gunshot wound. It was late April and I remember sitting in my quaint on-campus apartment, Copland's "Appalachian Spring" wafting through the rooms. I was gazing through an open window at a rich expanse of greening grass and here and there a flourish of bright forsythia. If I stepped outside, the hills would appear lovely and significant. At that moment the life of a school teacher at the Martha Greer Academy, an all-girls school in Virginia, seemed idyllic.

In most regards it was a very pleasant place to teach although some of the students were not convinced the proper side had won what they called The War of Northern Aggression. In fact, at Greer, a white girl's prestige was markedly enhanced if she were a confirmed member of the United Daughters of the Confederacy.

I knew something of this august organization, having been hatched by one in the previous generation. A product of Richmond society, my mother had been able to shed most of the South's endemic prejudices but still retained a charming patrician hauteur and a pleasant though slight southern drawl. As a highly successful attorney, she had hoped I would receive my B.A. at a prestigious southern university, head off to law school, and follow her footsteps into the courtroom.

But I was a bit of a rebel myself and had other ideas.

I had visited Philadelphia and had become interested in the historical background of the old city. The ghosts of Franklin, Adams, Jefferson, and Washington beckoned me northward to the University of Pennsylvania where I could study their historical spirits more closely. When I told my mother, she was disappointed but eventually accepted my choice, admitting that Penn *was* Ivy League and therefore prestigious enough for me. I had garnered a few partial academic scholarships, but she wrote a check for the tuition balance.

While I was at Penn, my interest in American history continued, so rather than applying to law school I told my mother I wanted to pursue an M.A. at the University of Virginia. By this time she had developed a grudging respect for my academic interests, convincing herself that my education would establish a firm foundation for my eventual legal career. She congratulated me on my choice of schools and wrote another check.

During my final year at UVA, she had called and emailed a few times inquiring about whether I had taken the LSAT and what law schools I might be applying to. I had responded by saying that I was still considering my options. Fortunately, she had been distracted for months by a highly complex and protracted legal case involving multiple plaintiffs and defendants, so she was not as attentive to my future plans as she had been before. Then, a month or so before I got my M.A. and without consulting my mother, I accepted the teaching job at Greer.

I was on spring break and we were standing in her newly renovated kitchen when I broke the news to her. I didn't think it would go over too well. And it didn't. She looked at me as if I had dragged a cheese grater across her face.

"Are you trying to torture me?" she asked.

"Not deliberately," I said. "I appreciate everything you've done for me."

"Well, that's a comfort, I guess."

"It's a Virginia school," I said. "I thought you might like that."

"I'm familiar with the school. We used to play them in field hockey. Trounced them every time, as I recall."

She opened a bottle of chardonnay and we went outside to sit on the stone patio. It was a mild afternoon and her garden was just beginning to bloom. As we finished off a few glasses of wine, she commented about some promising new roses she had planted and the possibility of entering them in a floral competition. She was also looking forward to the Roland Avenue House & Garden Tour, an annual event that always stopped at our house and her gardens. With all the wine and optimistic garden chatter, her dismay ebbed and she turned mellow and reflective.

"You know, Paul, it's one thing to go to a private school. It's quite another to teach at one."

"I take it you don't approve?"

"It's not a question of approval. For some people teaching is fine. Noble in fact."

"But not for me?"

"No, not for you."

"Well, that's what I'm going to do."

"I'll give you three years," she said.

She was half right; it took six.

Despite our occasional squabbles, I had a grudging respect for my mother's judgment. At a time of male domination in the legal world, she had managed to become the first woman associate and later partner in the venerable Baltimore law firm of Edgar & Abernathy. That is where she met my father, a man eight years older, and, when she arrived, already a partner himself.

By all accounts, my mother was a superb litigator. Once, during spring holiday when I was about twelve, I saw firsthand what she did for a living. Unbeknownst to her, I had taken a bus downtown to the Mitchell Courthouse in Baltimore, found the courtroom, and sat in the gallery behind what looked like other attorneys with briefcases. I can't recall the exact circumstances of the trial, something about an insurance claim I think, but I do remember my mother firing questions at a red-faced gentleman who sputtered angry responses and looked up helplessly at the judge who glanced at him as if he were an annoying insect.

Later, at home, my mother came up to my room.

"Did you enjoy the show?" she asked.

"You saw me?"

"I have spies," she said. "How long were you there?"

"About two hours."

She was actually smiling. I realized later that my independent act of going to the courthouse must have been gratifying to her, a first major step toward my law career perhaps.

"Did you see the last witness?"

"The guy with the red face?"

"He was the defendant. I was cross-examining him."

"What did he do wrong?"

"Let's just say he had a tenuous relationship with the truth."

My mother often spoke that way when I was younger, trying, I suppose, to expand my vocabulary and test my inferential thinking skills.

"He was a liar?" I asked.

"Pretty much."

She leaned over and kissed me on the forehead.

"Try to remember what he looked like today," she said.

I was never completely sure what she meant by that. I assumed she meant I should never allow myself to be put in such a humiliating position.

Although my parents never admitted it directly, I am certain that my conception was a surprising and not particularly festive moment for the Simmons household. My mother was thirty-seven, my father forty-five, and I have no doubt they both would have been content to lead their lives unencumbered by a child. In fact, my mother once told me she thought her morning sickness was incipient stomach cancer.

I grew up in a tidy Tudor-style home in northern Baltimore, an affluent neighborhood of spacious green lawns and dense shade trees. I was sent to fine private schools – first a coed primary school, then an all-boys prep school – and I spent my summers as a country club rat scurrying from swimming pool to tennis court to golf course.

Until I was fourteen, I led a safe and uneventful life. Then one winter day my father committed suicide. The maid found him in his den, lifelessly watching the DVD version of *Lonesome Dove*. He had taken a lethal overdose of his prescription medication for sleep and depression.

The story later leaked that my father had possibly been mishandling a client's funds. Although no legal action was taken or even threatened, he apparently could not bear the thought that a rumor of his impropriety or incompetence might spread through the sacred corridors of the Baltimore legal establishment. That seemed to be the prevailing theory about his suicide. And, since he left no note, it may well be true. But in the months and years that have passed, I have wondered if there were a better explanation. When I recall my father I see him as a tired and timid man, bested by a beautiful and more talented wife. Exhausted and consumed by envy and ennui, he might have simply called it quits.

Whatever the reason for his suicide, the loss of my father had little personal impact on me. Listening to the funeral liturgy of the Episcopal priest, I realized that I hardly knew the man. I couldn't recall one poignant moment I had spent with him – not a drive to the beach, not a game of catch, not a serious reprimand. Even now I remember him settled into his private den, submerged in his favorite leather chair, admiring his collection of western fiction. That was his singular eccentricity – a fascination with cowboys.

I have often wondered why my parents ever got married. They seemed to float about the house like mere acquaintances, often oblivious of each other and the rapturous potential of marriage. My father had his cowboys; my mother had her tennis matches, art club activities, and rose gardens. Occasionally they attended social functions together, but even then they seemed to depart separately, my mother leaving early to wait in the car, my father searching for his glasses or keys. I never saw them kiss or embrace; I am baffled that I was even conceived.

In only one aspect did my parents seem to share a genuine passion: their mutual desire that I enter the legal profession. They undoubtedly had their own private vision of me, Paul Everett Simmons, carrying the family legal torch into the twenty-first century. Lawyer, judge, Supreme Court Justice perhaps. My father, however, didn't live to see me forsake the legal torch and become a teacher. My mother did. And I think she viewed my divergence from a law career as family treason.

But in the past six years, when my mother made occasional disparaging comments about teaching, I didn't argue much. Nor was I inclined to tell her that I was involved in the molding of fragile young psyches, that my nurturing would help my students become fine citizens and patriots. I didn't think she would buy it, and I wasn't sure I believed it anymore myself. The truth was I had grown tired of teaching and had begun to ponder other directions for my life.

Then, on that fateful day last April, just before the school year ended, my mother called me from Florida where she had retired.

"Do you remember your cousin Ethan?" she asked.

A hazy picture of a youngish man with light brown hair came to mind. I remembered meeting him at the funeral of my grandfather when I was about ten. He hadn't come to my father's funeral; there seemed to be a feud of sorts between the two sides of the family.

"Yes," I said. "Vaguely."

"He may have a job for you," she said.

"What happened to the feud?"

"That was between your father and his sister."

"You didn't like her either, did you?"

"No. But that's all in the past. She died last year."
She paused a second.

"The point is I called Ethan. To make amends."

"Really?"

"Yes, *really*. I do have a heart you know."

"I didn't say you didn't."

"Well, in the course of the conversation I mentioned that you might be looking for a change. And he said he had an opening coming up."

"What kind of job is it?"

"He's taken over his family's printing business. He needs a salesman."

"And you think sales is better than teaching?"

"Not much," she said. "But you're not ready for law school are you? At least a sales job will give you some grounding in the real world."

"You don't think teaching is 'real'?"

"You know what I mean." She sighed into the phone. "We don't talk much," she said, "but I can tell when my only son is bored to death."

I made a lame comment about her mind-reading ability, but she ignored it.

"Just call him," she said finally and gave me Ethan's number.

After I hung up, I thought of the new career she was proposing. I imagined myself trapped in a windowless office, mountains of paperwork piled on my desk, the screeching sounds and burnt-metal smell of printing presses assaulting my senses all day long. The whole image nauseated me.

But I called Ethan anyway. We agreed to meet the

next Friday night and he'd take me to D.C for dinner and we'd discuss the job.

"Pack a bag," he said. "We might spend the night."

2

That Friday night, Ethan Canton picked me up in a silver Mercedes. In his early forties, Ethan had a receding hairline, flecked with gray at his temples. His face was youthful, with the honed bone structure of a male model. He smiled a warm glad-to-see-you greeting that was the mark of a genuine friend or an unctuous con man.

I tossed my overnight bag in the back seat, and Ethan reached back and grabbed two beers from a small cooler. He popped them open, started the engine, and jolted out of the gravel parking lot. After we had driven off the campus, Ethan noticed two pretty young women jogging by the side of the road and he honked his horn. Startled, they turned toward him and as he slowed down, he waved and gave them a big smile. For a second I thought he was going to stop, but he accelerated ahead, still smiling.

"Nice scenery," he said.

Once we got on the highway, Ethan started talking in elaborate terms about the Mercedes, how it was his third, new this time. He pointed out its various features, the bells and whistles, all with a beer in his hand. I was a bit concerned by how fast he was driving, not to mention the beer, but he seemed in control. He discussed the various merits of other luxury cars, the choices one has to make. I had little interest in cars myself and was generally satisfied with my aging Honda Civic though its air conditioning had died a year ago.

About twenty minutes into the trip, Ethan finished with the subject of cars, and broached the subject of the job.

"Paul, I was amazed when your mother called. I don't know how much you know, but to my family she was like the wicked witch of the South."

"I knew there was a feud."

"All about money," he said. "Your father got a bigger cut of Grandad's estate. Didn't amount to much, a few thousand bucks, but it really pissed mom off. My whole life I heard about how you guys lived like kings in a rich neighborhood."

He told me that as a teenager he had actually driven to Baltimore, driven right up to our house to see for himself how we lived. But he never came in; he just looked. It wasn't that great, he told me. We didn't live in a mansion – in fact it looked kind of small to be honest. He apparently walked around back and discovered we didn't even have a pool or a tennis court. Not much of a yard either. Just a really nice garden, he said.

We drove a while, the spring dusk and the envious past flying by in the wind outside.

"Did your mother tell you anything about the business I'm in?"

"Just that it's a family printing business."

"That's how it started. Three generations in a small dead town in Western Maryland. Federton. Ever heard of it?"

"No."

"No one has. It's dead."

He seemed to stare through the windshield to poor dead Federton. I imagined a frail little town that you might see in a Christmas train garden.

"I worked in the business from the age of ten," he said. "Still have ink stains on my fingers."

I knew it was a figurative comment, but I glanced at his hands anyway. I didn't see any stains, but the cuticles looked a bit chewed up.

He told me that after he finished college –"Frostburg State, I'm not an Ivy Leaguer like you" – he made some business suggestions, the firm expanded and eventually moved nearer to Baltimore and D.C. They made him vice-president, and when his father and uncle retired he took over and became president. About seven years later they both died, two months apart, and he inherited the business. With his mother, that is.

"She died last year," he said solemnly. "Now I own it all. Lock, stock, and barrel."

He drove silently for several miles. Sipping his beer, his jaw clenched, he looked as if he were contemplating the massive weight of his corporate responsibilities.

"That's the background of Canton & Canton," he said a few minutes later. "But since I took over, I've been redefining the company, re-configuring it. We're not a Mom and Pop Shop anymore. We're regional, active in seven states, going national really, ready to go bigger, much bigger. I see us entering the North American markets soon – Canada, Mexico. Europe in a few years ... Asia.

"We're not just into printing, you know. That's a big part of it, sure, but we can handle almost any publication or communication need. Marketing, public relations website development, programming, you name it. We sub-contract a lot, but our customers can call us for almost anything.

"What I'm trying to say is that it's a great place to start as a sales rep. I have two other reps besides myself and one of them's quitting in July. Anyway, I need a guy to replace him. You've got the education, you know, experience working with people." He tapped my knee. "What do you think so far?"

I felt unsure. I was still imagining the horrors of a printing plant.

Sensing my reluctance, Ethan launched into an all-out sales pitch. In essence he said Canton & Canton would offer me the world and the moon. Not only a great salary but commissions and "out of sight" bonuses. My monetary compensation alone would surpass a measly teacher's income by "a country mile." Incredible benefits, paid holidays, paid vacation, "the best health insurance on the planet," company car – a Ford Fusion, "brand new, just off the showroom floor." Not only that, he said, but I'd get a company iPhone and laptop that were both "state of the art."

"Plus, there's no clock punching, no required office hours really. You pretty much make your own schedule. Most days you're on the open road, driving through beautiful countryside, free as a bird."

It was a wonderful image and I actually pictured a carefree bird flying over golden highways and lush green meadows. He must have noticed the serene look on my face because he smiled reassuringly and went in for the close.

"Besides," he said, tapping me on the leg again, "I'm an only child like you and you're family. We take care of our own."

He was definitely a salesman. I had the effervescent feeling I was with the big brother I never had. Sipping my beer, feeling the light buzz, I realized that Ethan hadn't ever tried to interview me. I wasn't a candidate for a job. I was a customer.

"What do you say? The job's yours if you want it."

I thought of the past six years, the adolescent drama of teenage girls, the piles of uninspired papers to grade. I hated to admit it but perhaps my mother was right; perhaps I was ready for something more *real*. Something different at least. I could feel the nightmarish images of the printing plant dissolving, and I gazed through the windshield to the pink hues of the horizon.

"Okay," I heard myself say.

Ethan turned to me, smiling, shook my hand, and reached back to get me another beer.

"Congratulations," he said. "You won't regret it."

I was still dubious about taking such a big step. But Ethan didn't appear worried at all. During the whole ride to D.C. he sipped his beer, smiled, and chattered about the glorious future I had ahead of me.

We stopped in Washington to celebrate at an Irish saloon on the ground floor of a hotel. "Colin's Pub" the sign said as we walked in. We ate in a cozy little dining room adjacent to the bar. Irish heroes, maps, flags, coats of arms dotted the walls.

Just as we were finishing dinner, a burly man of fifty-something approached the table. Ethan stood up and they shook hands.

"Paul's my new sales rep. And a long lost cousin."

My hand disappeared in the massive grip of Colin Doyle.

"Colin used to be a boxer. He broke a guy's jaw at the bar once."

"That was back in the day. English bloke. Called me a gun runner."

Colin led us out of the restaurant into the bar, a long room with a make-shift stage jammed into the corner. A bartender appeared with a bottle of Irish whiskey and suddenly three shot glasses were full.

"Here's to your new career!" Colin toasted and tossed down the booze before Ethan had taken hold of his glass.

I sipped mine. Colin eyed me skeptically, then looked at Ethan.

Ethan chugged his shot. Or tried to. A drop of liquid dribbled down his chin, and his eyes were watery.

Colin shook his head. "Would you look at him? One shot and he's crying his eyes out."

It was after this light banter that I discovered another reason Ethan had come to Washington. A young woman with light brown hair long enough to tuck in her skirt walked in. We all stood and watched her for a moment, and then Ethan walked over to her. He stroked her hair, letting his fingers slide down the silky slope until they rested comfortably on her right buttock. He whispered something in her ear, and the pretty face blushed.

"She used to work for me," Colin said. "I tried to have a go with her, but I guess she prefers pansies like Ethan."

We both watched as Ethan had a go at the girl.

"Lovely creature," Colin said.

"She looks young."

"Mental age of twelve, I'd say. I mean she is with Ethan."

"Does Ethan come here a lot?" I asked.

"When he can get away from his wife."

I recalled that Ethan *was* married; my mother had told me on the phone. Even had a young son. They lived somewhere out in the Baltimore suburbs. I began to realize I knew very little about my cousin or my new employer.

Ethan decided to bring the girl over. Closer, she looked mid-twenties. Ethan introduced us. I took the girl's long velvety hand, and, as she leaned closer, I could smell the dense perfume that filled the air between us, almost as intoxicating as the Irish whiskey.

"Listen," Ethan said, drawing me aside, "Shauna and I are going to disappear for a while. I made reservations at the hotel under your name in case I don't get back before last call. Here's a little spending money." Ethan jammed a wad of bills into my hand. "Call it a signing bonus," he said.

A moment later the love birds waved goodbye, and my new big brother was gone. I counted the money – more than three hundred dollars. Life in the real world was moving fast.

I must have looked a bit dazed because Colin grabbed my arm and pulled me back to the bar.

"Looks like you could use another drink," he said.

I had two more whiskeys and felt the bar whirl. Colin disappeared too after a few minutes, but I remained in the bar, watching it fill up with all sorts of delightful people including a few straggly members of a band. Feeling a little blurry, I switched to a water and was sipping it when Colin walked by. He grabbed my glass, sniffed, and put it back in my hand.

"Not much of a drinker, are you?" he asked.

"I'm not Irish," I said.

"We'll work on that," he said. "You do fuck, don't you?"

"Absolutely," I said.

"I mean women."

"Yes, sir." I said. "Morning, noon, and night."

He smiled at that before he disappeared again, seemingly reassured that I was masculine enough to sit at his bar.

But the truth was the last time I had been with a woman was in December, another teacher at school, a divorcee with two children. On a faculty ski trip, a few glasses of wine, a spark of fire light, and months of embarrassed glances. Even before that my record with women was dismal. I lost my virginity at the belated age of twenty-one. Since then only short-lived flings and ill-fated dalliances. Like most men, I guess, I was reluctant to admit I yearned for something more than copulation. Deep down I was a hopeless romantic.

That night last spring, however, I was alone in Colin's Pub. I switched back to beer, and as time passed, the bar filled and dancers began to swarm the small dance floor. The music was Irish-American at first, evolving into pure Irish with a fiery strain of revolutionary fever. The crowd, few genuinely Irish, I'm sure, whooped it up. I sipped the beer, the crisp carbonation resurrecting me. I felt a surging hope in the life that lay beyond the bubbles, a feeling of relief that I was no longer a role model, a spiritual guide, a caretaker of sensitive souls.

About an hour later, the band took a break and I happened to glance to my left and noticed the couple that had been sitting next to me had been replaced by a single woman.

"You seemed caught up in the music," she said. Or rather she slurred.

She was a woman in her early fifties, well-dressed but strands of her expensive hair style were slightly askew.

"I guess I was."

"Can I buy you a drink?" she asked.

She had a pleasant drunken smile on her face.

"I'm fine, thanks."

She looked at me closely, her smile somewhat altered by surprise.

"Well," she said, "maybe you can buy me a drink."

I said sure and ordered her a drink. While we waited, she kept smiling, studying my face.

"You look like someone famous," she said.

"I do?"

"I just can't think who it is," she said.

Her drink came.

"On the house," the bartender said, gesturing to the

end of the bar where Colin Doyle raised his thumb as if to indicate my current bar companion had earned me a virility bonus.

"I know the owner," I said in explanation.

"Maybe you *are* someone famous!"

"Not in the least."

She leaned forward, examining my face again, so close I could smell alcohol and tobacco on her breath.

"I know," she said suddenly. "The guy on that soap opera. The guy with the dreamy blue eyes. He's a cop. On the show, I mean. Are you a cop?"

"No," I said. "I don't even have blue eyes."

She leaned over, staring at my eyes.

"Maybe not," she said. "But you still look like him. I'll Google him for you."

While I sipped my beer, she started tapping away on her phone.

"Here he is." She held the phone in front of me. I saw a small picture of a guy smiling back at me.

"You look just like him."

"I'll take your word for it," I said. But I didn't really see the resemblance.

"Well, you're really cute even if you're not a famous star."

She sat there smiling and I think I was supposed to tell her how cute she was too, but I hadn't had enough to drink for that. So she did it herself.

"You know, you might not believe this, but I was a beauty queen once."

It *was* hard to believe.

"Miss Franklin County."

"I've never met a beauty queen before."

"Actually, I was just runner-up. So I guess you still haven't."

"Maybe next time."

She laughed, "Yeah, next time."

I thought the conversation was coming to an end, and I had started to look around for the band again. But she tapped me on the arm.

"Tell me something. And I want you to be honest."

"I'll try," I said.

"Do you like sex?" she asked.

I smiled. "Is that a trick question?"

"It's not a trick question at all. I was married once to a man who didn't like sex."

She turned to the bartender and ordered us both new drinks.

"Of course, he's my ex-husband now."

"He didn't like sex at all?"

"A little bit at first. Then nothing," she said staring into her empty glass.

"That's hard to believe," I said.

She looked up, smiling. "I know. But he had oodles of money. I mean *oooodles!*"

The fresh drinks came.

"Let's toast to sex," she said. And I clinked my beer bottle against her gin and tonic. I took a sip; she chugged hers about halfway.

"Was there a second husband?" I asked.

"There was. But he didn't like sex either."

"Was he rich?"

"He was queer. Or gay. Or bi. Whatever. But I think he was more queer."

"I guess that might hinder your sex life."

"Yeah. It's a shame," she said sadly. "A real shame. I mean he was an incredibly beautiful man." She paused and looked at me dreamily. "And you know what else?" She leaned even closer to me. "He had the biggest cock on the face of the earth."

I burst out laughing. I couldn't help myself. And then

she started laughing too, and we sat at the bar laughing so hard people started turning around and staring at us.

A minute or so later, after our laughter had subsided, the beauty queen let loose a loud belch, probably from all the tonic water she had consumed.

"I'm really sorry," she said. "I think I need to walk back to my hotel."

"You aren't staying here?"

"Here?" she asked as if this hotel were several social rungs beneath her. "No. Down the road."

She started to gather her belongings and signal the bartender.

She turned to me. "Would you like to walk me back?"

I wasn't sure what she had in mind, but she appeared in poor shape, so I reluctantly agreed and settled up. As we were walking toward the exit, Colin Doyle came up to me and patted me on the back.

"Well done, son," he said.

She held my hand as we walked. Unsteady in high heels, she actually took them off and walked in stocking feet the two blocks to her hotel. After we walked in, she asked me to walk her to her room. When we were in the elevator, she put her arms around me and kissed me, her breath so unpleasant I almost gagged.

"You're not queer too, are you?"

"No."

When the elevator opened, she grabbed my hand again and dragged me down the hall to her room. She fumbled with her room card, but her hands were shaking so much she couldn't get the door to unlock.

"I hate these things," she said, looking up at me.

"Let me help."

I slid the card down, the green light flashed, the door opened, and she held it open for me. But I stood outside.

"You're not coming in?" she asked.

"I can't."

"What's wrong?"

I looked at her a moment and in the dim hall light she seemed almost ghostly.

"I'm engaged," I lied.

"I won't tell anybody," she said. "It'll be our little secret." She put her fingers to her lips and giggled.

"I really can't."

She studied my face a second.

"You *sure* you aren't queer?"

"I'm sure."

"Too bad," she sighed, "You're going to miss a great time."

She smiled coyly and stumbled inside.

When I returned to Colin's bar, my appetite for the night life had dissipated. I checked into the hotel room Ethan had reserved for me and lay on the king-size bed, staring up at the empty white ceiling. It was all rather funny. I go to D.C. with my cousin, accept a job, and end up with a drunken ex-runner-up-beauty queen while my older cousin was most likely making love to a twenty-five year old goddess. I had a lot to learn from Ethan.

To assuage my loneliness, I turned on the television, but the reruns and news broadcasts began to blur and I shut it off. Just as I was about to doze off, the hotel phone rang.

"That you, Paul?" It was Ethan.

"Yes."

"You all right?"

"I'm fine," I said.

"You alone?"

"Yes."

"Stop it, Baby. I'm on the phone."

I heard a high-pitched giggle in the background.

"Where are you?" I asked.

"Shauna's," he said. I heard some muffled sounds, giggles. In that instant I formed an image of Ethan's wife and son nestled in their respective beds, alone, as I was.

"Listen, you going to be all right there?"

"Of course," I said.

"I'll pick you up at nine tomorrow." There was another pause, another muffled sound, Ethan finally back on the line laughing. "Make that eleven. I think that's checkout time."

3

When the school year came to an end, the administration gave me a set of Martha Greer Academy wine glasses, and I was politely reminded that I would have to vacate my campus apartment before the end of June. Some of my colleagues threw a goodbye bash at one of their houses, and the woman I had slept with on the skiing trip in December took that moment to tell me how much she admired my taking a step into "the harsh world of reality," a statement that reminded me too much of my mother.

Ethan had also called a few times to confirm our business arrangement and tell me he would be sending brochures and materials about Canton & Canton. His sales rep, the one who was quitting, had decided to stay on through the second week of July, so I had a month to find a place to live and prepare for a new career.

After hearing of my job plans, my mother sent me a check for $5,000. "Find yourself a decent apartment," she said. "And buy some proper furniture and business clothes."

I decided to move back to Baltimore; the whole Inner Harbor area was teeming with activity. I found a new apartment in a renovated warehouse a few blocks away from the Science Center and Harborplace, and after a week or so of shopping at discount furniture outlets I was a resident of Baltimore once more.

I still had several weeks before my new job started, so I took exploratory walks in my changing home city, renewed my library card, checked out several promising bars, visited some museums, and saw a few Orioles games.

One evening, while I was walking by the waterfront and gazing at the boats in the marina, I remembered a former classmate from Penn, Vince Catorro. His father owned a number of businesses throughout Cape Cod, and Vinnie had always worked in the resort areas during the summer. After graduating he had taken on the full-time responsibility of running his father's gift and novelty shops in Nantucket and Martha's Vineyard. He had always pestered me about coming up to visit him, but I had always found excuses to avoid it.

Vinnie was generous to a fault; he just had a cloying need to be accepted, to be reassured that got on your nerves at times. But despite that, I decided to take a chance. I wanted to visit someplace new and I'd never been to Cape Cod. He was living in Nantucket, he said when I called him, and almost instantly he began giving me directions and telling me what exotic women I'd be humping five minutes after my arrival. He talked so much, he was so eager that I almost backed out. He wanted me to stay for a month; I said a week, maybe two.

So on a hot July day, I made the long drive north. Vinnie greeted me in Hyannis Port and we dropped my car off at a garage where a business friend of his father's would look out for it and took the ferry to Nantucket. On the way over, he insisted that we drink Cape Codders, a pleasant combination of vodka and cranberry juice.

"They'll make a man out of you," he assured me.

"Good," I said. "I've always wanted to be a man."

Standing in the warm sun on the top outside deck, we enjoyed a few manly drinks while Vinnie pointed out a number of landmarks and gave me a brief tourist's guide to Nantucket history. But as we neared the harbor I was able to glimpse for myself the alluring charm of the old whaling town.

After we arrived in town, we stopped to eat at a small lobster restaurant that was swamped with very lovely college-age girls. When I mentioned this to Vinnie, his face lit up, and I thought he would utter a crude boast about how he was banging his way through the island's female habitat. But what he actually said astonished me.

"They're nice," he said. "But I'm spoken for now."

" 'Spoken for'?

He nodded happily.

"You mean you've got a girlfriend?" I had never seen Vinnie with a girlfriend. I had never seen Vinnie with a girl, other than his mother.

He smiled proudly.

"For a month now," he said. "Beautiful girl. We're living together. She's black. Bi-racial, actually. Dad's not too thrilled. But it's love all right."

After dinner Vinnie drove me to his house, a cozy two-bedroom bungalow.

He showed me to the guest bedroom and told me to make myself at home.

In the shower, I realized how much sun I had taken on the ferry; my face and arms looked pink and flushed. But I felt revived and alive. An hour later, we set out in Vinnie's Volvo to a happy hour in town.

We stopped at a gazebo-shaped bar with an outdoor deck, the sun descending into the bobbing masts and riggings. Reggae music trickled out from a few small speakers attached to the roof of the bar. Locals and tourists basked in the shade, and we all seemed to draw sustenance from the fresh sea air.

"Great place, huh?" Vinnie asked.

As we sipped our drinks, I took a good look at him. Somehow in the past few years Vinnie must have come to the conclusion that the key to his social failure had to do with his body, so he had started lifting weights religiously. Now, with new muscle and his already hairy arms, he was positively apelike.

"So," I asked, "when do I meet the future Mrs. Cattoro?"

"Tonight. She works as a waitress, gets off about 11."

He told me there was a party on the island that night. A guy named Silverstein who was in the music business in Boston came down every few weeks and had a party at his summer place.

After we had a few drinks at the gazebo bar, we headed to the party. Silverstein's home was a brownish-gray classic beach house. A massive wrap-around porch led to comfortable rooms of breezy open windows and durable furniture. There was even a band situated on the deck. But their amplifiers kept conking out so often they finally quit and left. After that, the music came from an indoor/outdoor sound system.

Vinnie and I wandered through the sandy lawn and positioned ourselves with a group of people near a volleyball court lit by makeshift flood lights. There were about ten bikini-clad girls swatting the ball around. We watched them leaping and falling, squealing and laughing. About twenty minutes later, they stopped and started to disperse, slipping on t-shirts or sun dresses.

"I wonder where Silverstein is," Vinnie said.

"He's over there," a voice said from behind us.

We turned to look.

A rotund man had appeared on the porch. He was wearing an Hawaiian shirt the size of a jib jail. Vinnie went over to greet Silverstein, but I took that opportunity to find a bathroom and went inside. Scavengers were gnawing on the remains of a table once filled with food. I snared an orphaned pickle and started on my search for the first floor bathroom. When I got there, I found an endless line of desperate girls who pointed up. So I made my way up the staircase, past a couple inhaling each other. I was reluctant to start opening doors, but I did find one ajar. A guy stood by the door; two girls were on their knees, their heads hovering above a toilet seat lid.

"Looking for a contact," the guy by the door said, eyes glazed, and a smudge of powder on his nostril. I'm sure there was another bathroom or two upstairs, but I was beginning to feel like a trespasser.

So I headed back downstairs and outside around behind the house and the lights of the volleyball court. I walked about fifty yards through sand and past numerous scrub pines until I thought I was safe by a clump of brush. After I finished my business and had started back, I heard a strange sound. At first I thought it might be an animal. But as I stepped closer I realized it wasn't an animal at all. About ten feet ahead, a guy was lying on the sand, and straddling him, riding him actually, was a naked woman with long blond-streaked hair, her back to me. Her upper torso gyrated and contorted, tossing her hair forward and back, while she moaned and groaned. I stared transfixed, amazed that I was actually watching live sexual intercourse. I had seen stag films, of course, and samplings of porn, but watching two people going at it in front of me was a first.

I glanced down at the guy on the ground. Instead of looking up at the young lady, he was gazing straight at me, grinning. He might have just passed his bar exam or made a twenty foot putt. I stared at him for several seconds, and then he winked. That action somehow unnerved me, made me aware of my own intrusion. I withdrew, hurrying back toward the party. I found Vinnie and was about to tell him what I had seen when I realized he was standing with Silverstein.

"This is Silverstein," Vinnie announced as if he were

presenting the Duke of York.

Silverstein stuck out his sweaty hand that seemed to hang in the air like a blowfish. I shook it and he mumbled something, giggled a bit, and waddled off toward the bar. He was stoned out of his mind.

"There's another game starting," Vinnie said.

Vinnie and I started walking toward the volleyball court where a co-ed group was beginning to play.

I was especially attracted to a strawberry-blond-haired girl. I watched her lean body soar and dive, her long ponytail flipping loosely as she moved. Twenty minutes later the game ended; the strawberry blonde walked to the far side, where a girlfriend handed her a drink. I couldn't help staring at her.

"Want a beer?" Vinnie asked.

I shook my head and Vinnie drifted off.

I was still staring at the strawberry blonde when she turned and looked my way. I must have been staring hard because she looked at me as if she thought she knew me. She smiled and gave a little wave. I turned around, thinking she must have been waving at someone else. When I turned back to look at her, she had slipped from sight. After Vinnie returned, a beer in his hand, he started talking about the music, but I wasn't paying attention. My eyes were fixated on the spot where the strawberry girl had vanished.

I was about to give up when suddenly she appeared in front of me, standing next to a friend. She had walked out of the trees on my right and there she was.

"Do I know you?" she asked.

"I don't think so."

"Too bad," she said. "You're kind of cute in a just-hatched-bird kind of way."

I gazed blankly into her sea-blue eyes, stunned by her loveliness and confused by her comment. She must have thought I was too drunk to respond because after a few seconds of silence she and her friend walked off.

"She's hot," Vinnie said. "Go after her."

"She called me a just-hatched bird."

"So what? She likes you."

"I'm not sure about that."

"Check her out then."

"I think I need another drink."

"Good idea," he said. "A little liquid courage."

But as I turned toward the bar there was a sudden outburst from the porch.

"You fucking asshole!" I heard a woman yell. "You goddam fucking asshole!"

We all turned around and looked toward the porch. Silverstein was leaning against a porch post vomiting copiously down upon a group of chairs, which moments before had been a group of people. The woman yelling was standing with her arms spread, revealing a lava flow of pinkish chunks on her bare shoulders and back. Some drunken bystander walked over to her and tried to wipe the mess off with his hands.

Silverstein was oblivious. His face hovered over the wood railing like a massive hunting trophy, vomit and sweat mingling on his chin. A few people tried to grab him and move him back inside. But as they tried to force his girth inside, he grabbed his massive belly, and his whole magnificent torso crashed to the floor in a heap.

"Heart attack," someone said.

A group surrounded Silverstein, so fully that I could no longer see him. I wondered whether anyone had the fortitude to perform CPR on such a ghastly creature. For a few minutes, the music from the stereo mocked the horror on the porch until someone snapped it off. Word spread that there was a medical student present who had run – or been shoved – to the rescue. The whole party seemed to have gathered now in the broad lawn, the night taking on an eerie silence. Soon we heard the bleating wail of an ambulance and saw the blinking red lights. We all watched as Silverstein was carried off; a few drunken guests even applauded. For several minutes after he was gone people mulled about, offering their uninformed medical opinions about his prognosis, murmuring about his relatively young age, the value of proper diet. But people suddenly realized there was still a beer keg on the porch and they began refilling their plastic cups. The music was turned back on, and for all intents and purposes the party resumed. The genial Silverstein became a misty drunken memory.

Soon after Silverstein had been hauled off, Vinnie suggested that this might be a good time to leave.

"I want to find that girl, the strawberry blonde," I said. "You go ahead."

"How will you get back?" Vinnie asked.

"I'll find her. She'll give me a ride."

"You sure?"

"I'm fine. Go meet your girlfriend."

After protestations that I would be hopelessly lost in the Nantucket night maze, Vinnie finally relented and left. Alone now, I moved around for the rest of the night like a ghost looking for a lost soul. I wasn't drunk but I felt compelled to find the girl. The party stretched into the late hours, and I watched from the porch as cars kicked up sand and left. But the strawberry girl had eluded me.

I fell asleep on a half-deflated rubber raft in a small screened-in porch. Nestled in a corner, atop the cushion from a settee, was a couple, their tanned arms and legs entwined, sweetly asleep.

When I awoke, the couple was gone. I felt gritty and stiff from lying on the lumpy shape and sandy floor. It was late morning, but the whole house was silent. I began to wander through the rooms of carnage. Sleeping bodies lay in odd angles – on sofas, across cushions on the hardwood floor, under the broad expanse of the dining room table. The remaining food was crusted over, surrounded by a hundred flies. It suddenly dawned on me: I was in a strange house owned by a strange man who might at that moment be deceased.

Outside, I realized it was later than I thought. I had left my watch at Vinnie's – but the sun was fairly high. All over the yard was the scattered refuse of the party – smashed cups, flip flops. Exploring behind the house, I found little except a sagging clothesline and an outdoor shower.

I heard a noise and coming toward me was a tall athletic man with light brown hair, wearing khaki shorts and a faded blue polo shirt.

We shook hands and introduced ourselves. His name was Ryder Scott.

"I spent the night," I said.

"So did I," he said.

When he grinned, I suddenly recognized him – the guy with the blonde on the sand dunes the night before.

"Good to see you again," he said.

"Sorry about last night," I said. "I didn't mean to spy on you. I was just looking for a place to pee."

"I'm glad you missed us then."

"Is she still here, the girl you were with?"

"No," he said. "It was a brief courtship."

By his expression I imagined Ryder had a lot of brief courtships. He pulled off his shirt and said he was going to use the shower. That reminded me of Silverstein; it was his house after all. I mentioned that to Ryder.

"He's going to be all right," Ryder said. "Some sort of gastric disturbance."

"You spoke to him?"

"No. Kim told me. His sister, " he said. "They called her from the hospital."

"She didn't go with him?"

"She was mad at him. He puked all over her."

"That was Silverstein's sister?"

He nodded and told me the hospital had called about three or four hours later to update Kim on his condition. But apparently she still didn't want to go see him.

"I would have thought she'd calmed down by then."

"Oh, she'd calmed down," Ryder said. "But I don't think she cared all that much."

"She didn't care about her own brother?"

"That's what it seemed like to me."

"You were with her?"

"I was in bed with her. When they called, she was riding me like a cowgirl."

I stared at him. "You mean you had sex with two women last night?"

"It was a pretty good night," he said, smiling.

I laughed. "Maybe for you but not for Silverstein."

"Oh, he'll be just fine. He just needs to knock off the carbs and cocaine a bit."

"So where's Kim now?"

"Still asleep, I imagine," Ryder said, adjusting the nozzle in the shower stall. "We had a wake-up session earlier. Then she conked out again."

"And her brother's still in the hospital?"

"I guess."

I shook my head.

"They have a complicated relationship," he said.

It must be complicated, I thought. Her brother is rushed to the hospital, possibly dying, she wipes off his puke and hops in the sack with Ryder Scott. Then in the morning she does him again. Either Ryder was God's gift to women or Kim was incredibly callous.

Ryder slipped in the shower and in a few minutes he stepped out. When he was finished with his toweling and combing, he put on his clothes, and offered me a ride to town.

He drove a weathered white Audi, dusty from sand, strewn with magazines, paperback books, empty beer cans – a charming disarray. He seemed to slide into the car seat as if it were a well-worn glove, and he drove effortlessly, casually, his right hand almost caressing the wheel, his left dangling outside. Riding with him I had the feeling the air would always be warm and clear, that life was simply a cozy drive through sunshine. In many ways it reminded me of the ride to Washington with Ethan.

"Where does Vinnie live?" he asked when we got near town.

"I'm not sure actually. I'll have to search about a bit."

"You have time for lunch?"

"Sure."

In fact, time seemed to be standing still.

We stopped at a marina restaurant near where Vinnie and I had gone for happy hour. Ryder recommended the lobster salad, and we sat under an umbrella, gazing out toward the sunny marina. There were more empty slips now in the middle of the day, and I imagined sails out on the Sound, breathing in and out, the water lapping, people smiling into the glint of the sea.

During the hour or so of lunch, Ryder and I chatted about my career move and a bit about his background. I noticed that Ryder had an accent, a hint of the South, something similar to my mother's. When I mentioned that to him, he said he had been born in Norfolk, Virginia, the son of a naval commander and Virginia debutante, and had been raised as a military brat, transported around the globe from Virginia to Hawaii to San Diego to Annapolis. He attended a private school near Annapolis and went to several colleges before graduating from Washington & Lee. At least that's what he said. But there was something in his tone, almost a dreamy quality, that made me wonder how much of it was true.

"What're you doing now?" I asked.

I didn't think it was a difficult question, but he paused reflectively as if I had just asked his concept of God and the universe.

"I presume you mean my career?" he said finally.

"Yes."

"Well, right now I'm enjoying the fruits of a recent business venture."

He flashed me his grin as if to validate the story.

At the end of the lunch, I mentioned that I had met a girl at Silverstein's party. I described her as best I could.

"Shelly Moran," he said.

"You know her?"

"I've met her a few times."

I wondered if she were another one of his brief courtships.

"Don't worry," he said, as if reading my mind. "I don't know her *that* well."

I breathed a little easier and asked him if she were involved with anyone.

"Involved?"

"In a relationship."

He looked at me benevolently, as if I were a different breed from him, a pitiful one-woman type of guy.

"I don't know," he said. "Would you like to meet her?"

"Sure," I said. "Officially at least. Our first meeting didn't go too well."

"Well, how about tonight? I'm having a little dinner

party. She'll be there," he said. "Can you come?"

"I'd be glad to," I said. "Is it a special occasion?"

"Not really. But I can make one up if you want."

I laughed and told him that wasn't necessary.

We walked back to Ryder's car after lunch – which I insisted on paying for.

"You going to be all right finding your friend?"

"I'll find him," I said. "But he's probably pissed off I abandoned him last night. He wanted me to meet his new girlfriend."

"Tell you what. Invite them to the party."

"Are you sure?"

"Absolutely."

"Is Kim coming?" I asked.

"Kim? No. Her husband's coming over on the afternoon ferry."

"She's *married*?"

"Didn't I mention that?" he said.

"You skipped that part."

"Oh, well," he shrugged, smiling again.

As we said goodbye, he gave me the name of the restaurant and its location.

"The official party starts at 7:30. But drop by early," he said. "We'll have drinks."

I had to call Vinnie but I didn't have a cell phone. I have had three in my life and have lost them all. It had been about a month since I had lost the last one, and I still hadn't gotten around to replacing it. Friends and work colleagues couldn't understand how I could survive so long without one, but that was probably because they texted and tweeted non-stop. I hadn't been caught up in that frenzy; I kept one only for emergencies.

So I did what I usually did when I needed to make a call and didn't have my own phone. I borrowed one, this time from a lovely sales clerk in one of the local shops downtown.

Before I dialed Vinnie's number, I prepared a fallacious version of the previous night's events to impress and irritate Vinnie, how I fell prey to three lovely female volleyball players. But when his Boston accent came on the voice mail, I just left him something simple:

"I'm still alive. See you later."

I had his address in my wallet and asked directions from my helpful clerk who drew a little map and told me I was only a half-mile away.

On the way there, I noticed that crowds were filling the streets – tourists on bikes, boaters, shoppers, a lovely sunny Saturday. Waitresses scrambled to restaurants and I thought of the strawberry girl, Shelly Moran. A "just-hatched bird," she had called me. Not the most flattering compliment, but I was excited by the prospect of seeing her again.

The door was unlocked at Vinnie's house and inside the living room was almost dark, the blinds down. I noticed some clothes thrown loosely on the floor and sofa.

I walked down the hall toward the two bedrooms and saw that Vinnie's door was closed. Pausing outside, I pressed my ear to the door and heard moaning and the rhythmic clink of bedsprings. Hard as it was for me to imagine, it was clear that Vinnie was screwing someone. I was torn between a sense of paternal pride and fraternal envy. Everybody seemed to be having sex on the island except me.

I tiptoed quietly back down the hall and stepped outside onto Vinnie's front porch. There were a couple of white Adirondack chairs so I sat down and watched the afternoon unfold.

And suddenly I saw Shelly – at least I thought I saw her – riding in an open jeep with another girl. As they sped away, I started to run and wave, but they didn't see me. I walked several hundred yards down the road, searching for signs of the jeep. But they had vanished.

Twenty minutes later, I was back inside, and the window shades were raised, drenching the living room with light.

"Hey, Paul!"

There in the kitchen and dining area was Vinnie, bare-chested. Next to him was a tall slender dark-haired girl with glasses, her hands buried in an enormous salad bowl on a small island. She was wearing the Penn t-shirt Vinnie had worn the night before.

"We're making a salad," he said.

"A giant salad," she said.

"There's nuts in the bowl over there."

"Pretzels, chips, all kinds of stuff."

"Beers in the fridge. Help yourself."

Their voices were like a lovely duet, full of romantic generosity. After they finished offering me everything in their kitchen pantry, Vinnie introduced me to Clara who said she had already heard a lot about me.

"What did he tell you?" I asked.

"Just the good stuff," Vinnie said.

Clara smiled. "Vincent said you helped him out a lot in college."

"We helped each other out," I said.

"True enough," Vinnie said, as he was leaning over Clara, nuzzling her neck.

"Stop, Vincent, we have company!"

Vinnie smiled happily and asked me what I had been doing all this time. I told him about staying at Silverstein's, that he was okay, that I had gotten a ride back with a guy named Ryder Scott. With that, Vinnie looked at me with some interest.

"No kidding," he said. "Ryder Scott." He said it with near reverence. "I didn't see him last night."

"How do you know him?"

"Well, he doesn't know me, but Ryder's something of a legend," Vinnie said. "A real cockhound. He's been coming to the Cape for years."

He casually strolled over and began to kiss Clara's neck again. It was hard to believe; the only women I'd ever seen him touch were glossy centerfolds in *Playboy*.

"Vincent," Clara said. "Not now."

"I just can't help myself."

"Try," she said.

Vinnie pulled himself away and grabbed two beers from the fridge.

"So tell me, where did you two meet?" I asked as Vinnie handed me a beer.

"In front of my shop," he said. "Saw this beautiful angel admiring one of our many works of art."

"It was just a bracelet," Clara said. "You guys don't have much art."

Vinnie looked at me. "Clara thinks we should stock some more fine art."

"Not *fine* art, " she said. "But some good local artists. I told you I'd be glad to help."

"She was an art history major," he said proudly. "Isn't she great?" Vinnie said, leaning over to kiss Clara again.

As she squealed "Vincent!" once more, I turned away and found a copy of the *Boston Globe* on a chair and began looking for the Orioles' score. They were on a brief winning streak, but who knew how long that would last.

"Here, you finish the salad," I heard Clara say. "I'm going to take a shower."

When she was gone, Vinnie came over to me.

"What do you think?" His voice was eager, the old

Vinnie, seeking approval.

"You mean Clara?"

"Yeah."

"She's sweet," I said. "Pretty."

He beamed at the sound of each word. "I know," he said, suddenly serious. "I'm going to marry her. She's going to have my babies."

I pictured a group of muscular hairy babies playing on a beach.

"I'll invite you to the wedding."

He sat down and leaned back, his own hairy hands clenched behind his head, his eyes fixated on the blissful future.

A few minutes later, I invited them to Ryder's party.

4

Ryder's dinner party was held at an old stone restaurant, a former seafarer's house. It was a fine, cool building with a handsome veranda and dark alluring hideaways inside. The dinner itself took place outside – a stone patio with wrought-iron furniture, glass table-tops, black gas-lit lanterns, and a lovely patch of a garden with a small fountain in the center of the lawn that spouted water through the snout of a leaping whale.

When I arrived that evening, it was still early and light. As I stepped inside, I didn't see Ryder at first. Then I heard the sound of a woman's laugh, and I instinctively turned. There was Ryder Scott, handsome in a madras shirt and blue jeans, standing at the bar, chatting with a woman. He waved me over as soon as he saw me.

"I just got here myself," he said as we shook hands and sat down.

The woman he was with was Marie, the owner of the restaurant. Dressed in a long floral dress and quite tan, she had a vibrant attractiveness that so many women in their middle years seem to have, a confident maturity enhanced by a hint of flirtatiousness.

Ryder ordered me a beer and once we had drinks, I listened in on their conversation.

"How do you like the arrangements?" Marie asked.

"I haven't been outside yet," Ryder said. "I was lured in by your ravishing beauty."

Marie laughed. "You were lured in by our ravishing barmaid."

"I hadn't even noticed her," Ryder said.

"You asked her for her phone number yesterday. She told me."

Ryder looked down the bar to where the barmaid was now serving another customer. She *was* pretty and I doubt she could have possibly escaped Ryder's notice.

"She must have misunderstood me," he protested. "I was asking for *your* number."

Marie laughed.

"You really are a first-class bullshitter."

"I would never bullshit you, Marie."

"I think you'd bullshit anyone."

He adopted a contemplative posture, then resorted to his all-purpose grin.

"Well, I'll just have to get over my hurt feelings," he said. "In the meantime why don't you tell Paul what we have planned for tonight."

"You mean that note you dropped off yesterday?"

"Yes. I'm sure you've committed it to memory."

"Absolutely," she said, smiling. "I have nothing else to do but memorize drivel."

Marie walked over to the hostess's stand and came back with an expensive-looking cream-colored envelope. She slid a single page out, slipped on fashionable reading glasses, and started reading.

> *Dear Lovely and Gracious Marie,*
>
> *I would like my dinner party tomorrow to be a shimmering aesthetic experience as well as a culinary delight. I want colors, music, and texture – an unforgettable symphony of sensory detail!*
>
> *I want my guests to soar – to savor life at heights unknown to mortal creatures.*
>
> *Sincerely,*
> *Ryder Scott*

"Magnificent!" Ryder raised his glass. "I expect a call

from the Pulitzer committee any minute."

We all smiled and Ryder took a healthy gulp of his drink and looked happily over to me as if to share the wondrous nature of his party and the heightened way he had described it. He was probably a little drunk already because his classic smile looked off-kilter.

"You really are something else," Marie said.

And he was something else – a dreamer, a charlatan, a seducer. Take your pick or choose one yourself, but you had to like him, at least at that moment, in the cool of the bar.

Part of Ryder's charm, I realized, was his ability to appear genuinely ebullient and ridiculously affected. Despite her critical comments, Marie was clearly taken by him, looking at him with wonder, perhaps asking him silent questions: Are you as ludicrous as you sound? Or maybe, where have you been most of my humdrum life?

"Listen, Marie, why don't you join us tonight?" Ryder said.

"Thanks for asking," she said, "but I do have to work."

"You're too beautiful to work."

"I'm too poor not to."

"I'm sure you can delegate your responsibilities for this one special night. After all, it's my last night on the island."

I wondered if that were true; he hadn't mentioned it at lunch.

She shook her head. "I really can't."

Ryder leaned back, sipped his vodka tonic, perused her a moment, as if he were reconsidering his strategy. Then he leaned forward, staring into her eyes.

"How about *after?*"

Her eyes widened in mock or real curiosity.

"After?"

"When the dining is over," he said.

"What do you have in mind?" Her voice had changed ever so slightly – now a coy but interested party.

"There's only one possibility on a night like this."

"And what's that?"

Ryder smiled, placed both of his hands on hers. "A stroll to the sea with a chilled bottle of champagne."

I was mesmerized by it all. Right in front of my face, I was watching a master in action. And it was all so outrageous and transparent. But when he uttered this last proposal, Marie didn't blurt out an expletive or laugh in his face. Not this time.

"We'll see," she said finally, lowering her eyes for a moment, almost as a concession.

"I can't wait," Ryder said.

He had her, I thought. It had worked.

A few minutes later she excused herself, and after she was gone, I turned to him.

"Is that how you do it?" I asked.

"What?"

"How you seduce women."

He almost looked offended.

"I don't seduce women," he said.

"What do you call it then?"

I wondered if anyone had ever asked him that. He looked pensive, even a bit serious.

"I suppose what I do is a form of magic."

"You're a magician?"

"I was actually. I had a magic act when I was kid."

"And that's how you learned to seduce women?"

He smiled and glanced down the length of the bar to where the ravishing Marie was now speaking with the ravishing barmaid. I wondered if he was thinking about how much magic it would take to escort *two* ravishing women on a stroll to the sea with a chilled bottle of champagne.

He looked back at me. "Women love fantasy," he said. "And fantasy is a form of illusion. When I meet a woman I create an illusion she can't resist."

"Sounds like seduction to me."

"Women can't be seduced. They just like to see the rabbit pop out of the hat."

He smiled broadly, apparently pleased that he had successfully transformed seduction into a justifiable and respectable magician's trick.

"That's impressive," I admitted. "But don't you think women expect more?" I asked.

"More what?"

"I don't know. Maybe some women aren't interested in seeing a rabbit pulled out of your hat. Maybe they'd like to date you for a while. Go out for a pizza. Fall in love. Maybe even marry you."

"I see where you're going, but you know, Paul, women think about marriage when they see a pink ribbon or an old dog."

I'm not sure what he meant by that; I'm not sure he did either. It occurred to me that Ryder must have built-in, ready-to-go expressions of nonsense for almost any occasion. He was a really fascinating man; so much of him seemed untouched by reality.

Ryder glanced at his watch. "Well, I'd love to discuss magic some more, but my guests will be arriving soon."

We strolled out to the outdoor patio where his party was to be held. The sunlight had lowered beneath the surrounding trees, and the garden grass was green and lush. Several wrought-iron tables had been merged to form one large table, the glass tops clear and reflecting the lantern light. Ryder walked around the table, inspecting the setting: solid looking china with blue trim and royal blue napkins. A string of Christmas lights gave the summer setting a surreal winter quality, and there was a faint tingle of jazz in the air. He looked over to me and gave me a wink, as if we were co-conspirators in his world of illusion and drivel.

When Ryder left to check on something, I walked out on the soft lawn and watched the whale spurt water, thinking back in time to the old Nantucket Island – rough, wild, primitive. That is what first drove me to study and teach history, the wonder about what life must have been like back then, whenever then was. What the people looked like; what they talked about, what they did for pleasure, how they courted one another, how they brutalized each other, how they survived physically and mentally. And it struck me that I was out of it now, out of the life of the past and into the business of the present. I wondered for the first time since that evening with Ethan if I would miss the world I was departing. But I looked around at the glimmer of the glass table, felt the coolness of the air, remembered that Shelly Moran was about to reenter my life, a new life, and history seemed very far away.

It was perhaps logical that the first guest to arrive would be Vinnie, his hair gelled GQ fashion. On his arm, sweet Clara, looking shy and awkward. We chatted a bit, Ryder reappeared, a few more guests came in, all unknown to me of course, and all strangely enough in couples. I waited for my girl, Shelly, half afraid now that she'd appear on the arms of another man. There were six, then eight people all milling about, a server carrying trays of champagne glasses, waiting fingertips reaching out for them. I chatted with Vinnie and Clara, then another older couple for whom the night was a reunion of sorts. They had dated thirty years ago, married different people, been divorced and now were newly acquainted on Nantucket. Ryder had met them on the ferry. They were both silver-haired, fit, and almost glowing.

"This wonderful young man was nice enough to invite us to dinner," the woman said, speaking of Ryder.

"A glorious night," the man said. He was practically floating, a smile so luminous you would have thought he'd discovered the fountain of youth. He looked at the woman as if he had; he seemed incapable of uttering anything but gushing bromides of happiness.

I glanced back at the door, saw Ryder smile, and there she was coming in the door, Shelly, her hair golden red in the lantern light, her neck long and tender, large dangling gold earrings catching the gaslight gently, provocatively. I started to suck my empty champagne glass as if it were an oxygen mask.

Ryder put his arm around her shoulder, kissed her cheek in cavalier fashion, whispered something that made her smile. She looked over at me, following Ryder who was beckoning toward me, and she smiled at me. All I could do was wave my empty champagne glass. She was gliding through the party, weaving her way over to me. As she did, I glanced behind her, still expecting to see her escort; but she had come alone, her smile and eyes on me. I felt a pounding in my heart; I wished I had drunk more; I was too clear-headed for this.

"I was wrong," she said. She was inches away.

"Wrong?"

"You don't look anything like a just-hatched bird."

We shook hands and the smoothness of her fingers thrilled me.

"I'm glad," I said.

A server with champagne drifted by and we each took a glass.

"So, Paul, what do you do?" she asked.

I actually had to pause to think of the answer. "I'm a salesman, I guess." The term seemed unnatural on my tongue.

She was smiling. "Are you sure?"

I was beginning to feel a trickle of perspiration make its path down my armpit.

"I used to be a teacher," I said. "I'm starting a new job in sales in a few weeks."

I am not exactly suave in the presence of women, but I was staring into Shelly's blue eyes, and those laughing eyes were focusing right back.

"How are you two doing?" It was Ryder who had appeared out of nowhere.

"We're doing fine," Shelly said. She put her arm in mine.

Ryder leaned over to Shelly.

"Watch this rogue. He seems innocent enough, but his appearance is deceiving. He can charm the panties off a nun."

"I don't have anything to worry about then," she said. "I'm not a nun and I'm not wearing any panties."

Ryder smiled and winked at her. "That's the spirit," he said, slapping me on the back again before departing for another group.

We watched Ryder go off.

"Have you known him long?" I asked.

"Ryder? Everyone knows Ryder. I'm probably the only woman on the island he hasn't slept with. That's why I was surprised he called this afternoon to ask me to the dinner party."

"He called this afternoon? He told me at lunch you were already coming to the dinner."

"That's Ryder for you," she said. "He called about three o'clock. He told me he knew someone who was absolutely crazy about me."

I blushed.

In a few minutes, Ryder tinkled a glass and called the

party to the table for dinner. It was perhaps the irony of ironies that Ryder, ladies' man, stud extraordinaire, was the only person present without a date. He sat alone at the head of the table, cheerful and proud. At the time, I wondered why a man would take on the expense of having a dinner party for a series of couples he apparently barely knew. He seemed to thrive on the romance of the moment. Whenever I glanced at him, he was always smiling, chatting, and gesturing.

But what I remember most is Shelly. Sitting next to her, I had ample opportunity to admire her profile – a lean jaw line that led to the tender ears and dangling gold earrings; the wisps of gold filament that fluttered at her temple; the crinkle at her eyes when she smiled. Sometimes, when she was talking across the table, I would simply stare at her. She seemed to realize it too; for in those moments, she would reach beneath the edge of the glass table-top and squeeze my hand or thigh. It did not seem real – her floral halo, the taste of Chablis and lobster bisque, the gentle trickle of the fountain, the faint cooling summer wind, the shadowy teasing lantern light.

As the wine flowed and the evening wore on, we turned more and more toward each other, and words seemed to flow from our lips. I spoke about my family, my father's premature death, my mother – the legal careers of my parents, which especially interested her since she was approaching her third year of law school at Boston University. She spoke about the pressure she felt from her family to succeed, to somehow match her parents' PhDs, her brother's MD. She was even interning this summer at a prestigious law firm in Boston to get a head start on the fierce competition to come next year. Our whole futures hovered in the candlelight that night, and I think our nervous anticipation generated a sort of giddiness. We laughed and chattered breathlessly – about the Orioles and Red Sox, our mutual disdain for Facebook and Twitter, the subtle flavor of fresh muffins dipped in drawn butter, the Kennedy mystique, why champagne tastes better sipped under the stars – a desultory stream of subjects that seemed to draw us closer. It was as if for that precious moment we were amassing our collective thoughts and wits to steel ourselves against the awesome obstacles of life to come.

The evening drifted on and soon we were all rising, saying various goodbyes. Shelly and I strolled to the fountain, watched the whale spurt water. As we turned back toward the veranda, we saw Ryder talking to the hostess, smiling, his arm caressing her shoulders. We thanked him, but he waved us off, shooed us out the door of the restaurant.

We strolled through the hum and whir of Nantucket night life, the cars, the lights, the chatter surrounding us, too mundane to be relevant. I had no idea where we were headed; it didn't seem to matter. Feeling her hand in mine, listening to her talk about a summer job she once had on Main Street, I felt I wanted to carve the moment in the bark of a tree. I could not reproduce the route we took that night if I were offered a million dollars, nor could I tell you how long it lasted, but somehow we ended up on the dock of a marina, the boats deserted now, just bobbing in the black water.

She was standing away from me now, her back to me, and the light from the dock shone on her hair making the gold-red shimmer.

"Don't you just love the smell of the sea," she said. "It always reminds me of my grandfather taking me out on his boat."

"Was he a fisherman?"

"No. He just loved to sail. I remember when I was

little I used to draw pictures of sailboats and mail them to him. I liked to draw the clouds and the sun and the water, all different, unrealistic colors."

"Were the pictures good?"

"I thought they were." She paused, looking out to the boats, as if remembering the child of her past crafting crayon sailboats.

"He died rather suddenly. He had just come in from sailing. He was sitting on his porch having a drink. They found him slumped over, his drink spilled on his old khaki shorts."

Shelly visibly shuddered; her eyes moist. I put my arm on her shoulder and moved against her, my chin resting on her head. She leaned back and my arms came around her.

"I'm sorry," I said. She squeezed my hands.

We walked back in silence, my arm around her, and I felt as if I had known her for years. She seemed to fit so snugly under my arm, leaning against my body, that it seemed impossible that I should not know her, that I should not be with her.

She was staying with two other female law students at a small apartment house near town. We stopped by a lamppost outside; the air had cooled, and Shelly was almost shivering. She hugged me suddenly, holding my body firmly.

"I've had a wonderful night," she said.

I felt a shiver too, not from cold, just nervousness. I wasn't sure if she wanted to see me again. She pulled back gently, grabbing my hands in hers, kissing them, gazing up at me. Smiling.

"Do I still look like a just hatched bird?" I asked.

She smiled and shook her head. "I guess I'll never live that down."

Her arms went up around me, and I stepped into her

embrace as if I were entering a warm fire-lit room. We kissed for a long time. When our lips parted, she stayed close, smiling.

"Want to go bike riding tomorrow?" she asked.

"Sure," I said.

"Bring a swim suit and towel," she said. "Eleven."

She was holding my hands now, staring up at me. She moved close.

"I'm very glad I met you," she said.

Her hands slipped from mine and I watched her walk up the steps to her apartment, her golden-red hair lit by a solitary porch light. After she inserted her key, she turned and waved before drifting inside. I watched the closed door a few moments before I turned away. All the way home I was walking on air.

5

The next morning I woke to loud moaning from Vinnie's bedroom. Later, lying in bed, I heard running in the hall, a giggle or two, a squeal of "Vinnie, don't!" and then the muffled sound of water in the bathroom, a shower for two and more laughter.

I didn't see Vinnie or Clara that morning, not since the dinner the night before. They vanished before I got up, but he left a note that they were going to Hyannis Port for the day.

On the way to Shelly's apartment, walking down the shaded streets, I felt a queasy lightness – as if the night before had been illusory. But when I turned the corner of her street, I caught sight of her standing on the porch of her apartment, looking out from the shade to the sunny side of the street, adjusting her ponytail and checking her image in a small compact. I stopped, stared at her, awe-struck that she was there waiting for me.

That day we biked around the island, getting lost a few times, eventually finding a route to the beach where we sat, talked, and swam. She insisted on applying a special lotion on me, and I savored the tender touch of her fingers on my back.

When we returned, I asked her to have dinner with me.

"You're asking me out on a date?" she said.

"I suppose I am."

"You're turning into a real lady killer."

On my way back to Vinnie's, I asked a local man

about restaurants and he gave me the name of one on the water, The Sea Gaze.

"It's expensive," he said.

"Good," I said.

And that's where Shelly and I went that night.

She was wearing a cornflower blue sun dress that complemented her eyes and burnished tan.

"You look beautiful," I said.

"I hope so," she said. "I splurged on a new dress."

About sunset we sat down at the restaurant's outdoor deck, and I ordered a bottle of chardonnay. The price was outrageous but I didn't care; I was sitting with a dream. That is a bit how I felt – as if this lovely bright young woman across from me, the one who was clasping my hand, might dissolve at any moment.

"I'm a sucker for sunsets," she said. She was gazing out over the water at the sun which now was beginning its hovering motion near the western edge of dark blue water. "They're quite different from sunrises, don't you think?"

I was so entranced by her and her voice and the wine and the still coolness of the perfect sky, I didn't realize it was a question.

"In what sense?" I heard myself say.

"Sunrises always seem so delicate, so subtle. The water is calm; it looks safer in the lightening sky. I guess it reassures me in a way."

"What about sunsets?"

"Well, look," she said, pointing toward the horizon. "So many colors. So dramatic. Mysterious too. It's exciting but there's an anxiety there too." She looked out at the colors, and I could almost picture her as a little girl, trying to capture the image with her paints and crayons. "It's as if," she continued, "the excitement, the drama comes from whether .... "

She paused and smiled, almost embarrassed.

"Go on," I said.

"I mean each time the sun sets you wonder if it will ever rise again."

"It usually does."

She looked back at me and laughed.

"God, I must sound like a complete idiot."

"Not at all," I said. At that moment her observations seemed the insights of an angel.

When we came back to her apartment, she stopped and turned toward me.

"I want you to walk around the block for a minute. Then come back."

"Why?"

"Go."

She went inside and, befuddled, I began my little walk. I wondered if there were someone inside she had to get rid of – a visiting boyfriend, perhaps.

When I returned, the door was ajar and I heard the sound of classical music. Pushing open the door, I came into a darkened living room illuminated only by a half dozen candles, wavering ever so slightly.

"Shelly?" I called, feeling a bit uneasy. But she didn't answer. I turned to my right and nearly jumped. Shelly was standing about twelve feet away, behind one of the candles. She was completely naked.

"Hi," she said softly. "Like the music?"

I didn't answer at first.

"It's Vivaldi," she said.

I must have looked confused.

"*The Four Seasons,* you know."

I nodded.

She began walking over to me and with each step I think my breathing quickened.

She took my hand.

"There are more candles in the bedroom," she said.

And that night the carnal festival began.

The next six days I was with Shelly almost constantly. I virtually moved into her apartment. We slept together, ate, drank, rode bikes, shopped, swam, all in a dewy, summery daze. I couldn't help touching her —to entwine her fingers in mine, pick her up in the air, kiss her long sleek throat, flip her pony tail.

One early morning, while it was still dark, she woke me.

"I want to see the sunrise," she said.

And we jumped on bikes and pedaled out of the town through the dim edge of dawn, down dark gravelly paths and a long stretch of tree-lined streets, our bikes cranking their rusty chains. Once there she threw her bike to the sand and raced to the center of the beach. The sky was changing already, the water lapping, the air still cool. And we stood holding hands, trembling as we watched the horizon. It was all as she said – a subtle reassuring rise in the clouds, a soft and comforting light that began to suffuse the damp quiet beach.

"Oh, Paul," she said.

We kissed and started clutching each other's clothes, and suddenly we were on the sand naked, writhing, hard, rough, pounding and wild. Sweaty and scraped, we finished as the sun bloomed on the gray edge of the sky.

Those were six magical days. I was undeniably happy, without a doubt the happiest I had ever been. Yet even during the passion and dreamy romance, I felt a tingling worry, a doubt, especially as the date of her departure time approached. During our conversations, whenever I broached the subject of the future, she'd deflect the issue, absorb herself in the present moment. But the time finally came when there was no avoiding the subject. What were we going to do? What was to develop out of all this?

Unfortunately, on the morning she was to leave, she and her roommates were scrambling around, trying to put all their belongings together to make the morning ferry. Tension sparked and the voices were angry – her roommates displeased that she had virtually abandoned them during the week. Shelly was irritable too. I stood around on the porch helpless, watched them drop luggage and bags out by my feet as they packed. I tried to catch Shelly's eye, but she was absorbed in packing – or at least she pretended to be. Frustrated, I went inside and grabbed her arm.

"Can we talk?" I asked.

"In a minute," she said. It was a tone of voice I hadn't heard before.

Finally, when I heard a vacuum cleaner start on the inside, she came out, a sad look on her face. We walked away aimlessly for a while; her head was down, her eyes focused on the pebbles she kicked. What was there to say? She seemed almost a different woman.

I stopped her, holding her arm.

"Listen," I said. At first she stood looking away. I still wasn't sure what to say. Her eyes finally turned to me; they seemed gray now.

"What?"

I looked into her eyes and tried to see the glimmer of feeling that I had seen for the past several days, tried to find the warmth that could make me speak in a coherent fashion.

"We haven't talked about this before," I said, feeling the inadequacy of my words.

" 'This'?"

"This," I said, stupidly beckoning to the traffic.

She looked around – at nothing.

I tried again. "Whether we'll see each other. When we'll see each other."

"I'm sure we will," she said. "Someday."

" 'Someday'?"

She looked up at me.

"These past few days have been wonderful," she said.

I must have looked like a child whose puppy had been smashed by a truck because at that moment she put her hand to my face.

"They've been very special for me. You don't know how special," she said.

But, as I looked at her through the growing cataract of a tear, I sensed a finality in her voice that I didn't want to hear.

"I'll be in touch," she said.

"Soon?" I managed to say, but my voice was the pitiful chirp of a newly hatched bird.

Then we kissed, smoothly, a hint of the warmth of the days before.

"I have to get back and get ready. My friends are going to kill me."

And that was how she left me. She squeezed my hand once more, turned, and ran back to the apartment. I felt the glare of the harsh sun pressing against my burned neck as I watched her disappear.

That night I got drunk with Vinnie. Clara had left to visit someone in Falmouth, so we ended up drinking shooters and beer at a bar called "The Chicken Box." All Vinnie could talk about was Clara, his dream girl, wedding bells, the whole spectrum of romantic bullshit. The next thing I remembered was jolting awake in the middle of the night, lying in a puddle of sweat on Vinnie's living room sofa.

I escaped Vinnie and the whole Nantucket and Cape Cod scene as soon as possible. And one of the worst memories of the departure was the look of pity on Vinnie's face as he watched me step on the ferry.

The whole trip back to Baltimore was horrendous. The ferry ride was nauseating; a heavy gray sky brought high waves and a rocking deck. And driving to Baltimore was just as bad, a dreary descent into a liquid hell. My air-conditionless car sucked in humidity, and I sweated as if I were in a tropical rainforest.

I had never soared so high and then plunged so far into confusion. At times during the ride my stomach would flutter with hope. I would suddenly see Shelly in the light of a rising sun, golden and supple, the crisp salt water licking at her legs. But then I would nosedive into a gray despair, realizing that it had all been a teasing glimpse into the demented world of romantic love.

6

The next day I spent three hours sitting on the walls of Fort McHenry, staring up the Patapsco River where nearly two centuries before British warships pummeled these very grounds. I imagined bombs bursting around me, the ear-jarring blasts, fireworks of orange and white, the whole world rumbling. I wondered what it felt like to be literally shaken by exploding metal, to be hit by flying shrapnel, to feel a sharp wedge of hot steel pierce my chest, lop off the top of my head. Under the blue sky and pleasant sun, I felt a lightness, an intimation of sudden violent death. Sitting alone with my morbid historic imagination, I felt that it might be rather glorious to perish defending the walls of our new nation.

I don't know whether it was the heroic imagery of the past, but when I walked the few miles back to my apartment that afternoon, I felt inspired, perhaps like Francis Scott Key, to take literary action. At first, I thought about sending Shelly an email. But electronic communication seemed too emotionless and cold. The historian in me wanted to evoke something of the past when people communicated more humanly with pen and ink. I had to reach out to Shelly through the older, more traditional means of an actual letter.

That night I played a classical tape of Vivaldi, sat at my kitchen table, a newly-purchased stationary pad in front of me, and tried to compose a missive that would rekindle in her the spirit and passion of Nantucket. Unfortunately, as I wrote I discovered I had become completely inept in writing at length in cursive. I realized that during the past twelve years the only cursive I had written were notes for my college and graduate school classes and brief remarks on students' papers. During that time my penmanship had atrophied so much that the inky scrawl on my pad was unreadable. I had to abandon the romance of the handwritten letter and turn to my modern laptop.

About midnight I finished and printed it out. I was convinced she would read this letter and immediately board a plane to Baltimore. I hand-wrote her name and address and sealed the envelope with my tongue. So intense was my need to mail it that I decided not to wait until daylight; I had to mail it that very night, to seize the advantage of time.

I strolled through the thick July night, the dark sky stained by a tangerine-colored haze absorbed by the soft street lights leading toward the harbor. Traffic was still pulsing; the bars emptying and half-blind drivers were blinking their way home.

The letter seemed to burn my fingers as I walked. I passed two or three mailboxes that seemed too isolated, too vulnerable to theft. I gripped the letter more tightly and decided to walk all the way to the central post office, that great edifice of American government, safeguard of communication and now romance. When I arrived I stood for a moment with the letter in my hands, rereading her name. *Shelly Moran.* I checked to see if there was a stamp, saw a yellow bird commemorating something; and with a nervousness that bordered on paranoia, I dropped it in.

For days afterward, I sat alone in my cool monastic apartment, drinking quarts of iced tea and reading an assortment of magazines and books – one a history of Fort McHenry. I wondered how she would respond to my letter. Would she succumb to the impersonality of an email, would she call me on my home phone, would she write a real letter? I still didn't have a cell phone so she couldn't text. Maybe she wouldn't respond at all.

During those agonizing days of limbo, I found myself recalling incidents from my past, a faded newsreel of the Paul Simmons autobiography of ill-fated romance.

I remembered fifth grade, the last year before college that I attended classes with girls. Meredith arrived at school after spring break, and throughout the first few weeks of class, there were moments I nearly fell down entire flights of stairs, blinded by her actual presence.

One spring night while my parents were out, the phone rang. It was Meredith and in her sweet shy voice she asked if I could come over, her parents were out too, apparently at the same social function as mine. So that evening I dabbed my cheek with my father's Old Spice, stole a tulip from my mother's garden, and made the most heroic trek of my young life.

When I arrived, Meredith was thrilled by the flower. Holding my hand, she led me into a large family room, paneled in knotty pine and carpeted in luxurious beige, so thick we could barely hear ourselves move. A gigantic blue marlin hung over the sofa watching us. I was so nervous I thought I'd urinate down the side of my leg.

We sat together on the sofa and watched television – I can't remember what it was – I was too conscious of Meredith. But we were holding hands and sitting close together. One moment during the nameless show, I felt her lean toward me, so close I could hardly stand it. I turned and looked into her face, hypnotized by the light of her eyes. Then we kissed. Just once.

That was my one and only night with Meredith. She told me her mother had discovered my flower and interrogated her until she confessed. As a result of our tryst she was forbidden to see me or any other boy. I was crushed.

The next year I went to a different school and Meredith moved; there were never any other romantic encounters between us. But I did do some research at the Enoch Pratt Library, studying the human anatomy from an academic perspective. Much of it boggled my nascent mind, but I had a fundamental comprehension of the facts of life.

Not that it helped me much. In sixth grade I went to an all-boys school. During my middle school years my only contact with girls was at the cotillion dance lessons my mother insisted I attend. In high school I did manage to kiss a few girls from Bryn Mawr and Roland Park on the isolated sun porches of their abandoned houses.

My classmates, meanwhile, were having no problems at all. George Van Houton screwed Matty Stuart in his parents' hot tub one November night while his parents were entertaining guests, including the city's mayor. Demetrius "Demo" Aristes enjoyed Megan Cahill in his attic bedroom, his parents' boudoir, the sewing room, atop a pile of dirty laundry in the basement, and underneath a chestnut tree overlooking the seventeenth green at the Elkridge Country Club. These were the masters, the leaders of the pack that girls were warned about. It all passed me by.

In college, the same pattern persisted. I briefly had a girlfriend my freshman year, but she was a good Catholic and she had sworn to her Mother, Father, Godparents, Aunts, Uncles, Jesus, every other mortal or deity she could summon up, that her virginity would be preserved until her wedding day. We gave it a whirl, got within centimeters of damning ourselves with the fleshiest of all sins. After we broke up, she abandoned her celibacy vow and turned into a libertine, bedding down with pot dealers, visiting poets, and the son of a Kuwaiti sheik.

But everyone assumed I had had her first; in fact, everyone assumed I had had a number of women. Perhaps it was my casual attitude, the fact that I didn't seem to boast about non-existent conquests that made my college friends assume I was getting my share of female treasure. Of course, I didn't feel the need to set them straight; their belief in my phantom sexual achievements enabled me to allay my fears that I was a sexual failure.

Then in my senior year it happened. We had decided to go to a mixer in September at an all-women's college just outside Philadelphia. I rode out to the campus in the back seat, sipping cheap beer and listening to Vinnie crank out juvenile jokes and boast about some freshman from Cape Cod with breasts the size of ripe cantaloupes. Of course, I knew better. He had confessed in very drunken moments his feelings of inadequacy and the fact that he too was a virgin. At least he had the guts to admit the truth; I never did.

The mixer was the typical plastic cup beer and wine kind of function that four years of college life had inured me to. But the setting was quite different, what looked like an authentic European castle. I wandered about quite a bit, sneaking looks into the cavernous rooms on three levels and getting fairly sloshed on tepid beer. Sometime late in the evening I lost sight of my companions. Some had wandered off with girls of their choice; others had just slipped away into the night. Alone, I drifted into an unoccupied corner room large enough to hold five beds and desks rather comfortably. Feeling tired and noticing no one around, I decided to lie down, letting the beer spin merry scenes in my mind.

Sometime later, my eyes heavy, I felt a presence.

"You're sleeping in my bed," a voice said.

I looked up and started to rise. In the dark all I could

see was a lovely face with long dark hair.

"I'm sorry," I said, beginning to stand up.

"I know you," she said. "I saw you downstairs. Are you with anybody?"

"Some guys from school."

"I mean a girl."

"No."

"Good. Lie down," she said.

She pulled another bed over to mine so the two were abutting, what amounted to a double bed. When she pulled off her sweater, her naked breasts flopped out like round mounds of fresh dough. She unsnapped her blue jeans, her stark white panties appearing above solid legs. Disrobing completely, she lay down next to me, drawing so close her long hair fell across my chest.

"Is there some medical or religious reason why you still have your clothes on?" she asked.

She was reaching over and stroking my hair.

"Not that I can think of," I said.

"You're not a virgin?"

I laughed.

"I suppose that *is* ridiculous," she said.

I blushed secretively at just how unridiculous it actually was.

"You want me to take off my clothes?"

"Yes, I do," she said. "I prefer guys to be naked when I fuck them."

"How about your roommates?"

"They're gone," she said. "It's just you and me."

And it was. She slithered onto my body and made love to me with a passion I had only dreamed about. My inexperience must have been apparent, but I remember her saying, "Thanks I needed that" when we were finished.

I never really dated Lisa. I slept with her off and on

for most of the year, in between her visits to her psychiatrist and her other boyfriends. She was a free-spirited girl and an enthusiastic instructor. There was little she wouldn't try once or even three times, and I was a willing participant in her imaginative forays into sexual experimentation. She would often ask what I thought of a particular activity, how it ranked in the pyramid of pleasure, as if she were conducting research in erotic studies.

Except for the occasional smile or hug, she seemed uninterested in romantic gestures or chatter. Her pet name for me was *Mr. Simmons.* After intense sex, she would often turn over in the bed and begin perusing a volume of Dostoevsky or one of her favorite feminist authors. There was no handholding or cuddling; our only walk through the woods ended up as wild copulation on pine cones. Her indifference to monogamous romance even led her to try to set me up with a few of her college classmates whose hormonal urges needed to be satisfied, she said. But I always declined the offers – it was too much like being pimped out.

When she graduated, she left for Europe and I lost track of her. I envisioned her as a long-term student, writing deep probing essays about deconstructionism, dropping in and out of universities, and scattering lovers of all ages across the European continent. That, I thought, was her idea of romance. In the end, though, she would probably settle for a nice stock broker in New York who could indulge her whims in exchange for her sexual expertise.

There were other girls that year. I actually went on dates, held hands, and whispered the occasionally sweet nothing. But none of these relationships ever developed into love; the spark just wasn't there and we parted ways without any acrimony.

One girl I went out with briefly was a part-time model. She was tall and lovely with aspirations of becoming a star in television and film. But she was too obsessed with her career and appearance. Every time she looked me in the eyes I was convinced she was trying to see her own reflection.

7

The letter from Shelly finally arrived on a lovely Wednesday afternoon. After opening the mailbox, I sifted through advertisements, and it dropped out of the colorful glossy layouts, a solitary rectangle of icy white. I reached down and caressed it, gazing at my name inscribed in royal blue ink. Upstairs, I struggled with the door handle, my heart pounding away, and sat down to read.

> *Dear Paul,*
>
> *I am now sitting in my meager walk-up apartment, having just spent ten hours researching an obscure precedent for the biggest asshole in the entire firm who said he had to have my input like ASAP. Then the idiot went home early to play golf.*
>
> *I want to thank you for your letter. It was really sweet. Nantucket seems so distant now, almost like a dream. I too had a wonderful time with you. I'll never forget that sweet rose you plucked from that poor lady's garden. It was so spontaneous, so right. I would love to see you again. I've thought of you often.*
>
> *But there's a problem, I'm afraid, a rather large one. When we met I wanted to be free, I wanted to be single and wild, open to whatever, not entangled. I thought it was over when I went to Nantucket and when I met you I dismissed it from my mind. At least I tried to .... I saw no reason to tell you; it would only spoil the special*

time we had. But then he called me the night before I left. You were out getting wine. It threw me off; I thought I had shut him out. Then he called me when I got back here to Boston. I guess what I'm trying to say is that I'm not sure about things. I think there is still feeling between him and me, some residual bond....

The proverbial bottom line is, I can't see you right now. I have to live this situation through.

At this point I stopped reading, my stomach having lurched. But I took a breath and read on.

I hope you understand my dilemma. I truly care for you, but I can't take that step right now. Please stay in touch; I'd love to hear from you. And try not to hate me.

She wanted me to "stay in touch."

That was a provocative figure of speech. She wanted *me* to stay in touch while her Boston boyfriend was still screwing her brains out. I wonder if she appreciated the irony as much as I did.

To celebrate the irony, I stood up and went into the kitchen, opened the refrigerator but I was out of beer. Then I remembered the goodbye party at the school and looked in the top kitchen cabinet, and there it was: a nice new big bottle of Absolut Citron vodka. A gift from my one-night-stand teacher lover. There was an irony there too, I guess.

I filled a large plastic cup with ice and poured a healthy dose of vodka. The first swig was rough. The next several sips were much smoother, a light kick of the lemon flavor lifting my mood. The second cup was even better. When I finished my third drink, I was almost a new man. But then I made the mistake of returning to the living room and re-rereading the letter. Though I was a bit foggy by this time, it still sounded the same.

I had to get out. I had to escape. So I put on my Orioles t-shirt, dragged on my running shoes and headed outside into the bright July afternoon. I started out walking but accelerated into a jog through the heckling glare of Inner Harbor Baltimore, down the edge of Pratt Street, past the high rise on my left and a couple of silver buildings of commerce. I broke against traffic lights, heard the howling horn reaction, and slowed down as I arrived at Harborplace.

At the amphitheater there was a modest crowd sitting on the concrete benches watching a street performer juggling bowling pins. I stood in the back of the concrete steps, sweating and watching him mount a unicycle and ride around the outskirts of the crowd making jokes that I couldn't quite hear.

I was about to sit down when a homeless-looking man approached and asked for some change. His eyes appeared almost opalescent, quite beautiful if you have an appreciation for the macabre. He was wearing very loose stained blue jeans and a deeply faded polo shirt. He could have been Ryder Scott in thirty years.

I searched my shorts for change and found a quarter. Holding the paltry sum in my palm, I glanced over at my new friend who was staring at my hand with perhaps the same thought: *That won't buy shit.* I had to agree. So I looked through my wallet and saw several twenties.

A phrase came to me then, a time-worn aphorism perhaps, but nonetheless appropriate: "Charity begins at home." Well, I thought, Baltimore was my home again and this was one form of charity.

"Here," I said, handing the man a twenty.

I watched him disappear with my twenty dollars. I wasn't completely sure, but I had the suspicion he was going to invest his new-found fortune in a bottle and enjoy an afternoon's worth of alcoholic ruminations. Perhaps, I thought, he might find the key to amending his life; perhaps his whole spirit might be renewed by my one act of kindness. After all, anything was possible in America. You make love to a girl for a week, hold her hand, gaze lovingly into her sea-blue eyes, cradle her in your arms in the salty-sweet air of Nantucket, succumb to the most ethereal dreams of romance and love. And now she's back in Boston keeping in touch with her boyfriend's penis.

I decided to watch the juggling show for a while, so I moved forward and sat in the middle row of the concrete seats. The show was amusing, the performer cracking irreverent jokes at the expense of the tourists who sat watching and enjoying his verbal abuse. For a while I forgot my own troubles. When the show came to an end, the modest crowd applauded, and the performer laid out an immense top hat for tips. Feeling generous, I walked up to his hat and dropped in another twenty.

After the performer and crowd were gone, I was left alone on the concrete. I stared out at the dark dirty water and *The Constellation*, the old historical ship that presided over that end of the Harbor. It was a lovely spot actually. Beyond the great old ship, Federal Hill loomed in the background, with its defunct cannons a reminder, like Fort McHenry, of Baltimore's historic significance in the nineteenth century.

I was thinking about making the walk up to Federal Hill to contemplate history and take in the majestic view. But as I stood up and started walking, I noticed an outside bar on the Harborplace promenade that I had not been to before. Uplifted by the show and my previous three vodkas, I decided to prolong the uplift and enjoy the harbor view with a few more drinks. It was certainly better than reading a Dear John letter from an ex-lover.

I sat at the bar which was about half full on this delightful afternoon. I ordered a double vodka and gazed out to the marina. After a very rough start with my mail delivery, the day was turning rather pleasant. The drink was crisp and a surprising number of lovely girls were walking down the promenade.

As I was enjoying my cocktail, I noticed a gentleman standing slightly behind me to my right. He was wearing rose-tinted sunglasses and a tight black polo shirt. Up close he had crooked teeth and a crop of frizzy hair. He reminded me of one of The Three Stooges.

"May I?"

I think he was asking to sit down next to me. I don't know why he needed to ask; that whole side of the bar was empty.

"Be my guest," I said.

As he sat down I was greeted with the fragrance of cheap cologne and body odor.

When the bartender approached, the new gentleman ordered a frozen rum concoction and asked if I wanted another drink. I said okay and soon I had another fresh vodka cocktail with a pretty lime chunk. I admired the drink and sipped fully of its wondrous essence.

"Thanks," I said.

"My pleasure," my benefactor said. "It has been a very warm day indeed."

He spoke formally with an accent I couldn't identify.

I noticed he was looking at my Orioles shirt rather closely.

"I'm an Orioles fan," I told him.

"I see, " he said, smiling. "It is a very becoming shirt."

I followed his eyes down to the front of my sweat-stained orange t-shirt. It didn't look very becoming to me, but perhaps it was a problem with translation from his native language.

I think he said his name was Ott but I could be wrong. After mentioning the fact that he had a PhD in Molecular Something, he launched into a serious and meandering description of the nature of his work which sounded rather esoteric and way too technical for me, especially in my state of mind. I noticed a badge on his polo shirt, and he told me he was attending a conference at the convention center about something or other, and that these meetings were especially significant and vital. Unfortunately, I was just a bit too vodka-addled to appreciate his contributions to mankind.

Once he had convinced me of his importance to the future of the world, he expounded on his experiences in Baltimore, the "glorious" tourist sites, the ball fields, the museums, the restaurants, the ships, the monuments. All rather pedestrian chamber of commerce stuff until he made some excited utterances about strip shows and the prevalence and conviviality of the local prostitutes. He smiled crookedly and became especially animated about those particular field trips.

I wasn't in the mood to discuss the seedy life of Baltimore, however, so I stopped listening to Dr. Ott and gazed out to the promenade and the passersby.

After a few more minutes of pleasant drinking and gazing, I noticed a girl with strawberry blond hair strolling by. I leaned forward and stared, following her with my eyes as she walked down the promenade. From a distance she looked like Shelly, too much like Shelly – same hair, same figure. Even her walk was the same. Unfortunately, as I watched her disappearing in the distant crowd, I started thinking of the letter and the mysterious boyfriend in Boston. I formed a sickening image of Shelly lying naked in bed with this strange man climbing on top of her, his dark hideous penis hovering above her pale spread legs.

As the image intensified, I felt the vodkas doing a bit of a tumble in my stomach.

"Are you all right?" Dr. Ott asked, his hand touching my arm.

"I just need to go to the men's room," I said.

I was a bit wobbly at first but I managed to stand up and stagger away from the bar.

Inside the men's room, I stood for a moment and stared in the mirror. A disheveled, pathetic freak stared back. Sickened even more by the reflection, I went into the stall. As I kneeled down, the disturbing image of Shelly with her mysterious boyfriend began to form again. But just as it was beginning to turn horridly vivid, I heard a knocking sound.

When I glanced back through the open stall door, I saw the face of Dr. Ott.

"Can I be of any help?" he asked.

I looked up at him. He was smiling with his crooked teeth.

I turned away and heaved into the toilet bowl.

A minute later, I got up and Dr. Ott jumped back out of the way as I left the stall.

I hobbled out of the men's room and restaurant, onto the promenade. Half blinded by the bright sunlight, I started to jog toward where the girl had been walking, but I couldn't see her. I entered the Pratt Street Pavilion and started glancing into the shops.

Finally, I saw her in a toy shop talking to the sales clerk. I entered the shop, knocked over a plastic "20% OFF" sign, and then I was right there in front of them. They both turned and stared at me with a look of surprised disgust. Maybe it was my heavy breathing and the vomit stains on my becoming shirt.

The girl obviously wasn't Shelly.

I mumbled some sort of gibberish, left the store, and ran two blocks. Standing on the corner of Pratt and Charles, plying his trade, was the homeless man with the polo shirt. Feeling a strange kinship, I walked over to him and touched his arm. He turned around, his body stench and alcohol-breath palpable in the heat. Like mine, I guess.

He had no idea who I was.

"Don't you remember me?" I asked.

He muttered something that sounded remarkably like "Fuck you."

Around us people were watching the exchange.

"I gave him some money," I said to one woman who was standing nearby. She appeared appalled and began quickly walking off. The homeless man staggered further away too. Even he couldn't stand me.

I drifted about the harbor, my head beginning to ache from the effect of the booze and the steady sun. Eventually I found myself standing in front of the apartment building where I lived.

"Are you all right?"

I looked up and saw a tall black man who had just exited the front door. I recognized him as one of my neighbors, a nameless face I had seen maybe four or five times before. He looked concerned.

"Fine," I mumbled.

He nodded doubtfully, smiled, and left.

When I went inside, I picked up the letter Shelly had sent. I decided to read it again. Perhaps there was some subtlety that I had missed, a turn of phrase that I had misinterpreted. But the letter was still the same. Despite some nostalgic allusions and dubious expressions of affection, she was still casting me out. I was just another romantic fool left fluttering and twisting in the wind.

I was about to tear the letter into shreds when I

decided it deserved a more dramatic disposal. So I carried it into my kitchen. A moment later, matches in hand, I burned both the letter and envelope in my stainless steel sink.

But as I washed the ashes down the drain, I realized that the cremation was a petty and ineffectual sacrament to my own jealousy and stupidity. I didn't feel any better at all.

8

I managed to avoid hurling myself off any bridges for the next few weeks, and then I started my life in sales.

The Canton & Canton office was centrally located in Catonsville, Maryland, with easy access to Baltimore, Washington, and the mid-Atlantic region – and only a twenty minute drive from my apartment.

I was bit surprised by the facility. I had imagined a modern warehouse, perhaps in an industrial park. But it was located in a rather dilapidated part of town and looked warn and squalid, like an old country school or an abandoned firehouse. The gilded "Canton & Canton" signage on the front of the building seemed excessively ornate, like lipstick on a pig.

After I entered the creaking main doors, I was greeted by a very attractive young secretary at the front desk who offered me a quick smile and pushed a buzzer. In a few minutes, Ethan emerged grinning from another door and shook my hand as if I were a visiting celebrity.

"Welcome to Canton & Canton!" he announced and began escorting me through the dusty dim hallways and offices, introducing me to a handful of employees on the way to the warehouse and loading docks.

"It's got old bones but a really great heart," he said proudly.

During the tour, Ethan told me that the "plant," as he called it, had served several purposes. It had been a moving and storage company, a greeting card factory, a weekly newspaper, and a few other enterprises that I soon forgot. Ethan said the Canton family had owned it for almost seventeen years and had put in "substantial improvements" although those improvements were not particularly discernible. As we strolled back to his office, I noticed a few overhead fluorescent lights flickering on and off.

Later I was given a laptop, a cell phone – and yes a car with air conditioning. My office turned out to be small but rather cozy, with a window, desk, computer terminal, and a painting of geese flying for their lives in some Chesapeake Bay marsh land.

I spent a week learning the fundamentals of the printing, publishing, and communications business from two of Ethan's key employees, Herb and Gracie. Herb showed me the production machinery, from the bottom to the top, you might say, showed me how the materials were created and stored and shipped. I worked a few days doing warehouse work, even a brief stint on the fork lift, nearly rupturing an entire shipment to Staunton, Virginia. Gracie showed me the company website, the basics of the computer programs, hovering over me with each step, demanding that I repeat steps over and over, assigning me tasks to cover the spectrum of possibilities, how to access inventory, manage business accounts, marketing materials, prices, etc. One day I told her that she would have made a great teacher.

"Teaching is bullshit," she said.

Exactly what my mother might have said if she weren't a former Richmond debutante and daughter of the confederacy.

After Gracie's expert training, Ethan took over. He explained different marketing and sales strategies, running me through mock sessions with potential clients, how to approach them on the phone, in person, lead-in, sales pitch, closing techniques.

Ethan could talk for hours, sometimes in a circuitous

manner, often going back to the days of his father and uncle, transitioning into current jargon about profit margins, changing demographics, marketing strategies, and future conglomerate activities that would catapult Canton & Canton into *Fortune* and *Forbes*. When he talked, you were included; you were part of the vast potential of his financial fantasy.

"You're going to be part of something big someday," he would say to me. "I mean truly colossal."

Of course, many of these dreamy declarations came at the end of a business day and after several cocktails.

But Ethan's business passion seemed genuine, and he certainly would have been more successful if he had not had another passion that consumed him equally as much. For Ethan, the subject of women and sex was seldom absent from his conversation for long, even when he was expounding on what was ostensibly a strictly business topic. He could detour from a discussion of a promising new billing system to the sleek firmness of a woman's legs he once saw in the Jungle Club at the Baltimore-Washington airport.

"That's my biggest weakness, Paul," he confessed. "I just love pussy."

We were sitting in a Rockville restaurant one night in my second week of on-the-road training. Ethan kept an apartment nearby (a "business expense" he called it because one room contained a few boxes of overflow inventory) that he used for entertaining his "special customers."

"You know I got married at thirty-five. Married a woman ten years younger," he said almost mournfully. "And to tell you the truth, I am not sure I would have gotten married at all except my father said that only a married man with responsibility could be trusted to run a business. So getting married was actually a business decision."

I wondered what his wife would have thought of that comment.

"Not that I don't care for Cindy. She's great. Did I ever tell you how I met her?"

"No," I said. He had barely mentioned her at all.

"Let's have another drink."

The waitress came and took his order. He watched her come and go.

"I took a short vacation to Jamaica. That's where I met Cindy. One day I was standing at the bar looking for snatch and I saw her. She was about twenty feet away and had a ponytail. And I just love ponytails."

He sipped his drink and smiled.

"What happened?"

"Nothing right then."

He had turned his attention to the waitress who had brought new drinks. She too, I noticed, had a ponytail.

"You were talking about your wife."

"Yeah, right. Well, later," he said, still watching our waitress walk away, "there was a group playing reggae at this club. I saw her there. Her face was a bit round for my taste, but her skin was clear and she had these big expressive eyes. So I did what I usually did, I sent a note over with a drink."

"A note?"

"A song lyric. '*You are the woman that I've always dreamed of. I knew it from the start.*' From an old group called Firefall. Works really well.

"Anyway, she raised her drink as if to thank me and I went over. I told her I was president of my own company. She told me she was working in the Carroll County Library. Still is, in fact." He drained his second glass of whiskey, swirled the ice, and stopped to think.

"Well?" I asked.

He was enjoying my interest as much as anything, I suppose. Having recently failed at love, I was eager to hear a good romantic story.

"So," he continued, "about midnight I took the librarian for a walk on the beach."

"What happened?"

"That's for another day," he said, smiling.

After my in-house education, I traveled with Ethan or Charlie Kohler, the other sales rep, through most of the Mid-Atlantic region for the next several weeks, zipping along through the parched summer landscape, alighting at various businesses, hotels, restaurants, and bars along the way. I met the customers, learned their backgrounds and idiosyncrasies. Then I'd call on a few myself. After a while it became easy. I didn't really have to sell so much as service the customers' needs.

Charlie was thirty-eight, a former tight end for UNC. About six-four, he sported a boyish expression, a slow southern drawl, and the sexual fidelity of, well, Ethan. Charlie was married for the second time to a receptionist and lived in Laurel, Maryland. His first wife had once been a cheerleader for East Carolina before she flunked out.

"A brainless twit, Paul," he told me one day as we were driving back from a trip to Harrisonburg, Virginia. "When we first got married, we lived in Chapel Hill and she worked in a bank. A teller. She got fired. You know why? She had a habit of cashing people's checks and giving the checks right back to them. Once she quit doing that, she started screwing up something else. But I'll tell you, Paul, she was one sweet piece of ass.

"I can remember our second date together. She had been working at this insurance agency as a secretary for a few months and one of the agents was retiring. They were all taking him to some striptease place in Raleigh. And she invited me along. So during the course of the evening one of the dancers came over and sat down next to us. The dancer was about buck naked, her tits just popping out over this little bra-like thing. And then the manager came over too. And you know what he said? With a straight face, he asks us if we wanted to go to an orgy. Just like that. 'Do you want to go to an orgy?' I mean just like you and I would say, 'Would you like another beer?' I nearly fell off my chair. But Carolyn was a bit shy. So she said no. But this is the killer. Get this. You see we had driven up there in her car. Anyway, she says to me in the sweetest voice you ever heard, 'Well, Charlie, if *you* want to go to the orgy, you can borrow my car. I'll go home with one of the other girls.' Do you believe that? I think I fell in love with her right then.

"Of course, it wasn't til later that I figured out she probably didn't know what an orgy was."

It was Happy Hour, an almost sacred time for Charlie, and so we pulled into the Sheraton near the airport, home of the Jungle Club, one of Ethan's and Charlie's favorite spots. You never knew what kind of crowd you'd get there; it depended on the arrivals and departures, but Ethan and Charlie seemed to know pretty well when to stop. On this particular evening, we were a little early, but by seven a crowd began to swarm in.

Charlie drank beer like tap water and scoped the crowd for women. Time drifted by. Fortunately, I had learned over the first week or so that if I didn't switch from beer to softer drinks after a certain point, I'd have a liver that looked like roadkill. Ethan and Charlie had apparently built up immunity; they could drink for hours. Sexually rabid to begin with, they were only goaded more by the alcohol.

At eight-thirty, Charlie's hormones were virtually airborne. We were positioned at the bar to face the entrance and the tables leading to a dance floor. There were all sorts of people crowded in by now, overnight businessmen in suits, secretaries, airport personnel, and flight attendants. Music started from a DJ, the lights seemed to darken, libidos trembled and shook.

He fell in love about 9:15. I know because I had checked my watch about ten seconds before he turned to me, and, with those large brown eyes twinkling, said, "Paul, I think I'm in love." This pronouncement, I had learned, was Charlie's way of announcing to the world, usually me or Ethan, that within the range of his penis had appeared a suitable target for his attention. Often this declaration of love would be uttered several times in an evening, love to Charlie being something less than a permanent emotion.

At this particular moment, on a Thursday night, love was a blond flight attendant sitting about five yards away with two other friends from the same airline. As we were assessing the flight attendants, our attention was suddenly drawn to the entrance. One of the largest human beings I had ever seen stood there for a moment, almost as if he were trying to figure out the nature of the smaller species in front of him. He began moving forward, consuming space as he did, ducking his head underneath a hanging plant that seemed about twelve feet off the floor. Dressed in a massive striped polo shirt and what must have been special-order blue jeans, his hair combed back in long oily ringlets, he looked to be a good six-ten and 400 pounds. He had a ragged beard that covered what appeared to be acne or knife scars. And his eyes were dark marbles of intensity under heavy brows.

He stopped at the edge of the bar where the tables

began, snapped his fingers, and in a few seconds a beer appeared. Leaning against the bar, he downed one bottle in less than a minute, and had another in his hand when a waitress came over and pointed to a table nearby. He sat down alone, the chair disappearing under his massive haunches. It soon passed along the patrons at the bar that the beast we had observed was a professional wrestler with the well-deserved name of "The Cretin."

Not long after that ripple of excitement, the DJ commenced his show. Charlie sent a drink and note over to the blond flight attendant. As with Ethan, he occasionally used the Firefall lyric, but tonight he chose a line from Foreigner – *"I've been waiting for a girl like you to come into my life."* He and Ethan had a collection of lyrics and sometimes debated which lines produced the best results. I guess it was their idea of intellectual conversation.

Upon receiving the note and drink, the blonde looked over and waved in gratitude. That was all Charlie needed as an invitation.

"Come on," he said.

"Not tonight."

"It's a sure thing, man."

I shook my head. I really felt uncomfortable in the role of predator. Besides, I think Charlie really liked going on the hunt solo; it increased his chances of scoring. He usually had only one night or even a few hours so he had to strike quickly.

In a minute he had positioned himself at the table so that the blonde was aware that although her friends were undoubtedly delightful company, it was she and only she that made the furnace of his heart roar with heat. It was an education of sorts to watch Charlie from afar, to see his electric smile and hear the booming rebel yell of laughter stir up a crowd.

Unfortunately, with Charlie's departure, I was left alone and the inevitable boredom that set in. I was never sure if I would have to wait thirty minutes and then head home or if we would have to take a room and spend the night. It all depended on the quantities of alcohol Ethan and Charlie consumed and their luck with the ladies.

That night as Charlie pursued his sudsy concept of transitory heaven with a live Barbie Doll, I began to muse about other matters, most notably Shelly Moran. I had not heard from her since the infamous July letter, but she tended to rise up like a ghost at times like that night in the Jungle Club, when I was alone and had just enough alcohol and empty time to be vulnerable to nostalgia and hopeless romance. I had even mentioned her to both Ethan and Charlie, who had shown empathy for my lovesickness and spoken of their respective wives with similar reverence. Of course, those expressions of affection were rare. Love had its place – at home. Out in the world of travel and sales, free-spirited promiscuity was the respectable path to follow. It's all right to praise the women of the hearth, they seemed to imply, but it should be done quietly and not after the first three drinks.

I watched Charlie start dancing with the blonde, his suit coat off now, and his body showing whatever athletic rhythm he had retained after sixteen years of self-indulgence. In a moment they blended in with the crowd and I looked elsewhere.

At the bar, people were absorbed in their cell phones, compulsively tapping out text after text. Across the oval bar, I saw a woman who resembled my mother. She seemed to be alone. Dressed impeccably and sipping white wine, she wasn't texting and wasn't interested in the twitching on the dance floor either. After she took a final sip of her wine, she paid her check and strode in her high heels out of the bar. Impressed by her cool dignity, I felt like following her out to get her autograph.

But then I might have missed the action. Because soon after she left, I heard a scream and looked toward the sound. From my seat at the bar all I could see was a small crowd of heads gathered near the edge of the dance floor. So I moved forward to see the action firsthand. And there on the dance floor stood The Cretin holding Barbie's hand like King Kong with tiny Fay Ray. Facing them was my colleague Charlie. As near as I could guess, the two men were discussing in rather sharp tones the relative merits of their claim to Barbie who apparently was the one who had screamed. She was flailing at Cretin who seemed barely aware of the blows; he was a bit more concerned with the threat posed by Charlie who moved forward to claim Barbie for himself. Around me was a circle of bar patrons, many of them actually taking pictures or videos with their phones, more concerned with their potential YouTube classics than with the plight of Barbie.

It was at this moment that someone – it appeared to be the bouncer – came running through the crowd from behind me and tackled Charlie, driving him about five yards away. Undoubtedly, he was a bit reluctant to take on Cretin.

"Get off me, you fucking pig!" Barbie yelled, slapping at Cretin's massive chest.

"Shut up, Bitch!" he yelled back. "You're mine."

Barbie was clearly terrified; her face was only about ten feet away from me now, tears and mascara mingling in streams down her cheek. Suddenly, without really thinking, I took a swift step forward. While Cretin was looking away, I grabbed Barbie's hand, wrenched it away from him, and we started running through the crowd. I expected to be snared at any time from the rear, but I only heard a smash of glass behind me and The Cretin screaming, "Get back here, you faggot!"

I think he meant me.

We raced out of the bar into the dull lights of the lobby.

"Come on," she said, leading us past the elevators to the stairwell. "I'm staying here."

We ran up the stairs to the third floor and down the hallway, still half expecting the monster to attack us from behind. But we found her room and dived in safely. Barbie jumped on the bed, grabbed a pillow, and hid behind it, trembling.

I latched the chain lock and stood listening by the door for any movement, but after a minute or two I heard nothing.

"I think it's safe now," I said. "Are you all right?"

She raised her head and peaked out.

"I can't believe it. Two assholes in one night," she said.

Two? For a second I thought she was referring to me. Then I realized that she was including Charlie with The Cretin.

She related what had happened on the dance floor, that it was Charlie who had drunkenly begun to paw her while they were dancing. She had to swat his hands away from her ass and push his drooling mouth off her neck. When she tried to walk away, he grabbed her and held her.

"He kept calling me 'sweet pea' in that whiny southern accent," she said.

She said he was squeezing her hands and arms and that he was totally intoxicated. He called her a bitch and a whore. That's when The Cretin stepped in. He and Charlie began the argument that I saw, with The Cretin grabbing her as Charlie had, telling her that she was with him now, that Charlie could go fuck himself, she was his bitch, and so on.

"You really saved me," she said. "Thanks."

She smiled, a beautiful messy smile, and started wiping her face with a tissue.

"God," she said, "I must look like a witch."

She went into the bathroom to clean up. While she was inside there was a loud knock on the door. I jumped nervously and Barbie stuck her head out of the bathroom door, a frightened look on her face. For a second neither of us moved or said anything.

"Sarah, are you there?"

"It's my girlfriend," Sarah said. She came out of the bathroom.

"I'm here."

"Are you all right? Let me in."

"Are you alone?"

"Keisha's here too."

When the other flight attendants came in, they took a quick unflattering glance at me and both hugged Sarah.

Apparently the police had arrived a few minutes after we had made our escape. They had taken both Charlie and The Cretin outside where the whole episode was related. The police wanted to talk to Sarah, but a guy had appeared, Cretin's manager or agent, and he was able to get Cretin to agree to pay some sort of restitution for the bar damage he had caused (He had thrown a bottle and broken a light fixture.) The police still wanted to talk to Sarah, but the girlfriends wanted to come see if she was all right first.

"I don't want to see any cops," Sarah said.

But she finally agreed and after the other girls left, there was another knock and two policemen entered the room. After glancing at me, they asked Sarah if she needed any medical attention. She said she was okay physically, just upset. They asked her what happened, and she told them the story she had told me. When the part about my grabbing her from The Cretin came up, they looked over at me incredulously.

"You know who that guy was?" one of them asked.

"Some sort of wrestler," I said.

"Some sort," the cop said. "Guy weighs about five hundred pounds. Took a lot of guts to do what you did."

I was still shaking. The more I thought about it the more insane I thought it was.

They asked Sarah if she wanted to press charges against either guy, but she shook her head; she'd had enough of both of them. After the cops left, the other flight attendants came back.

"Well," I said, "I guess I better go."

"No," Sarah said.

I think we all three looked at her in surprise.

"I mean, could you stay a while? I'd feel safer."

I was about to tell her about Charlie, that he was my friend, but I wasn't sure I wanted to ruin my status as a savior.

"We'll stay with you, Sarah," the girls said. "You've got a flight tomorrow."

It was clear they didn't trust me because they lingered there for a moment, fussing over Sarah while I stood there like a piece of loose furniture.

When they were gone, Sarah said she was starving and grabbed the telephone.

"What do you want?"

"I'm not hungry," I said.

I wasn't sure what I was. But I was very much aware that I was alone in a hotel room with a very attractive woman with especially appealing legs. She ignored me and ordered sandwiches.

She walked over to the bathroom. "Watch out for

room service. I'm going to take a shower."

Feeling very strange and left to my resources, I decided to flick on the television. Sarah finished her shower before the food arrived and reentered the room in a long t-shirt with a sailboat and the words *St. Lucia* in faded blue. A towel was wrapped around her head like a turban. Without make-up she looked paler and a bit older. Her eyes were lovely, a cat-like green. I watched her gather things up and rearrange the room in an efficient manner.

"So what's your name?"

I told her my name and then I told her about Charlie. She looked a bit surprised.

"What are you doing with that loser?"

She went back to the bathroom. I heard a hair dryer, and a few minutes later, she returned, hair damp but combed out smoothly, face enhanced nicely. She was really very pretty.

We ate on the floor and watched a mindless comedy station, sipping soft drinks, all compliments of the hotel manager who had heard about the incident. When the show ended, I got up to go.

"Could you stay?" she asked timidly.

I looked at her.

"I really would feel safer," she said.

And so we slept together – and that is all we did, Sarah slipping off into deep slumber a few minutes after getting into bed. At first, watching her sleep, smelling her sweet feminine presence, I was disappointed. I had begun to feel a deep longing for her. But as my own fatigue began to consume me, I felt myself growing warmer, prouder, I suppose. I felt like a tired warrior who had spent the night protecting the innocent from wild and uncontrolled beasts.

The adventure at the Jungle Club became, like all

legends, subject to alteration and embellishment. Proud of what they viewed as my heroism, Charlie and Ethan retold the story countless times, varying it each time, to assorted employees and barflies. Charlie's role was expurgated substantially; my participation was elevated to Olympian dimensions. In the lexicon of Ethan and Charlie, I became the Boy Hero or Boy Wonder.

The only inexplicable element of the whole episode was why I had not taken advantage of my heroic status and fucked Sarah.

"You should have closed the deal," Charlie said.

We were sitting in Colin's restaurant. I had been training with Ethan all week and we had met Charlie after a call in Silver Spring.

"Maybe I will," I said.

"You won't," said Charlie.

I told them I would have had sex with Sarah had she shown any interest. But they didn't accept that. In their minds, the girl was right there in bed with me so I should have fucked her. When I told them she had a boyfriend in Hartford, that didn't change their minds either. So what if she had a boyfriend in Hartford or anywhere else for that matter. I made the final mistake of telling them that she seemed shallow and superficial. Basically, I told them, she wasn't my type.

"Not your type!" yelled Charlie. "She was gorgeous. What other type do you want?"

"He has a point, Paul," Ethan said. "Besides what is this about being shallow and superficial?"

"Yeah," said Charlie. "Those are virtues in a woman."

I thought they were kidding me, but I tried to explain what seemed to be obvious.

"Well," I said, "they aren't the qualities I'm looking for."

"We're talking about fucking!" Charlie said. "Christ,

Paul, she was a flight attendant! Her whole job is flying and fucking. It's part of their employee manual."

Just then Colin Doyle approached the table.

"Colin, you remember Paul?" said Ethan.

"I do."

"He thinks Charlie and I have twisted values."

"I didn't know you had any," Colin said.

Ethan ignored him and raised his beer.

"I think," said Ethan, "it's time for a toast."

So we hoisted our beers, and Colin commandeered a water glass from a nearby table.

"To the Boy Hero. And soon-to-be graduate of Canton & Canton Academy for Sales Representatives."

"Does The Boy Wonder know about his graduation present?" Charlie asked.

"Not yet," Ethan said.

"Tell him," Charlie said.

"Paul, we're taking you on a trip."

"A wonderful graduation trip," said Charlie.

"Three little words," Ethan said. He leaned forward, grinning proudly, like a father about to bestow a grand gift on a deserving son.

"Dewey Beach, Delaware," he said dramatically.

9

As a boy I spent most of my summer vacations on the Outer Banks. My mother regarded the nearer resorts of Ocean City, Rehobeth, and Dewey as too plebeian. On certain occasions, however, when scions of Baltimore society invited me, I was allowed to go. But Dewey Beach had remained foreign to me, a mere speck on the map, sandwiched between Rehobeth to the north and Ocean City to the south.

The trip to Dewey that Labor Day weekend – my graduation gift – was reminiscent of an amusement park ride with two sexually depraved adolescents. Whatever mature instincts Charlie and Ethan possessed vanished with the wind that whipped over Ethan's convertible.

Charlie was in the front passenger seat, scanning every car in search of women, occasionally bellowing his rebel mating call. At those moments Ethan would drumbeat his horn and join in with Charlie. I couldn't help thinking about their wives, neither of whom I had met. What were these guys like at home, in the confines of domesticity?

When we crossed the Chesapeake Bay Bridge, I thought Charlie would convulse with joy, the blue-gray water below a first skirmish line to pass on the way to weekend debauchery. A few miles later we were driving through farmland and vast empty spaces that might well have been Kansas or Nebraska except for the occasional billboard announcing sun and fun at various shore hotels.

As we entered Delaware, Charlie pulled out a bottle of

iced champagne, the spray from the bottle striking me in the face like a cold kiss of ocean wave. We raced through Rehobeth first, getting a sniff of salt air, and in a few minutes we were at the scruffy edges of Dewey Beach.

No doubt there are genres of literature, erotic travel books perhaps, that document the hedonistic excesses of certain resort locations, but Dewey Beach deserves at least a footnote. At one time apparently drinking was permitted on the beach, and, according to Ethan, life was superb; but sometime in the modern era, hordes of barbarians on motorcycles descended upon the beach sparking a civil war between the Regulars and the Barbarians that was resolved by local bureaucrats who passed an ordinance banning drinking alcohol on the beach. This legal maneuver discouraged the invasions of the barbarians, but it had little impact on the regulars who continued their riotous drinking at the bars and clubs and houses that dotted the thin strip of a municipality, some quite respectable, others just shabby.

Having never been to Dewey, I was impressed by the lack of any clear organization to the town. It was more of a patch of shops, bars, and restaurants, with adjacent condos, houses, and hotels, all dropped on the edge of the Atlantic for human frolic and mischief.

According to Ethan and Charlie, and virtually anyone else I had ever talked to about it, Dewey was now a summer mecca of sorts. From Memorial Day to Labor Day, every Friday afternoon, the caravans from D.C., Baltimore, Wilmington, Philadelphia and points between and beyond, would begin their eager treks. Deserting their desks and offices, perhaps deserting loved ones and families, the weekend hordes would toss their beach gear in their trunks, chill down some brews, and set sail for this shimmering world of irresponsibility. After a few hours of travel, they would check their inhibitions at the border of Dewey Beach and commence to follow their base instincts.

And nowhere were the wretchedness and sinfulness more in evidence than in a bar called The Dead Duck. The entrance to the Duck is a touch unpretentious: you make your way down a path between a dumpster and parched vegetation to a gate manned by steroid addicts with shaved heads. You inhale the mingled scents of sweat, beer, and vomit that seem to hover like a mist as you wait to enter. Of course, you might not notice this at all since it's considered rather gauche to enter The Dead Duck in anything resembling a sober state.

Inside the gate there is a scruffy open courtyard with a few starving trees stretching their skeletal limbs toward the heavens as if desperate to escape. A band is usually on hand under a corrugated roof about to collapse, and the amplified music from multiple decades reverberates the hours away. Nearly every summer night The Duck is filled, over two hundred perspiring torsos, pinched and shoe-horned in at every conceivable angle. The drinkers drink ever more and the destruction of brain cells rages on until 1 a.m. when the patrons spill into the alleys to pursue more self-abuse and affairs of the flesh, or to pass out for the evening.

The contingent of three from Canton & Canton arrived Friday about 4:30 in the afternoon, a quiet time at The Duck, populated only by a few seedy customers and the staff preparing for the night's drinking.

The owner of The Dead Duck and host of the Canton group for the weekend, was Sam Bannion. According to Ethan, Sam had been thrown out of all the premier prep schools in New England, finally graduating from a public high school in New Haven. At that point he joined the army where he enjoyed a brief but eventful tour of duty in Iraq. After suffering a leg wound a few months into his tour, he was discharged.

After graduating from the University of Maryland, Sam landed a job with Canton & Canton where he became an immediate success. When he retired from sales, he started bar managing and a few years later he had enough money to buy a bar in Baltimore. He sat on it for a few more years, then sold it for an "obscene" profit when the property suddenly became essential for the erection of a "big ass corporation." With the profits he did some traveling and then bought another bar, this time in New Haven. He sold that bar and bought the Campus Beach Club in Dewey. He immediately changed the name and made a ton of money.

Sam was pushing fifty, his dark hair sprinkled gray. Muscular but harboring a slight paunch, he was nursing a beer and talking about his t-shirts. Each shirt had a picture of a dead duck lying next to an empty bottle, with "The Dead Duck" across the top.

"You see these shirts everywhere," he said. "I was in L.A. this past winter. I knew this guy who worked for a studio and he invited me to this movie shoot. Anyway, one of the actresses was waiting around for her scene and she was wearing one of my shirts. I asked her where she got it and she said a girlfriend back east. Then I asked her out."

"What'd she say?"

"She said she didn't fuck men."

Sam probed Ethan about the business for a while, even seemed to put in an order for something. But the business talk didn't last long.

"You two," he said, shaking his head at Ethan and Charlie. "Married and still sluts."

He turned to me. "I remember when I met these guys, Paul. It was about 1896 or something like that. Charlie was banging all this confederate crack. But Ethan was an absolute dweeb. He couldn't tell the difference between a pussy and a brillo pad. Right, Ethan?"

Ethan laughed. "Not quite. But you can believe what you want."

"I believe it because it's true."

"Speaking of the truth, why don't you tell Paul about the time you were engaged."

Sam shook his head. "Nope. Not tonight."

"It's a funny story," Ethan said.

"That's because it didn't happen to you."

"Come on," Ethan said. "For the Boy Hero."

Charlie prodded Sam as well, and after they all did a few shooters he told the story. It was a rather long cautionary tale, laced with pornographic elements, but I am abridging it here for the sake of brevity and decorum.

Sam had met this legal secretary named Carrie and they became engaged after a month-long whirlwind romance. Sam was convinced he had found his soul mate, that they would live happily ever after.

Life was sublime for several months until one day another sublimity walked into Sam's New Haven bar, a gorgeous coed named Shannon who expressed in no uncertain terms her disenchantment with her long-term Yale boyfriend. Though deeply in love with Carrie, Sam couldn't deny himself the spectacular Shannon whom he regarded as "ambrosia from the Pussy Gods." Soon he was intimately involved with both women, arranging his life to meet the needs of his bifurcated desires.

It had to end tragically. And it did around Christmas when Carrie discovered a pair of bright green boxer shorts – apparently a Christmas gift from Shannon to Sam – that had an indiscreet message sewn into them. Intrigued by that discovery, Carrie looked deeper into Sam's chest of drawers and discovered a not too well hidden stash of lust letters that Shannon had sent to her war hero, letters that Sam confessed were raunchy even by his standards.

Carrie slapped him across the face and walked out. That was it. The engagement was over.

"What happened with Shannon?" I asked.

"She got tired of screwing a war hero," Ethan said. "Went back to the Yale asshole."

There was a postscript to the story as well. A few years after the Christmas incident, Sam was driving his new Mustang in New Haven when he was pulled over by a patrol car. When the police officer approached his car, Sam found himself face to face with his former fiancé, Carrie. He couldn't believe it; his sublime little Carrie, all five foot two of her, was a New Haven cop.

"She sticks her sweet little head in the car window and says, 'License and registration, sir.' In her cute little police uniform. Christ, she looked like a doll dressed up in an S&M costume. So she goes back to her patrol car and comes back with a wad of tickets from speeding to driving with a faulty brake light.

"But you know what," Sam said. "Even then, even when she'd just dumped all those traffic tickets in my lap, I think I still would have married her."

The Dead Duck kicked into high gear about eight, the professional ladies and gentlemen having arrived from their assorted home bases, perhaps after a stopover at their condos for a spurt of firewater. Bodies flowed in and began to blur as the golden oldies band bounced from Rolling Stones to the Four Tops and into a blitz of blue collar Springsteen. I lost the older Canton boys in their rush to cash in on the throng of nubile young creatures.

In my new Dead Duck t-shirt, I circulated through the mob. Not long after my first circuit, I saw a neatly dressed young man pull down a girl's halter top. For a good three seconds her breasts hung full and pale under the rafters of The Duck before she nonchalantly tucked them back in and smiled.

In a back corner, there was a large group of thirty-something guys sitting at a table piling up cans of Bud Light, creating a pyramid, talking loudly. From what I could gather they were reminiscing about the events at a bachelor party. One of the guys, who was wearing what looked like a Burger King crown, suddenly stood up on his chair, waving his beer can, splashing foam all over himself.

"I come to tell the truth, the whole truth, and nothing but the fucking truth," he proclaimed. "To be the king, you've got to beat the king. You've got to put the dildo in your mouth."

Everyone roared and he ceremoniously raised the beer can to his lips and chugged it, his cardboard crown toppling off his head, his shirt and shorts a frothy mess.

Sometime later I found myself standing next to a little thatched bar where a different ritual was taking place. One girl in a bikini was lying on the bar while a feverish crowd of beaver-sniffers jiggled and bobbed. The girl was served a shooter poured directly into her navel. The liquid having been deposited, a crew-cut gentleman suddenly lowered his bull-like head and began slurping the fluid and mouthing her lower abdomen until the girl squealed with delight. Girl after girl – I stopped counting at seven – let her navel be suckled in like manner. Tongues and mouths followed the fluid into the crevices of abdomen lard and to the naughty edge of swampland.

Much later I caught up with Sam hovering by the upper bar. I told him I needed some air, and he gave me directions to his house.

"Find yourself a woman," he said. "You got your own

room."

I nodded thanks and slipped out into the summer air. I walked away from the lights, away from the frantic festivities. Perhaps I had had one too many nights with cretins of all types. I needed something placid. At least I thought so at that moment, on that night.

I walked up to the beach, a half mile from the howling hysteria of Dewey night life, kept walking until I couldn't see one town light or hear one tremor of an amplifier.

There are dunes south of the town's main beach, and I sat down on the cool sand, my head on the blurry rim of intoxication. Looking out over the stretch of beach and moonlit sea, I thought of Thor Heyerdahl and *Kon Tiki,* one of the first history books I could distinctly remember reading as a child. But I couldn't remember what he was trying to prove. Something about whether one group of people could have possibly made a crossing somewhere. Suddenly, I thought of Shelly in Boston. I would have given anything to see her emerge from the darkness, her hair glowing like the phosphorescence in the sea.

As I was thinking of Shelly, I noticed a young couple strolling down the beach. They appeared to be drunk and were playfully swinging their clasped hands up and down. They stopped for a moment and I watched them kiss. It lasted a long time that kiss, long enough for the young man to slide his right hand down to the girl's thigh and up her sundress where it seemed to linger and probe. A moment or so later, the girl pulled back, the guy's hand coming out from her legs. She spoke to him and they resumed walking again, hand in hand. Twenty yards later, they stopped and kissed once more in the darkness. I couldn't tell whether he was stroking her thighs again. I hoped he was. I hoped they would stop and make love on the beach.

As I watched them in the distance, I was reminded of

the beach walks with Shelly. I closed my eyes and remembered her lithe body pressed against me, her long hair in my fingertips, the taste of her lips and tongue, the smell of her smooth tender neck.

But when I opened my eyes I realized that it was over. She had someone else. There had always been someone else. All that week. Secrets of the female heart. When I looked toward the beach, the couple was gone.

I decided to find Sam's place. I trudged on through the sand back into the hellish lights of the town. The bars seemed to be emptying, the glazed denizens of the Dewey night life creeping homeward toward trysts and slumber.

"Hey, we haven't got any girls yet!" I heard someone yell.

After an hour so searching, I arrived at the beach home of Sam Bannion. The door had been left unlocked so I went inside. It was a modern beach-front spread with area rugs and nautical paintings under track lights in the living room. I followed the sound of voices to a deck that abutted the kitchen. They were all outside sitting on deck chairs, the master lovers all alone, while the grand expanse of the dark Atlantic rumbled in the background.

"Who the hell's that?" I heard a voice say.

I didn't announce myself; I just stepped forward.

"Dear God. It's the Boy Hero," said Charlie.

They were all sipping beers, their feet propped up on the wooden deck railing. They offered me one from a nearby cooler. I shook my head and sat down.

"You guys look lonely," I said.

"You get laid, kid?" Sam asked.

"Let me smell your prick," Charlie said.

"Smell your own prick," I said.

"Jesus Christ," Sam yelled. "I invite you guys here for a good time and you're talking about smelling pricks."

He stood up and downed his beer.

"You know, that reminds me of something."

We all looked at him.

"When I was in College Park, my roommate and I were working at this campus bar. Anyway, this guy and I had the hots for this fine, truly aristocratic Wasp chick. Tall, natural blonde. Model type. So we made this bet: first guy to score with her buys the other a steak dinner. So one night he comes into the bar when I was working and he had the night off. The girl's there and I see him go over and sit down with her, buy her a few drinks. I didn't see them leave, the bar got packed, and I worked to about midnight.

"The next day I wake up late and go into the kitchen to get some coffee. I see my roommate sitting there with a shit-ass grin on his face. 'What're you smiling about?' I ask him. He points to the table and there in the middle is a pair of black panties. 'Guess whose?' he says. 'No way,' I say. 'Yes, way," he says. 'Take a sniff.' And so I did.

"A week later I took the sonofabitch to The Prime Rib in D.C."

"Wait a minute," said Ethan. "You didn't actually believe he fucked her?"

"I did," Sam said.

Ethan stared in disbelief.

"You're kidding? Panties on the kitchen table? That's your proof? I'd have gotten a DNA test before I paid for that dinner."

"It was a gentleman's bet," said Sam. "He wouldn't lie about that."

Charlie howled.

"It's true," Sam said. "I believed him. I probably would have believed him without the panties."

"I wouldn't have believed him *or* the dirty panties," said Charlie, laughing.

"Me neither," said Ethan clinking his beer can with Charlie. "You got played, pal."

Sam just shook his head and turned to me.

"That's the problem with these guys, Paul," he said. "They don't believe in anything."

The next day the religious discussion continued. Charlie, Ethan, and I were all sitting on beach chairs on a cheerful spot in front of Sam's house, somewhat isolated from the main beach crowd. Ethan and Charlie looked hung over. I felt fine. It was a blue, clear day; the heat of late August calmed by low humidity, the surf regular and rhythmic.

"There are two types of people," Ethan said out of nowhere. "Those who love the sea and those who love the mountains. You know I spent a week in Colorado once."

"Christ, Ethan, what are you talking about?"

"Aren't we bitchy this morning?" Ethan said. "You go one night without getting laid and turn into a miserable bastard."

In fact, they both looked pretty miserable.

"As I was saying," Ethan continued, "those people out west used to get up in the morning and check to see if the mountains were still there."

"What the fuck's your point?" Charlie asked.

"I just couldn't see much to those mountains. I mean the worship of the mountains. Even when I was skiing."

"Who's doing all this worshiping?"

"The way people go to the mountains, the way they go to the ocean."

"They like to swim," Charlie said irritably. "Which is what I'm going to do." He lumbered off toward the sea, clad in a Carolina blue suit.

"He doesn't appreciate the spiritual side of things," Ethan said.

As I was watching Charlie dive through the surf, Ethan said something about his wife.

"I'm sorry. I didn't hear –"

"I said I called my wife last night. I really missed her."

He laughed and looked at me, almost embarrassed by uttering such an endearment.

"She said she's had enough."

"Enough what?" I asked.

It was a stupid question. I knew the answer. We all knew the answer.

Ethan shrugged.

"She doesn't know about the women."

"I wouldn't be so sure," I said casually. He turned to me quickly, almost in a panic.

"What do you mean?"

I was startled. "Nothing. I just imagine she must be suspicious." That seemed to relieve him.

We watched Charlie lumber back from the surf.

"Feel like a new man," he said, spraying sea water all over us. "You ought to take a dip, Ethan. You look like shit."

Ethan turned to me, smiling now, all thoughts of his wife seemingly expunged.

"We're both old, Paul. On the slippery slope toward our last rewards." He clutched his breast as if to simulate a heart collapse. "Okay, Tar Heel God, I'll take a dip."

With that, Ethan was gone. But he gave me a wink before he walked off toward the surf. I interpreted the wink to mean that I should keep our conversation about his wife confidential. We were kinsmen after all.

Sometime close to three Ethan and Charlie gave up on the benefits of sun and sea, and went inside to sleep and refresh themselves for the coming night's activities, a house party hosted by Sam Bannion himself, with the Canton contingent serving as guests of honor. I closed my eyes and lay back on my beach towel, and had just about drifted off to sleep myself when I felt the presence of a shadow. I opened my eyes and saw our genial host smiling down at me.

"Hi, Sam," I said.

"Sorry I abandoned you guys today. I had to make some arrangements for the party."

He looked out to the sea. "Beautiful day," he said. "Why don't we take a walk?"

We started off north toward what I imagined was Rehobeth. For a good while Sam was quiet, almost a different person from the night before. After a half a mile or so, the houses on the beach thinned out, the beach widened, the crowd reduced to small groups here and there. One isolated group caught my eye. Man. Woman. Both thirty something. Girl about six. Boy around three. Parents in beach chairs reading, glancing at the children who were popping about in the sand, making piles with shovels and buckets. Sam stopped, tapped my arm, looking at the family.

"I thought that would be me once," he said.

"Family man?"

"Hard to imagine, huh?"

We walked a half mile or so further, and on the way back we saw The Family again. This time the father was tossing a beach ball that looked like a globe to his little girl while the little boy was lying asleep under the shade of a green umbrella. As Sam and I drifted past, his eyes remained cast over his shoulder.

Whatever he was actually thinking, he felt the urge to chat about Ethan.

"Things aren't going too well at home," he said.

"What do you mean?"

"I heard him talking to his wife on the phone." Sam shook his head. "Great woman, isn't she?"

"I've never met her."

He seemed surprised.

"Our family isn't close."

"Lovely girl."

"Ethan said he met her in Jamaica."

"Jamaica? He didn't meet her in Jamaica. He was shit-faced one night in D.C., chasing a piece of ass all night long. Cindy was staying at the hotel, some sort of convention, saw him in the lobby staggering around helpless. She took pity on his soul. He's lucky as hell he met her."

I could imagine the scene, but I wondered why Ethan had lied.

"Anyway. There's problems at home. She's pissed off. Shit, the guy lives like he's single. And the man's got a kid, for Christ's sake."

Sam's voice was almost hoarse, and the effect from such a gruff man surprised me.

We stopped in front of Sam's house. He looked up at it admiringly.

"Always wanted a house on the beach," he said. "Ever since I was a little kid. Used to take long walks up in Cape Cod with my father. He used to point out houses he'd like to buy. Talked about taking summer vacations, living on beach-front property."

"Sounds wonderful," I said.

"Yeah, it did. But when I was twelve the bastard packed up and left. Haven't seen him in forty years."

He turned his gaze out toward the sea.

"What the fuck," he said. "I got it all now."

He pulled his Dead Duck shirt over his head, tossed it on the deck of his house, and headed for the water. He sprinted the final yards into the waves, dived straight in and swam steadily out through the breakers until he was far out into the deeper peaceful sea.

10

Evening settled onto Dewey Beach like a cool cotton shirt, and guests began to shuffle past Sam Bannion's vibrant American flag out to his large wooden deck now nestled in shade. The hypnotic notes of a steel band were accompanied by the soothing percussion of the steel-gray sea.

A lovely night, guests in fresh clean styles unlike the vagrant wharf-rat look of the Dead Duck. Collared shirts with logos, sundresses, Hawaiian bursts of color, tans of all shades lit by an inner glow. There were a number of couples but mostly singles, generally middle-aged men, younger women, some clearly college-aged. A graybeard or two also checked in, better dressed, yet looking every bit as thrilled by life.

Ethan and Charlie had revived, their torpor washed away by sun, surf, and afternoon sleep and no doubt the anticipation of quivering women in all their sweet finery.

"I think I'm in love," said Charlie.

It was a bit early for this routine to start, Charlie having barely sipped his first cocktail; but his eyes and glands had been stirred by the arrival of a bevy of young women.

"Which one do you like?"

The voice belonged to a tall, hawk-like gentleman who spoke with an Eastern Shore twang. He was ogling with his mouth open. Canton & Canton's elder sales force had found a compatriot. I listened to their discussion for a while. The relative merits of artificial hair color versus natural coloring; the distribution of height to weight, more specifically breast size to waist size; the contours of calf and thigh muscle; the wattage of smile and the glitter of eye.

Having been bored by this kind of discussion before, I walked over to the bartender.

"You work for Sam often?" I asked. He poured my beer.

"Five nights a week at the bar," he said. "Sometimes here for private parties."

"How are these affairs?"

"Parties? Pretty good. Sam scouts the Duck and other bars, invites the best chicks he can find, some big shots and regular customers, locals mostly. Good for business, I guess."

A while later, I was drinking beer, leaning against the deck wall, absorbing the sounds of the music and surf when Charlie approached me.

"Come on over. We need you," he said.

What they needed was a third male to occupy the attention of a third girl, an artificial red-head with large brown eyes. Her friends were blond and pretty and were apparently already claimed by Ethan and Charlie. I was going to recommend the hawk-like gentleman, but I didn't see him around. So I walked over myself.

"Do you own your own company too?" the third girl asked me.

She was chewing gum, I noticed. A strange thing to be doing while drinking a frozen daiquiri.

"No," I said.

"What do you do?"

"I work for Ethan."

"Oh," she said. "We work at Social Security. We help people find themselves." She laughed. Some sort of inside Social Security joke, I guess.

"Do you have a boat?" she asked suddenly.

"I'm afraid not."

"I love boats," she said dreamily, casting her eyes out toward the sea as if one were buzzing by in the darkness.

I guess I was supposed to say that I loved boats too, just couldn't get enough of them. But I wasn't sure what that might lead to. She might say she liked Corvettes and I would have to pretend that I did too. Then types of food, songs by U2. Pretty soon we would be announcing our engagement.

"What exactly do you do at Social Security?" I asked. I wasn't really interested, but I knew what my assigned role was. The gum chewer, however, was looking over at her friends.

"I'm sorry," she said, glancing back at me. "They always do this to me." I didn't know what *this* meant, but I assumed it meant abandoning her with a loser like me. "What did you say?"

"That you have lovely eyes."

She smiled and talked a few minutes about how that was probably her best feature, that her sister also had big beautiful eyes, that it ran in the family, you know, like genes or something, all the while chewing away at her gum. Just when I thought I was trapped into a recitation of her genealogy, I noticed that the hawk-like gentleman had reappeared a few yards away. I waved and he came over.

"He owns a fleet of cigarette boats," I whispered to the gum chewer.

She flushed happily and I slipped away, promising to return. I don't think they heard me, their conversation having accelerated into the fast lane almost from the beginning.

I found myself drinking and drifting through the deck, lingering here and there, absorbing patches of conversation and glimpses of comely women. In my meanderings I caught sight of a tall silver-haired man conversing with Sam. Just as I made my way to them, the elderly man slipped off toward the bar.

"Find a wife yet, Paul?"

"Window shopping," I said.

"You see that guy I was just talking to? He's been shopping a lot. Most of his adult life, I'd say. Been married four times. Has about ten million bucks, but he fritters most of his money away on ex-wives. He has a taste for young snatch."

"He's very distinguished looking."

"Absolutely. Money, charm –"

The silver head returned. Sam introduced us. Arthur Pace. Not Art. Arthur. He had a wonderful smile that creased his tanned and wrinkled face. Firm business-like handshake.

"I'm sixty-eight years old and haven't learned a damn thing about women," he said as if he were picking up the conversation where he had left off with Sam. He also seemed rather drunk.

We stood drinking for a moment in silence, nearly three generations of men who couldn't fathom the feminine mystique yet were now coveting them in a corner of a deck.

"When my first wife divorced me, I was still quite young," Pace said. "About twenty-four and dirt poor. But I had gotten married far too quickly. She was a pleasant girl, but I was too wild and stupid to appreciate her. Looking back, I wished I had stayed with her."

I wondered what had prompted this confession. Perhaps Sam had broached the subject before. In any event Sam said nothing in response, so Mr. Pace kept talking. It might have been therapy.

"My next wife was a model. At least that's what she considered herself. She reached the pinnacle of her career by posing nude for some cheap muscle magazine. The name of the rag escapes me now, but it was gloriously slimy. I thought she looked like a slut. I didn't mind her being a slut while she was with me, you understand. But her flings with other men became just a tad tiresome. One day I came home and found her fornicating with a car mechanic."

Sam looked over at him.

"You're surprised, my friend?"

"How long ago was this?"

"1988 or thereabouts. Truly wonderful time. I made over three million dollars that decade. Of course, that was real money then."

"But money couldn't buy love?"

"Oh, it could buy love, sex, people, property – just about anything. Loyalty and devotion too – up to a point."

"What point was that?"

"Car mechanics, I suppose. Hell, Sam, I would have bought that girl a Caribbean Island if she had asked."

"You never know what they want."

"Indeed you don't." Mr. Pace punctuated his remark by draining his cocktail, the ice clinking crisply against the glass. "I believe I need a fresh drink. May I get you gentlemen anything?"

We shook our heads and Pace strode off.

"Pitiful story," Sam said.

"Have you heard this before?"

"Regularly. He ought to go on tour. Or talk shows. 'The Lamentations of Arthur Pace.' You know, his last wife he met at the Duck, if you can believe that. She'd left her husband and two kids to become a free spirit. Then one night old Pace comes in and they hit it off right away. They even had their reception at the bar. I was best man, for God's sake. Marriage lasted about six months. She got bored. He was heartbroken, the poor bastard."

Pace returned.

"I must say, Sam, you have an attractive group of young ladies tonight."

"All for you, Arthur."

"Did I ever tell you about what happened with the last girl I met at one of your parties?"

Sam winked at me.

"No, Arthur."

"Well, it was an absolute catastrophe for me. I took her to the Marina Deck for dinner. One of my favorite places. But I'm afraid the clientele was a little old for her. She was getting rather antsy, I could see. So I asked her what she wanted to do. She said, 'Get a bike and race down Coastal Highway.' I said that would be easy, I knew someone who had a bicycle shop in Ocean City. Then she leaned over and said, 'I mean motorcycles. I love riding motorcycles.' Well, I hadn't been on a motorcycle in decades. But she seemed eager.

"I made a few calls. And there we were near the inlet with two ominous-looking Harley-Davidsons. She was experienced and she revved up in this parking lot and took off. It was quite dark and I was really having trouble getting the hang of the machine. By the time I got it started, she rambled on back and skidded to a stop. 'Come on,' she yelled. So I revved up and suddenly I found myself moving – very fast. But the damn thing was too much to handle, I couldn't get the gears straight and when I looked up all I saw was the end of the pier and I drove straight off into the bay. Lucky I didn't drown. Damn embarrassing." Pace sipped hard on his glass. "Never saw her again," he said finally.

With the music and the sea and the drinks, I began to feel rather cheerful – especially after Mr. Pace left. I watched the pairings form for the night, and with that spontaneous spark of libido that occurs to most of us men, I felt an urge to join in. The hour was approaching eleven, and most of the eligible young ladies seemed to have grown scarce.

So I departed Sam Bannion's house party to go to Sam Bannion's saloon. I made my way to the alley next to the Dead Duck where I had to stand in line next to a fresh pile of vomit and the dumpster. For a moment, I nearly walked back, but the line moved quickly and before I had time to reconsider, I was thrusting my ID in front of the Neanderthal doorman.

Inside, bodies were thick patches of tan vibrating and lurching to the sounds of a new band, something wild and manic. Elbowing and slithering, I made my way through to where the navel slurping was in full swing. I swigged a fresh beer and found myself caught up in the uproar as men nosedived into female belly flesh, amidst the cheers of the horny crowd.

A slender girl with long dark hair and a deep tan was suddenly thrust upon the bar, her breasts peeking out under the skimpy pink top, her stomach firm and inviting. A man with graying hair was upon her at once, his head bobbing up and down, slurping away. She squealed; the crowd roared. Finally, the bartender said time was up, and the man raised his flushed head, a wet smile on his face.

The girl climbed off the bar, swayed slightly, and tossed down a bright red shooter. She was directly in front of me, her gorgeous wild hair falling midway to her back. After her shooter, she swayed again, this time backwards, and the full torrent of her silky hair fell against my face and I reached out to grab her before she fell. For a second she seemed nearly limp in my arms and her fragrance aroused me. I held her until she had her full balance, and then she turned around. A pair of giant warm-brown eyes greeted me.

"Thanks," she said, smiling.

"Are you all right?" I asked.

"I am now," she said.

I started to speak. But she put her arms around me, thrust her wet breasts against my chest, and kissed me, an all-out oral assault. She tasted sweetly of alcohol. Finally, a few centuries later, she pulled her lips and tongue away, her eyes still focused on mine, young and almost dewy.

She took my hand and led me to the dance floor. Still high from my beers and the adrenaline of passion, I held onto her as we grinded against each other on the beer-soaked wooden platform, the band noise electrifying my desire. I felt as if I were lost in a funhouse of sticky lust.

The band took a break, and we stood sweating on the dance floor, holding each other.

"You want a drink?" I asked.

She said yes and we drank two quick shooters apiece.

"Oh, wow!" she said pulling me against her and sticking her long tongue down my throat again.

We stood kissing hungrily, our arms around each other and our legs pressed tight.

"Let's go," she said.

We left holding hands and ran to a nearby series of condos piled indiscriminately behind a food market and a liquor store. On balconies above us, stereos blared and bodies swayed. The Dewey police patrolled the area in strait-laced amusement, ready to haul in anyone with open beer cans, while all around them drunken fools staggered and stumbled home.

She pointed to an entrance near a garage and we fell up the stairs and into a well-lit kitchen area and then into a living room with a few other people playing an air hockey game and watching a ball game to the tune of some unidentifiable rock music.

She waved to her friends, and, dragging me by the hand, led me upstairs. We entered a dark warm bedroom and all I could see was a pile of clothes, hair curlers on a chest, and the glint of perfume bottles. The bed was a jumbled mess, and after she shut the door, we were in utter darkness.

We started kissing passionately, desperately; and suddenly we were tearing at each other's clothes. She pushed me onto the bed and the rest of our clothes were somehow yanked off. There was no need for foreplay. She climbed on top of me, a wild sweet mass of fragrant hair and flesh. After she mounted me, she started grinding slowly and then, finding her rhythm, rode me faster, wilder, louder.

The sweaty frenzy lasted for several minutes until I felt a hot urgent sensation and a deep feeling of losing myself into her. She went on a little longer and then let out a whimper before she finally rolled off me. She lay on her back, breathing deeply, her wondrous breasts rising and falling.

She didn't say a thing as her breathing slowed; she just slipped off into a blissful sleep. I lay next to her listening to her breathing for a few minutes, thought of kissing her good night. But it was over. So I turned away from her and fell asleep myself.

Several hours later I woke. The girl lay sleeping next to me, snoring lightly. I looked at her in the darkness. She seemed younger now, more sweet and innocent. Her face appeared rounder, her hair still a glorious mess. My head spun, my mouth was dry. I didn't even know her name.

I dressed and took one more look back at the tan sleeping torso. I thought of writing a note. But what could I say? "I'll always remember you"? Had I been less hungover I might have thought of something, but I decided just to leave. In the morning she probably wouldn't remember me at all.

Outside a bank clock read 4:50 and 68 degrees; the air still dark, on the verge of dawn. The whole carnival world of Dewey seemed shut down. At first, not a single moving car; then after I had walked a block I noticed some movement, a headlight, a jeep careening out of a parking lot, the screech of gravel. Another escaping lover?

I headed up to the beach. The ocean was still there. Still cresting white and rolling waves. The sand still grainy and moist. As I stood there gazing out at the sea, I thought of Nantucket again, of Shelly on the beach at night. For a moment I wondered what she was doing right now. Had she just rolled out of bed with her lover in Boston? I bent over, nauseated once more by that same nightmarish image that continued to haunt me. After a few moments, I stood up and took a deep breath, the brisk sea wind whipping me back into shape.

I let myself into Sam's house with the key he had lent me. All was quiet; the living room lit by a solitary lamp near built-in bookshelves. I paused to look for a moment. There was Grant's memoirs – right next to a copy of Henry Miller's *Tropic of Cancer*. Eclectic tastes. Imagine those two at the Dead Duck, maybe slurping a few navels.

I grabbed a biography of Jefferson and went up the stairs to my room. Silence throughout, doors closed, everyone encased in slumber. I lay on my bed and began thumbing through Jefferson's life, but I fell asleep.

A few hours later I heard a sound at my door, and when I woke up I saw the door open and the hall light flooded into the room, along with the dim image of a naked girl. Her hair mussed and eyes blinking, she looked a bit dazed as she walked up near my bed.

"Sorry," she said and giggled. "Wrong room." And then she tiptoed out.

It took me a few moments for the realization to set in: the girl was Kristen Duboisier. I had taught her as a junior five years before. I got up quickly, walked to my door, and peaked out, just in time to see the door to Ethan's room close.

11

September slipped by quickly, the first time in twenty-five years that I was not facing an upcoming school year. I was in real time now, functioning in a new, vast, and complicated financial universe.

According to Ethan, Canton & Canton was a company taking on the world. No longer was it a mere printing firm; now it was an "enterprise" capable of handling all the needs of an ever-increasing digital and technological world. The key, Ethan said, was to establish in our customers the belief that Canton & Canton could solve all their problems. Knowing next to nothing about business, I naively accepted this quixotic notion as I did most arcane pronouncements.

Ethan had begun gradually shortening the company name to just Canton. It was simpler and cleaner. After all, he said when he was quite drunk, "You don't call God, God & God. You just call him God." So he began promoting a new slogan and encouraged us to use it in all electronic and print correspondence. "Call Canton – the problem solvers." He was even thinking of changing it to "Call Canton – the problem solvers of the universe." I facetiously suggested he amend it to "Call Canton – God's problem solvers," but he thought that was bit too risky.

Whatever occupied Ethan's business mind, I must admit my job was rather easy. I had the responsibility of calling on established customers, those needing printing and publishing services. These customers remembered the elder Cantons and respected the company and the family. As a member of that family, I was routinely trusted and accepted. I usually traveled four days a week, dropping into the main office in Catonsville once a week for meetings. My business contact with Ethan and Charlie was mostly via phone; and sometimes Ethan didn't even attend his own sales meetings.

I discovered I liked traveling or perhaps the freedom of the open trail. On longer trips I'd careen across the beige byways, mostly interstates and the Baltimore and Washington beltways, listening to music, talk radio, books on tape. At times I would become so immersed in the music or the voices that I literally forgot what county or state I was in.

At home, I'd take walks along the Baltimore harbor and stop in at bars or attend other events that occurred downtown. I even went on a few dates, but they never seemed to go anywhere. I fell into bed with one of them, but it was an alcohol escapade not much different from the Dewey Beach encounter. I considered an online dating agency but it was too costly and too unromantic. Even Grace tried to fix me up with one of her nieces, but after I met her in the office one day, I knew that would never work out. She was too much like her aunt in all the wrong ways.

I met my neighbor, Chad, fashionably dressed, artsy, and slightly neurotic. He flirted with me at first, but after I made my preference clear, we became friends without the encumbrance of romance. Besides, he said, he had a long-term boyfriend named Davey. Chad was a set designer for several local theatres and through his encouragement and free passes, I expanded my cultural experiences over the next several months. One evening in mid-October Chad rapped on my door and offered me a ticket for a gala opening night at the Lyric Theatre. He had to be out of town and couldn't use it.

And so, on a pleasant Friday evening, wearing a tuxedo, I rode the elevator downstairs and stepped into a waiting Uber car for the ride to the theatre. I hadn't been there since my second year of college when I had attended with my mother who had season tickets.

Unlike my mother's orchestra seats, Chad's free ticket led me midway up the balcony, an indication that he was somewhat low in the artsy pecking order. The play was a comedy starring an aging television personality named Edgar Fletcher. It had a few light moments, but like so many modern comedies it depended on sight gags and predictable one-liners. It was, in short, television on the live stage. During the intermission, the gentleman sitting next to me, a black man about thirty-five, waited for his female companion to leave and turned to me.

"Rather dreadful, don't you think?" His voice smooth with a British accent.

I agreed.

"My sister dragged me here." Indicating the woman who had just left.

"Where're you from?" I asked.

He smiled.

"I was born in Jamaica, but I went to school and university in England."

He introduced himself as Stevenson La Plante.

"You don't recognize me, do you?"

I looked at him and felt a dim memory.

"We live in the same building. I remember seeing you once this summer. You looked rather distressed."

I remembered: the day I had heard from Shelly, the drinks with Dr. Ott, and arriving back at the apartment building.

"Yeah," I said. "It was a bad day."

A few minutes later his sister returned and the play

resumed. Mercifully, the second half was short.

As we headed out of the balcony toward the lobby where the opening night reception was to be held, Stevenson's sister informed us that she had to work early the next day and had to leave.

We joined the crowd swarming into the lobby and crowding the hors d'oeuvres tables and bars. Servers were also circulating with canapés and champagne. It was a pleasant affair. The mayor was there, a handful of television personalities, athletes, even members of the Baltimore legal establishment.

"This stuff is atrocious," said Stevenson, speaking about the champagne we were sipping. "I need a real drink." We walked to the bar and he ordered a gin and tonic and I had a beer.

"So, Paul, what brings you here to this rather dubious production?" he asked.

"A free ticket," I said. "And something to do."

That was the truth. Despite my new life as traveling man I lived a more or less typical single man's existence, hours of agitated loneliness and exasperation. And sometimes, during those hours, the enchanting image of Shelly Moran occasionally haunted me.

"I came here for a particular reason," Stevenson said. "And believe me it wasn't my sister's company. Her husband dreads these affairs and she wouldn't think of coming alone."

"Why did you come?"

"Women," he said decisively. "I came here to meet women." He looked over at me. "You aren't gay are you?"

"No."

"There are a lot of that preference in our building you know."

"It's funny," I confessed, "at first, I thought *you* might be."

At that he raised his eyebrows and laughed heartily.

"Gay? That's a bloody good one."

He stood sipping and smiling at the thought.

"Now *that*'s why I came here!" he said suddenly and firmly. He was referring to a woman of about fifty in a long emerald gown. With frosted blond hair and taut jaw line, she appeared nearly twenty years younger than the ashen-faced man on her arm. She was chatting with a small group of people.

As we were staring at her, she glanced in our general direction, almost as if she could sense our interest. Stevenson raised his glass toward her and smiled. She looked at him with the slightest hesitation, smiled, and then resumed her conversation.

"Mark my word, my friend, I will have that woman," Stevenson stated.

"You will?"

"I have had women all over Europe and America. I can tell in an instant when I will have a woman."

I had experienced Ryder Scott, Ethan, Charlie, and Sam Bannion. But none of them had spoken with the absolute confidence of Stevenson La Plante.

"When do you think you will have her?"

"It depends. If I speak with her tonight, I will have her before Wednesday of next week." Then he paused a moment, looked at me. "Perhaps you would like to have her?"

"No, she's seems a bit too old for me."

"Nonsense, man. She's a lustful, vital woman."

"How can you tell?"

"I can tell," he said emphatically. "I see in her eyes a sense of longing."

"Really," I said. "She seems kind of content to me."

He stood admiring her for two or three minutes, his concentration steady and intense.

"She's never had a black man before," he said.

I smiled at him.

"How do you know that?"

"In all candor, I don't. Not for certain. But her look gave her away. She did not see *me*. She saw a tall black essence. I've seen the look before."

"What look exactly?"

He sighed as if he were reluctant to explain a rather obvious social phenomenon.

"Most white women enjoy a particular fantasy: that we black men offer a wild and unfathomable bedroom experience, that we are just a half species above animals, forged by our Creator especially for fornication."

"That's what her look meant?"

"Yes," he said. "When they see a black man, that's what occurs in their subliminal mind. Right now those subliminal feelings are stirring. Perhaps she is already wondering what it will be like with me, a black essence. She couldn't care less about me personally. I am merely the embodiment of her fantasies."

"You offer yourself solely as a stereotype?" I asked.

"Precisely."

"Isn't that a bit – "

"Self abasing?"

"Yes."

"Why? If a man has blond hair and blue eyes, would he not exploit the so-called beach boy image?"

I thought about that. Since I didn't have blond hair or blue eyes, I wondered what stereotype *I* could exploit.

"Of course he would," Stevenson said. "We all exploit our particular advantages."

"But yours isn't an individual trait. It's purely a racial stereotype."

"And by taking advantage of it, I am contributing indirectly to the oppression of my race?"

I had read quite a bit about racial oppression in my academic life, but I had never quite heard it discussed in this framework.

Stevenson was smiling now; clearly he was enjoying the discussion, as a tutor might enjoy an enlightening discussion with a pupil.

"Well," I said, "I wouldn't go that far."

"Personally, I exploit all black stereotypes," he said. "For instance, there are undoubtedly a large percentage of whites who view the black man as lazy. I do my own work very well; in fact, I am an excellent engineer. Those people who accept laziness or even stupidity as a black stereotype are amazed I can do anything. Doing anything intricate or complex enhances their estimation of my ability. I am even more impressive to them, the latent racists. To them I am an anomaly they can respect. As for those people, liberals usually, who feel personally guilty about the oppression of my race, my exploitation of them is even simpler. I simply present my blackness and they practically genuflect."

He sipped his gin. "Either way I have turned my skin color into a distinct advantage."

"Apparently," I said. "You seem very confident."

"I am," he said.

We gazed out to the woman whom he had claimed.

"How will you go about it?" I asked.

"The woman? Rather simple, I'd say. I will walk up to her and tell her I thought I recognized her. Perhaps ask if she was in the cinema or on the telly. It is an old ploy but flattering. I will then get her name, smile, and engage her eyes. She will definitely be impressed by my accent, believing correctly that I am well educated and worldly. Then I will give her my business card. Like this." He reached into his coat pocket and handed me one. "I will tell her she may call me if she wishes. I am new to the country and have few acquaintances here. She will then feel more comfortable about my solicitation without acknowledging that she is submitting to her desires. I think she will call me by Monday or Tuesday. If not, I will call her Wednesday. We will meet in a dark hotel restaurant downtown not far from my apartment. It will be a three o'clock meeting, so the crowd will be minimal. I will impress her with my choice of wine, she will imbibe freely, succumb to my compliments, and in two hours I will be mounting her."

"It seems rather mechanical."

"It's sex, my friend." He drained his drink. "I must be off."

Stevenson laid his glass on a nearby ledge, shook my hand, said to give him a call, and headed toward the crowd and the woman. I saw her look up at his approach almost as if she had expected it; she seemed to slip off away from the women she was conversing with, her husband not in sight. Stevenson positioned himself so her back was against the wall and they stood, with her head tilted up to him, a smile on her face. She had not taken her eyes off him. She laughed suddenly, casually touched his arm. They both seemed to be laughing, but their positions had become more intimate, more personal. I must have stood there for about five minutes watching the unheard conversation, but after a while, I left.

When I returned home that evening about midnight, I felt a gnawing kind of loneliness; the whole apartment seemed a quiet testimony to my solitary and dismal existence. In my bedroom, I checked my work phone which I had left at home. One message.

"Hey, Paul, Ethan here. Listen, I know it's late notice, but I was wondering if you could come up for a cookout tomorrow afternoon. Casual. About four. Give me a call."

His voice sounded a bit jittery, but I'd have to call him in the morning.

Then I checked my home phone. That too had one message.

"Hi, Paul. It's Shelly ... I was just thinking about you and thought I'd give you a call ... Anyway I just hope you're doing well ... Take care."

I paced the apartment marveling at the miracle of her call. But the pauses in her message seemed to scream out for explanation. She didn't say she wanted to see me, or please call me. I had the urge to call her back, even text her, but resisted it. For all I knew her boyfriend might have been away for the weekend and she was merely bored. With that thought, my elation turned to irritation.

I struggled through a rough night and woke to a fresh morning light flowing through the curtains. Clear blue October sky. I got up and played the messages again, listening to Shelly's about a dozen times, trying anew to decipher her true meaning through the tones of her halting speech. Perhaps, I thought, she was drunk. The courageous thing to do would be to call her. But I was in no mood to have my ego deflated again. Perhaps an email? That way I could control my comments; I would not be subject to the spontaneous quirks of my emotions as I would be on the phone. In written form, I could be confident and manly. So I started writing.

> *Shelly,*
> *When I heard your voice on my machine last night, I thought for a moment that I had picked up the soundwaves of a ghost...*

I deleted that. Tried again. Deleted. Deleted. Tried several more times, each effort ringing false: too cocky, too romantic, too pitiful. I just couldn't capture my true feelings. After about an hour, I took a break and called Ethan. He answered on the first ring.

"Paul? Are you coming?"

He sounded almost desperate.

"Yeah."

"That's great."

"Are you all right?" I asked.

"Sure," he said, "but it's just a little strange here."

"What do you mean?"

He didn't respond.

"Ethan?"

"Sorry. Yeah, well, it seems Cindy's been talking to a lawyer."

"A lawyer?"

"She dropped Bryan at her sister's for the weekend, and we tried to talk it out. I guess she wants me around more. I guess she felt out of the loop."

I thought of Ethan with my former student at Dewey Beach. Yes, Cindy was *way* out of the loop.

"So you're having a cookout?"

"Yeah. Thought that might reassure her a bit. Charlie is bringing his wife. Couple of neighbors."

"Do you think a cookout will do it?"

He disappeared for a second.

"Sorry. Yeah. I mean I don't know. Shauna's been calling too."

"Who?"

"The girl from D.C. You met her at Colin's place."

"Why is she calling?"

"She's late," he whispered.

"Late for what?" I asked.

"Christsake, Paul. Late for her fucking period."

"Does Cindy know about her?"

"Not for sure, I don't think. That's not the main thing anyway. It's me."

He had that right.

"So you think having a cookout —"

"Any fucking thing! I've got to make her feel she's part of my life, I guess. She mentioned the fact that she'd never met your side of the family. I told her it was just you and your mother."

"That's not your fault really."

"I told her that. But that's why it's so important you come up."

He gave me directions and hung up, apparently believing that a cookout and my appearance at it would somehow heal his marital problems. I couldn't quite grasp that sort of delusional thinking, so I returned to my own personal delusion: the email to Shelly. But I kept deleting again and again.

Frustrated, I decided to get out. I took the elevator downstairs, walked up the street to the Walter's Art Gallery, looked at a few ancient weapons, antique jewelry, stopped at the gift shop. About to leave, I got a great idea. Simple really. A postcard from Baltimore. Picture of the harbor, blue and lovely. Brief message:

> *Hi Shelly,*
> *Enjoying life in the city and my new*
> *job. Hope you are doing well in school.*
> *If you're going to be in the area, drop*
> *in. Love to see you!*
> *Best, Paul."*

It came to me in an instant. Cool, confident, and concerned. Wrote it out right there, got a stamp from the gift shop, mailed it on the way back to my apartment. I felt like whistling.

12

Driving to Ethan's house later that afternoon, I felt a rejuvenation matched by the blueness of the day and the crisp red and gold foliage that fringed the highway. I imagined myself driving to pick up Shelly for a date, an afternoon football game, and as I pull up to her house, she steps out into the light, running off the front porch and there in front of me, a fresh, rosy-cheeked wonder, her hair the color of the gold-red leaves, her eyes blue and clear as the autumn sky.

That fantasy propelled me along as I followed Ethan's directions a few miles south of Pennsylvania. A few quick turns later through tree-lined roads and I was there. A two-story stone house set back from the main road, with a neat white fence, a well-kept line of shrubbery, and an acre of lush lawn.

Walking toward the party on the back deck, I saw Charlie in a Carolina sweatshirt, his large hand clasping a can of beer. He saw me and waved.

"It's the Boy Hero!" he rebel-yelled.

I stepped up onto the deck and Ethan ran up to me. He was wearing a new apron and an expression of pure gratitude. I actually felt like a hero.

"Glad you could make it," he said and shook my hand. "Come on over and meet Cindy."

He led me across the broad expanse of the deck. Light rock music mingled with the smoke from an expensive-looking gas grill. It looked new and I wondered if Ethan had purchased it solely for this special marriage-saving event.

He led me past six or seven other guests to a woman leaning against the deck wall. Cindy was drinking wine and chatting with a white-haired woman. Ethan rushed through the introduction to the older woman, nearly shoving her out of the way so he could present me to his wife.

When I looked at Cindy up close, I was struck by her wondrous eyes – a vibrant, enchanting aqua color.

"This is my cousin Paul," Ethan said proudly.

"It's nice to meet you," I said.

"Yes. I was wondering if you actually existed."

Her smile matched her eyes, a teasing twinkle that made you think you were with an old friend with a wry sense of humor. She wasn't classically beautiful, but her fresh natural loveliness was just as captivating.

"I hear you went to Penn," she said.

"I did."

She told me she had gone to Drexel where her father was a Chemistry professor.

"I didn't inherit the science genes though. To me the Periodic Table is a piece of antique furniture."

"It is," I said. "My mother has one in her living room."

She laughed. "Another science moron. You're my kind of guy."

We chatted a bit about Philadelphia, the proximity of the schools, restaurants, bars. She told me she had been an English major and had taken library science courses. She had thought about teaching, she loved reading. How had I liked teaching? What books had I read recently? Sometime during the discussion, Ethan thrust a beer in my hand and patted me on the back again. But for most of the time Cindy and I were alone in the corner of the deck. I could have talked with her for hours. She was smart and witty, with an engaging flirtatiousness that made me think I was truly something special. I was disappointed when she excused herself to go inside for a heavier sweater.

When she left, I walked over to Charlie who was tending the grill in Ethan's temporary absence.

"Did you hear what's going on?" he asked.

"You mean Ethan and Cindy?"

"That's old news," he said. "The real news is Ethan has the IRS sniffing around."

"Why?"

"He wouldn't say. He keeps that stuff pretty hush-hush. He huddles with that accountant Igor."

"You mean Calvin?"

"Looks more like an Igor to me. Guy seems to be a little sneaky. Wouldn't surprise me if they both took a few short cuts here and there."

At that moment Charlie's wife came over. Dressed in tight designer blue jeans, heels, with pronounced make-up, Annette was the artificial counterpoint to Cindy's casual freshness. Charlie stared at his wife's figure as if as if she were a fine cut of beef. I didn't know much about his second wife; he only talked about his first.

"Hi," she said. "This sure is a lovely place, isn't it?"

She had an airy, breathy voice. Not so much southern as country. Close up, her eyes were embellished with so many eye-lining flourishes that I found myself counting the different colors. Her hair too was tinted with multi-colored layers, I suppose to hide signs of gray. There was nothing subtle about her appearance; she would stand out in a night club or bar, which is where I assume Charlie met her.

I met a few of the other guests and neighbors and was chatting to one about the Ravens when I saw Cindy come back out followed by Ethan carrying large grill tongs and still wearing his apron. She walked ahead of him, sipping wine while he was talking, seemingly uninterested in his chatter. She walked over to a guest, started talking to her, and Ethan was left standing with the greasy grill implement in his hands

A few drinks later the cool sunset drove us all inside the house, and we spread out throughout the kitchen and family room.

I was with Cindy and another woman talking about movies. I casually mentioned that I had just attended a play at the Lyric.

"We used to have season tickets," Cindy said. "But Ethan never seemed to be able to make it. Then we had Bryan and living so far out −"

"There are a lot of small theatres too," I said. "I never realized how many. I've gone to a few plays. Usually they're pretty inexpensive and small; never a bad seat."

"You know, I used to act in college," Cindy said.

"Really?" the neighbor said, surprised.

"Hard to believe. But I really enjoyed it."

"What were you in?"

She sipped her wine. Looked down at it with a wistful grin. "Oh, basically minor parts. I thought I had a chance at a major role once but didn't get it. I was dreadfully depressed." She laughed.

"What role?"

"Laura in *The Glass Menagerie*. It's probably best I didn't get it. I might be in Hollywood reading about my gentleman callers in *People* magazine."

"You ought to try out," I said. "Local theatres have auditions all the time. All kinds of plays."

Cindy shook her head.

"There's not enough time," she said. "With work and Bryan."

"I'd like to meet Bryan," I said.

"He's with my sister in York," she said.

Ethan came over and put his arms around his wife.

"How are you two getting along?"

Cindy ignored him so the other woman spoke up.

"That chicken smells divine, Ethan."

"Be ready in a minute," he said, giving Cindy a kiss beneath the ear as he left.

After Ethan was gone, Cindy laughed. "He's never cooked a thing in his life. He's never even made a bowl of cereal for his son."

The dinner was adequate at best, much of the chicken so overdone it was inedible.

As we were eating, I looked over at Cindy who was standing with an older male neighbor. She caught my eye, picked up a piece of burned chicken, and made a gagging sign. I laughed and held up a charred spear of asparagus that Ethan had apparently tossed on the grill to display his culinary virtuosity.

After dinner, the neighbors and non-Canton company guests gradually drifted out.

"Why don't we shoot some pool?" Ethan said.

"Oh, you have a pool table too?" said Annette in her breathy girlish voice.

I was standing with Cindy chatting, but when we heard Annette's voice, we both turned and looked at her.

"In the basement," said Ethan.

As we headed downstairs, Cindy whispered in my ear: "Is she for real?"

"I think so," I whispered back.

"She's like Marilyn Monroe doing Dolly Parton."

Downstairs was a large oak-paneled room with a gas fireplace, a bar, and a pool table situated in the center of the room. On the periphery were a sofa, a flat-screen television, and a musical console with speakers. Annette and I sat on the bar stools while Cindy went behind the bar, pouring herself another glass of wine and Annette a rum and coke. When she offered me a beer, I said no thanks.

Suddenly the room exploded into country music and Charlie let out his rebel yell. Ethan quickly walked over and adjusted the sound to a human level. Doing a bit of a dance to the music, Charlie came over, lifted Annette off the bar stool, and started twirling her about.

Ethan watched the dancers frolic about a bit before he walked over to Cindy and me.

"You playing, Paul?"

"You all go ahead," I said. "I'll watch."

He turned to his wife.

"How about you, Babe?"

" '*Babe*'?" she said, pronouncing the word as if it were a racial slur. "Since when have you ever called me *Babe*?"

"What's wrong with Babe?" Ethan asked.

Cindy laughed and sipped her wine. She looked over at me, smiling. "I'm a Babe, Paul. I was a bitch this morning. Now I'm a Babe."

I had to smile too but when I looked over at Ethan he wasn't amused. He grabbed a drink from the bar and walked away to watch Charlie and Annette.

Annette was squealing as her husband danced her around the room, grabbing her ass, nuzzling her neck and sticking his tongue in her ear. During one intricate dance move, she jumped up, wrapped her legs around Charlie's hips, and actually started dry humping him. It was almost too grotesque for words.

Cindy watched the antics a moment and leaned over toward me, laughing. "Look at Ethan," she whispered. "He just loves this low-class depravity. It can't get too slutty for him." Ethan did seem enthralled. Watching him, I wondered how much Cindy knew about Ethan's own personal depravity, the women he chased and screwed away from home. She must have her suspicions, I thought. That must be why she's talking to lawyers.

Cindy stepped out from the bar toward the pool table and racked the balls. After she chose a cue stick from the case on the wall, she looked over at the guests who were still at it, Charlie clutching Annette from behind now, a beer tucked in his hand, slurping her neck, grinding his loins against her ass.

"Hey, Bubba. The orgy's over," Cindy yelled to Charlie who appeared just a few minutes away from stripping his wife bare and banging her on the basement floor.

"I'm not sure they want to play," I said.

"Not pool anyway. Maybe *Hide the Salami.*"

Annette heard her and looked up, laughing.

" 'Hide the Salami'? What's that?" she asked.

"It's my wife's idea of a joke," Ethan said, grabbing a cue stick off the wall.

"Oh, Babe," Cindy said. "I've always thought *you* were my idea of a joke."

Ethan glared at her, gripping the cue stick firmly. For a moment I thought he might swing it at her. I started to get up.

"Ethan – " I said.

He turned toward me, his hand up.

"It's okay, Paul," he said. "Cindy's just full of jokes tonight."

"Maybe we ought to call it a night," I said.

"No, Cindy wants to play, so we'll play. First team to get fifty balls in wins. Any color."

"Teams?" Cindy said. "What teams?"

"Couples," Ethan said.

"Couples?" Cindy said, laughing. "I don't think so."

Annette squealed as Charlie seemed to be biting her ear. We all glanced at the spectacle.

"I know," Cindy said. "How about Babes vs Bubbas."

"Bubbas?" Ethan said.

Cindy ignored him and turned toward me. "Why

don't you keep score, Paul? I don't think these guys can count to fifty."

Cindy turned to the table. She took a practice stroke and slammed the cue ball hard, smashing the triangle of balls. Two dropped in.

"Good shot," I said.

She smiled at me.

"I played a lot in college," she said. "You remember Jimmer's?"

Jimmer's was a student dive bar in Philadelphia with several free pool tables in one of the back rooms.

"Sure," I said. "But I never played much."

"I did," she said. "I used to date the owner."

"You dated who?" Ethan asked sharply, his jealousy piqued.

Cindy ignored him. I knew she was joking, of course. Jimmers was owned by a seventy year-old lesbian.

"Your turn, Babe," Cindy said, turning to Annette, whose ass appeared firmly attached to her husband's crotch. Charlie gave Annette a final little thrust, and she let out a little high-pitched giggle. As she walked toward the table, she gazed into a Budweiser wall mirror and adjusted her hair.

"God, I look awful," she said, hoping I guess for a compliment. But Ethan was still staring at Cindy and Charlie was grabbing himself another beer. I just kept my mouth shut.

Cindy met Annette by the table. "This is a cue stick," Cindy said. "Just pretend it's a really big dick."

Annette laughed. "I've never seen a dick that big."

Cindy demonstrated how to hold the cue stick. But when Annette tried to strike the cue ball, she missed everything.

"Oh, damn," she said.

"Try again," said Ethan.

She did, nudging the cue ball into a minor collision.

"Way to go," Charlie said. "Another drink and you'll be knocking them all in."

Charlie poured Annette a strong rum and coke. That seemed to revive her spirits and he began nuzzling her from the back again while she drank and watched Ethan dab chalk on his cue stick.

Cindy turned away from the table and walked past me behind the bar. She poured herself another wine and put her arm around my shoulder. She smelled wonderful. An alluring floral scent.

She leaned toward me, nodding at Annette who was back with Charlie, grinning. "So what's your assessment, Paul?" she whispered.

"About Annette?"

"Yes," she said. "I don't know much about genetics, but my wild guess is in-breeding. First cousins, maybe. What do you think?"

"I don't know. I'm just a science moron," I said.

She laughed and patted my shoulder. "We both are. For all we know she could be a genius."

Ethan was a very good player and he ran several balls in a row. After each ball fell, he cast a glance over to the bar, hoping, I guess, to hear a word of approval from Cindy who appeared unmoved by her husband's pool prowess.

But Annette *had* noticed. She stepped away from Charlie's grasp to watch Ethan play.

"Wow!" Annette said loudly. "You're good," watching Ethan hit a few more balls in. "*Really good!*"

She was smiling at Ethan, clearly impressed.

Ethan smiled back at Annette. He waggled the stick some more, dabbed a bit more chalk, all the while examining the table as if he were a surgeon about to perform delicate surgery. Then he turned away, reached up, and dramatically pulled the bridge stick off the wall. With meticulous care, he started arranging and adjusting the bridge to set up his shot, his face a mask of intense concentration.

"Christ, Ethan, hit the fucking shot," said Charlie, who wasn't smiling and didn't seem too impressed.

"He's trying to show off," Cindy said in my ear. "For the country girl."

"Maybe for you too," I whispered back.

"How romantic," she said. "I'm practically swooning."

After he took about ten slow and deliberate practice strokes, Ethan finally let go. But the bridge shot missed completely.

Annette let out a very disappointed "Awww" sound, as Charlie approached her from behind to resume ass grinding.

While they were busy, Cindy walked to the pool table.

"It's not your turn," Ethan said, clearly miffed by his dramatic failure.

"I know Babe, but I just have to try one of those cool bridge shots. Like the one you just fucked up."

Ethan looked as if he were about to say something nasty but thought better of it. He just shook his head and walked to the bar next to me. Grabbing a bottle of Jack Daniels, he poured it straight into a rocks glass and chugged it down. Colin Doyle would have been impressed. He didn't dribble at all.

"I've never seen Cindy this drunk," Ethan said to me.

"She's just in a good mood."

"She's drunk."

He was probably right, she was drunk, but I felt the need to defend her. Maybe it was because I knew way too much about Ethan's outside life, maybe it was because I really liked Cindy.

While he poured another drink, Cindy made a simple

bridge shot and missed another.

"Your turn, Buddy!" he yelled to Charlie.

Charlie reluctantly let go of Annette, took a deep beer swig, and stumbled to the table. He dabbed some chalk, took some very masculine practice strokes, his eyes dark and hard. He suddenly struck the cue ball, but he hit it off center and the white ball squibbed weakly into a few banks and pitifully died.

Ethan laughed. "Great shot!"

Charlie stared at the table a second before screaming out "SHEEEIT," audible over the country music and possibly into the next county.

Cindy walked over to him and patted him on the back, walking him back from the table. He looked as if he had dropped a touchdown pass in the end zone.

"It's okay, Bubba," she said. "It's okay."

"My turn!" Annette yelled.

She clicked her heels over to the table and started practicing her stroke, her butt wiggling in front of Ethan. I was watching her butt and thought Ethan was too, until I turned to him and noticed he was staring at Charlie and Cindy who were laughing and slow dancing awkwardly between the sofa and television.

Annette stroked the cue ball against a clump of balls, and one miraculously fell into the corner pocket. She let out a yelp but nobody seemed to care. When she turned around, she noticed Cindy and her husband dancing.

"What are they doing?" she asked as she walked over to us.

"Dancing," I said.

"She's just trying to make me jealous," Ethan said. "Have another drink." He made her a stiff drink and she chugged half the glass.

"Well, why don't *we* dance?" she said.

"Sure," Ethan said. "Why not."

And so I sat and watched Annette and Ethan dancing at one end of the room and Charlie and Cindy dancing at the other end. The alcohol was flowing, the hormones were jumping, and I felt as if I were watching a slow train wreck rapidly speeding up. Fortunately, the song ended and the couples separated.

"Whose turn is it?" yelled Annette as Charlie grabbed her by the arm and pulled her away.

Cindy came over to refill her wine glass, and she and Ethan were standing in front of me at the bar.

"Why'd you dance with him?" asked Ethan, his face turning red.

"Oh, Babe," Cindy said. "You look so serious."

"Stop all this *Babe* shit for Christ's sake."

"I'm just having a good time, Babe. You know what a good time is don't you?"

"What are you talking about?"

Cindy turned to me and smiled.

"He doesn't know what I'm talking about, Paul."

I stared into her lovely aqua eyes and I thought maybe she *did* know about Ethan.

"You're just drunk," Ethan said. "To get back at me or something."

" '*Or something*.'? "

"Yeah. Something."

"Oh, Babe, what can I say. You're just so *deep*."

This colloquy was suddenly interrupted by a scream from the corner of the room.

We all looked over to Annette, in time to see Charlie slap her on the side of the head. Annette staggered on her heels and fell against the sofa.

I jumped off the bar stool and ran over and grabbed Charlie, pulling him away from Annette.

"Take it easy," I said to him.

"Goddam slut," he said toward Annette. It was almost

a growl. He pulled his arm out of my grasp, stepped back a second, looking at his wife on the floor. Red-faced and enraged, he turned and stalked away up the stairs.

Ethan was tending to Annette who was getting to her feet. Tears were running down her flushed face, her thick make-up smeared, her multi-colored hair wildly askew.

"Son of a bitch," she said.

Ethan helped her up and started escorting her to the nearby powder room.

I looked over to Cindy who seemed amused by it all.

"Nice cookout," she said to Ethan. "Great food. Lively guests."

"That was your fault," Ethan said to his wife.

"Of course it was. It's always my fault."

"You started all that dancing," Ethan said.

Cindy took a final swallow of her wine and stared at her husband.

"Oh, fuck you, Ethan," she said.

She looked over to me and smiled.

"Good night, Paul. It was really nice meeting you."

She gave me a brief hug and disappeared up the stairs as well. I didn't see her the rest of the night.

Charlie stayed at Ethan's that night, and I ended up driving Annette home. For the first ten minutes she sobbed, called her husband a no good prick and other names that I couldn't decipher because her head was in a wad of make-up-stained tissues. After she calmed down, she switched on my car radio, found a country station, and for most of the trip she sort of hummed, bobbed her head, tapped her toes to the rhythms. Her mood had completely changed. While listening to one song, she casually placed her left hand on my right thigh. But just as casually I placed it back in her lap.

The trip took about forty-five minutes, and when I pulled up in front of their townhouse, she asked me to walk her to the door. She held my arm for support as we went up the walkway.

"Listen," she slurred, "you want to come in?"

"No, thanks," I said. "I need to be getting back."

"You can spend the night if you want."

"No," I said. "I can drive."

"I bet you can," she said, smiling coquettishly.

"You get some sleep," I said, withdrawing. By her look, I could tell she wasn't used to hearing *no*.

13

For the next month, after the domestic fiasco at Ethan's house, it was hard to look at Charlie in the same way although the Sunday after the incident he had called me and apologized for his behavior. As for Ethan, he was faced with a bitter wife, a troublesome girlfriend, and the rumored IRS problem. As far as I knew, he was to blame for all of them.

I avoided both Ethan and Charlie as much as I could. In our work discussions I tried to maintain a business demeanor. When they planned happy hour excursions, I begged off. But one day, after our weekly meeting, Ethan asked me into his office.

"How have you been?" he asked. He greeted me with a smile, sitting forward at his desk. He beckoned to a chair and I sat down.

I said I was fine.

"Good," he nodded absently. His smile disappeared. "I've had it pretty hard recently." He scratched his head, frowned suddenly, and looked down at some printouts on his desk.

"Business?" I asked.

"Oh, always problems there." But he started shaking his head.

"Cindy?" I guessed.

"What?"

"Are you still having problems with Cindy?"

"We tough it out," he said.

"Bryan?"

He paused and for a second he seemed to have

forgotten his son. He shook his head.

"It's Shauna," he said.

"You aren't married to her."

"Try to tell her that." He paused. "She's definitely pregnant." Pause again. "She says she wants to have the baby."

His head was in his hands, his thinning hair making him appear suddenly older.

"That's impossible, of course. But you can't reason with her."

"What's unreasonable about wanting to have a baby?"

He looked at me with a queer expression.

"Are you serious? It's absolutely out of the question. She's got to get rid of it. That's all."

"Well, I wish you luck," I said and started to get up.

"Where you going?"

"I have an appointment." Actually not, but I wanted to leave.

"Paul, I need a favor."

"A favor?" I asked. "What?"

My voice sounded angry even to me; I think my tone surprised us both. He blinked a few times and then put his hand to his head and scratched.

"Don't tell Cindy."

"Why would I tell her, Ethan? I've only met her once. I have no idea if I'll ever see her or talk to her again."

"That's not the real favor anyway." He looked at me and visibly swallowed. "I'd like you to talk to Shauna."

I couldn't believe it. "For what purpose?"

"Try to convince her that abortion is the only sensible action she can take. For God's sake, Paul, if she has a baby my life will be shot to hell."

"You'll just have two kids instead of one," I said.

He jumped up.

" 'Just have two kids'? Are you serious? Don't you see

the repercussions?"

For a second, I thought about getting into an ethical discussion, but he was a bit too unhinged for that.

"Well, I won't tell Cindy," I said. "But I won't talk to Shauna either." I turned away to leave. As I neared the door, Ethan spoke.

"Paul, I'm sorry. I've been a little stressed. With Cindy and Shauna." He paused. "And business shit. I'm not thinking straight. I shouldn't have involved you. It's my responsibility." He walked around the desk over to where I stood and we shook hands.

Later I found out through Charlie that Shauna did have her abortion, that Ethan had not only paid for it but had given her some sort of cash settlement as well.

My own personal life was also less than content. After my postcard to Shelly, I was in romantic suspension. Why had she called? Would she respond to the card? As I had in the summer, I found myself incessantly checking my phone messages and emails, but there was nothing from Shelly and no letters. I occupied myself as much as possible outside of work. I even called my new friend Stevenson, and we played tennis together at an indoor club that he belonged to. Over beers one day I asked him about how his planned seduction went with the woman from the premiere.

"I must say I might be losing my touch."

"What happened?"

"I'm afraid I only had a few moments before her husband returned to her side. I did manage to flatter her and get her business card."

"Did you get in touch with her?"

"Certainly," he said. "Unfortunately when I invited her out she deftly deflected my invitation. I tried a few more times but she declined my offer. Most cordially."

"Well, there are plenty of women," I said.

"True," he said. "But I might have to start considering women more my own age." He sipped his beer, looking a bit morose.

I thought of suggesting that he might want to focus on romantic relationships rather than sexual conquests, but by the look of him I think he knew that. And as I got to know Stevenson over the next several months, I realized that his Don Juan persona was mostly an act.

One day in early November, my mother called to ask about my holiday plans. She had kept tabs with me during a few intermittent calls; she had even helped throw some business my way by making a few calls to connections in the area.

"Why don't you come down for Christmas?" she said. "Do you have plans?"

"No."

"How much time can you take off?"

"Four or five days," I said. "Ethan's closing the office for a few days. He said we can take off just about anytime we need to anyway."

"I doubt if he said that."

"No," I admitted. "He didn't say that exactly."

"You may be right," she said. "You may not be cut out for the law."

"I've been dating a law student," I said suddenly without thinking.

There was a pause. A rare moment: my mother at a loss for words. But not for long.

"I see," said. "What school?"

I told her a hazy and heavily amended account of Shelly.

"What are her plans?"

"I have no idea."

"Well," she said. "I'll book your flight."

Later that week I was surprised to receive a call from Cindy Canton, her voice readily recognizable, though I hadn't talked to her since the disastrous cookout. She sounded cheerful.

"Listen," she said, "I don't know whether you have plans or not, but I was wondering if you could come out for Thanksgiving."

I hesitated a moment, thinking of Ethan and Shauna and the nasty barbecue scene I had witnessed before. Cindy must have guessed as much.

"It should be peaceful this time. Ethan's been on his best behavior. Best for him at least. And I'll try to be a good girl too. I really enjoyed our talk. It's rare that I have an intelligent conversation with anyone. Besides I want you to meet Bryan."

"I'd be glad to come," I said.

"Great. Oh, guess what? You may not have realized it but you inspired me when I met you last month."

I thought about legal action. Divorce.

"I tried out for a play," she said.

"No kidding."

"Cross my heart. What's more amazing is that I got the part. It's a small part really. I'm an Irish maid. Been working on my accent."

"Where's the play?"

"Fells Point. Original production. A comedy. But my part is kind of showy, a few funny lines. Runs weekends in January. I hope you can make it."

"I wouldn't miss it," I said.

That week I went out and bought a bottle of wine to take up for the Canton dinner. I remembered that Cindy had been drinking a Chardonnay, so I purchased a brand I knew my mother would recommend.

On Thanksgiving Day I drove out to Ethan's house

after a brisk tennis match with Stevenson. Both of us were committed to family events, and both of us were less than enthusiastic for varying reasons. But as I drove I actually found myself looking forward to seeing Cindy and meeting Bryan.

On the way to the Cantons' house, I remembered my parents once arguing about country living. My father talked about a home in the country, spoke in wistful tones, as if living in the country could provide some spiritual solace for him. He had grown up on farmland in Western Maryland, and I guess he yearned to return to the richness of the earth, the rustic simplicity of life. Maybe that was why he liked western stories so much. In my mother's mind the "country" was populated by the less sophisticated. Even wealthy horse breeders and fox hunters who were established members of blueblood society perplexed her. "They dedicate their entire lives to the worship of beasts," she said.

I rapped on the door to Ethan's house about four. The sky was growing cloudy and the trees that I remembered as full and colorful were now rattling in the chilly wind. Looking up at the smoke unfurling from their chimney, I imagined the glow of the fire and the smell of turkey. I rapped again and stood for a few minutes, the chill creeping under my jacket. I tried to look through the curtains, but they were closed and the blinds shut out my view completely. Then I heard a movement from inside. The door opened slightly, six or seven inches and stopped. There was no other voice or sound. Sticking my head around the door frame, I was startled by the little face almost clinging to the door. A little boy's face.

"Hi," I said.

He stood by the door looking up at me.

"Are your mommy and daddy home?"

He nodded.

As I was about to ask where, I heard footsteps. Cindy Canton turned the corner, smiling in a strained but lovely face.

"Bryan, have you met your second cousin?"

"Hi Bryan," I said. "I'm Paul."

I put my hand out and Bryan and I shook hands.

"He's shy," Cindy said. She shrugged, turned to me and smiled.

She hugged me and I smelled her floral scent that I recalled the month before.

"I'm so glad you could come."

I handed Cindy the bottle of wine.

"I hope you like it," I said.

"Oh, thank you," she said. Her face seemed to light up and I looked into her eyes. "I'm sure I will."

I found myself staring at her, enchanted by the charm of her smiling face. But just then Ethan appeared. He looked flushed but he smiled his salesman smile.

"How you doing, Boy Hero?"

He shook my hand as if he hadn't seen me in ten years. "Let's get you a drink."

He patted me on the shoulder and headed off to the kitchen. After he disappeared, Cindy grabbed me and pulled me to where Bryan couldn't hear.

"We've decided to separate," she whispered.

"I'm sorry."

"Don't be," she said, waving to Bryan. "It's the best thing. I feel rather relieved. We've been arguing about it all week. Hell of a Thanksgiving note."

When Ethan returned, we sat in the upstairs family room and Ethan turned to watch a pro football game. He said he had some money on the outcome. Bryan sat on the floor, near his mother, playing with some toy figures.

"He's going to pass, Bryan. Look. It's third down, " Ethan said.

Bryan looked up at his father and then his mother.

"He doesn't know what third down is, Ethan."

Ethan ignored her.

"Can't understand it, Paul. The boy has no interest in sports."

"He's only five," Cindy said.

"Maybe in a few years," I said.

Ethan swigged his drink. It looked like whiskey. I had the feeling he wasn't really interested in me or the game, or even Bryan's lack of interest in sports. He seemed more concerned with his cell phone which he checked about every twenty seconds.

I looked over at Bryan who had returned to his toys.

"He's a good-looking boy," I said.

"He certainly is," said Cindy. She reached over and grabbed Bryan, ruffled his sandy hair. "He's my baby."

Ethan glanced over at the scene of affection.

"Come here, Big Guy," he said suddenly to his son. Ethan set his phone down, dropped to his knees, and beckoned with his hands out. Bryan, still clinging to his mother, looked back at his father; didn't move. "Let him go, Cindy." She released him but the boy didn't move. "Come here, Pal," Ethan coaxed. But Bryan still didn't move; just stared at his father. "Come on." Reluctantly, Bryan stepped tentatively over to Ethan who lifted him up like a doll.

"Going to be a tight end like his Uncle Charlie." Ethan smiled but Bryan looked baffled and cast a look back to his mother and to me.

"What's a tight end?" asked Bryan meekly.

Ethan hurled him up into the air and caught him.

"Don't let him fall."

"Jesus, Cindy. You can't baby the kid all the time."

Ethan started wrestling with Bryan on the floor. Bryan wiggled.

Cindy got up.

"I need to check dinner. Could you give me a hand, Paul?" I followed her into the kitchen.

"That's all for show," she said, reaching in the oven to pull out the turkey, without my help. "He *never* plays with Bryan like that." She set the pan with the turkey on the center island counter, started to baste it. I didn't know what to say. I must have appeared rather clueless, because in the midst of her ladling the turkey drippings, Cindy looked at me and laughed. A delightful laugh.

"I'm sorry, Paul. I promised you a peaceful dinner."

"No major blows yet," I said.

"Well, I don't think it will come to that. But I *am* sorry. The timing was bad but I couldn't take it any longer. "

We heard Ethan yelp from the other room. Cindy turned toward the door with a look of concern, but a moment later Bryan came walking calmly into the kitchen.

"Are you all right, honey?" she asked.

"I'm hungry, Mommy," he said.

"I bet you are."

She gave him some cheese and crackers from a tray. He sat at the kitchen table, still carrying a handful of toy soldiers.

"Who's your favorite guy?" I asked.

Bryan looked up at me, surprised.

"General Grant," he said.

"Oh, really," I said. I took a chair and sat down near Bryan. "Which guy is that?"

He handed me a man. A Civil War soldier that looked like Grant.

"Is he in charge?"

Bryan nodded.

"I like General Lee too," he said, offering me another

guy.

"Do they ever fight each other?"

"Not really," he said. "They send in their soldiers."

"Great strategy," I said.

He smiled for the first time.

"Do you want to see my other guys?" he asked, his face more animated.

"Sure."

He looked over to his mother. Cindy was smiling.

"You two go ahead."

I followed Bryan out of the kitchen and through the family room where Ethan was lying on the couch, his drink and phone perched on his chest. Bryan took my hand as we went down the hall.

"It's a little dark here," he said, guiding me.

We went up into his bedroom and we sat on the floor. He reached under his bed and dragged out a Tupperware container of men and weapons. He pulled each one out individually and began to name them.

"You got a whole army there," I said. "You really like the Civil War?"

"I guess." He paused. "Want to play Candyland?"

I smiled at his sudden transformation from soldier to kid. He put the men away and pulled the game off his shelf.

"You have to be the girl," he said. "I lost the other boy." He meant the figures that moved around the game board.

We played two games, mostly in silence, except when Bryan explained a rule to me or when we both anguished over sliding back down the candyland trail. Then Cindy appeared at the door.

"How are you two doing?"

"I won, Mommy."

"Well, take a break. It's time for dinner. Show Paul

where the bathroom is and wash your hands."

Throughout dinner Ethan was a virtual automaton, eating with perfunctory movements, hardly commenting on the food or the discussion which occurred between Cindy and me, his eyes periodically glancing at his cell phone next to his dinner plate.

Cindy was talking about trying to memorize her lines. Bryan remained quiet but every now and then I'd wink at him and he'd smile shyly. I told Ethan that Bryan was a first-rate Candyland player. Ethan nodded and looked at his son as if he were an alien.

When dinner was over, I helped Cindy with the dishes in the kitchen and Ethan wandered off to watch another football game. I asked her about Bryan's interest in the Civil War.

"Oh," she said, laughing. "That's from my Uncle Mike. We visited him in Ohio and he's a real Civil War fanatic. He was a reenactor and has a virtual museum of artifacts. Bryan just loved it. So Uncle Mike gave him all those soldiers and toys he plays with."

"It's surprising to see a kid his age interested in history."

"I know. But I'm sure he'll get into all those computer games soon," she said.

After we finished the clean-up, I decided it was best that I left. They all walked me to the door.

"Let me know about your play," I said to Cindy.

"I will."

She stepped forward and gave me a hug and kissed me on my cheek.

"Thanks for everything," I said to Ethan and Cindy. I shook Bryan's hand. "Take care of those soldiers," I said. "Maybe next time I'll beat you at Candyland." Bryan smiled and I bent down and hugged him. He held me tight. "It was great meeting you," I said to him.

"I'll walk you to your car," Ethan said.

We stepped into the chilly air, colder now with the dark windy sky. When we were away from the house, Ethan spoke.

"Did Cindy tell you?"

"What?"

"That we're separating."

I nodded.

"It was tough for me tonight," he said. "I'm moving out this weekend. Find an apartment."

"Things will probably work out," I said without much enthusiasm.

"Do you really think so?" he said.

"There's always a chance."

"I hope so," he said sadly. "She's great isn't she?"

"Yes," I agreed.

He looked a little sick and pale, but he managed a smile and shook my hand before I left.

After I returned home about eight p.m., I received a call from Cindy Canton.

"Paul, I couldn't say this in front of Ethan, but I want to thank you for being so kind to Bryan. Ethan hasn't much time for him and he needs some sort of male role model. You'll be a great father someday."

I traveled a lot over the next few weeks, and at various moments I would remember Cindy's voice on the phone, her compliment making me think of fatherhood and what it meant.

I only had dim memories of my own father: his tall awkward form ambling about the house in khakis and a button-down shirt, reading glasses perched on his head. He would occasionally drop by the den where I might be doing homework or watching television. Sometimes he would stand there a while and smile at me, maybe even ask me what I was doing. But then he would just drift away, wandering back to own private study to peruse legal documents or cowboy books.

14

One evening, after I had just returned from a trip to West Virginia, a drive through icy rain, turning to snow, I got my mail and went up to my apartment. Looking through the pile, I noticed two pieces from the Canton family address.

One envelope was addressed in a child's handwriting. I opened it and found it was a homemade Christmas card. On the cover was a crayon picture of a house with a Santa Claus standing next to it. Inside was a large multi-colored "Merry Christmas" with the name of "Bryan Canton" scrawled at the bottom.

The other card was more traditional and professional, a single Christmas tree standing alone in a field of snow, a few colorful adornments. Inside, on the right side, was the "Merry Christmas!" message again, with the hand-written phrase "Love, Cindy" and "We miss you!" at the bottom. Ethan's name was not mentioned at all, a sign I suppose that he was no longer present in their world.

On the left side paper-clipped to the card were four photos. Three were of Bryan in various positions and attire, one of him lying in bed reading what appeared to be a Civil War illustrated book. The fourth photo was of Cindy herself. I looked into her eyes, the color not quite true to life, not quite right, but evocative enough for me to stare at it for a moment or two. I posted them all in a prominent position on the bulletin board in my kitchen.

Several days later, on a Sunday night, I was reading in my living room when my home phone rang.

"Paul?"

It seemed like a light year since I had heard the voice, the real live voice.

"Shelly?"

"Did I call at a bad time?"

"No," I said. "Not at all."

"The reason I called was that I'm on winter break, and I was looking at your card and I was amazed at how beautiful Baltimore looked."

My first thought was to wonder why she was looking at a postcard I had sent almost two months earlier. But I guess it was better late than never.

"It's even more beautiful now," I said. "The whole harbor is lit up in thousands of white lights."

"Sounds gorgeous. Well, that's what I wanted to see about. I have this time off .... I have this girlfriend in D.C. I was going to visit, and you said to drop by if I were in the area. I thought maybe I could stop and see you. If it's ok?"

"It's fine," I said.

"This coming weekend? I'll be taking the train."

We settled the time, and I jotted some numbers on an old newspaper.

For the next two days I tried to remind myself that she had spurned me in the summer, ignored me in the autumn, and now had just etched me into her cramped winter schedule, wedged me between law school and a D.C. girlfriend. Where was the Boston lover? I had no idea.

At home at night, I underwent self-scrutiny. My once blond-streaked summer hair looked too mousy. The tan was long gone; I hoped that there was something she could see in me that would evoke the Nantucket passion.

Two p.m. on a Saturday afternoon, Penn Station, Baltimore. ETA for Shelly Moran: 2:35. Wearing my dark gray suit, I sat on the smooth wooden benches, working a crossword puzzle from the *Baltimore Sun,* casting glances at my watch. When I looked around the train station, I felt as if I were an extra in a black and white film noir.

At 2:25 I assumed my position on the platform with travelers and my fellow greeters who alternately wiped their runny noses and stomped cold and impatient feet. Then a rumbling began and we saw the train heading toward us, the rumble rising to full volume as it raced by, my eyes searching each window for the face that I had carried in my mind.

The train screeched to a stop and the bodies inside began to exit, mingling with the boarders, and the whole platform turned into confusion. I thought I had missed her, that I should have remained upstairs and greeted her as she came up. Then, from behind a clot of people, I saw her, dressed casually in blue jeans and ski jacket, her long hair pulled back in a red ribbon that matched the jacket.

"Shelly!" I yelled.

She turned.

I expected a beaming smile, a look of elation. But what I saw surprised me. She wasn't the fresh girl of summer; her face looked strained and her smile seemed tired. We hugged briefly.

"My," she said, stepping back to look at me in my suit. "Aren't you the portrait of corporate success."

Her voice was upbeat, but up close she looked more haggard. Even her pony tail looked frazzled.

As we drove to my apartment, she told me that the night before she had been persuaded to celebrate the end of the semester with a few friends. It had been a long night, she said. One drink led to another – beer, wine, shots – the celebration stretching to last call and beyond at a friend's place. The result was she got drunk as hell and hadn't had much sleep.

"I'm really hung over," she said, reclining against the headrest.

I glanced at her and I couldn't help feeling pissed off. If she knew she was going to see me the next day, why would she get so obliterated the night before?

But I wanted to try to salvage the situation, so I told her I was hoping to take her on a walk around the harbor and then go to dinner.

"A waterfront restaurant," I said. "Like Nantucket."

With her eyes closed, she smiled, almost painfully.

"That sounds great, Paul, but I think I need to lie down a bit first."

Inside my apartment she took a brief look around and rendered her verdict.

"This is a man's apartment," she said.

"Why?"

"Not one plant for one thing," she said.

"They tend to die," I confessed, remembering a fern that I had purchased in the summer and transferred around the apartment until it expired.

I showed her the bedroom where I had hoped to make love to her all afternoon. Instead, she flung her jacket onto a chair, pulled off her shoes, and crawled into bed, wrapping herself in my blanket and comforter.

"I'm sorry," she said, looking up at me. "I just need a few hours."

"Can I get you anything?" I asked.

"Not now."

"Sweet dreams," I said, closing the door.

So I sat in the living room still wearing my handsome suit and waited for my hungover summer dream to recover. I started reading a novel that I had picked up at the library. Four o'clock became five, then six. I opened the bedroom door quietly and glanced in, but there was no movement other than her gentle breathing. I closed the door again and walked over to the window. Evening was easing in and I watched traffic for a while. I thought about putting on some soothing classical music, maybe Vivaldi, but didn't want to wake sleeping beauty. I turned another light on and went back to my novel.

I had almost dozed off myself when I heard a sound and the bedroom door was opening. There was Shelly, wrapped in a blanket, her hair a tangled mess, awake but distressed.

"More bad news," she said.

"What?"

"I must have miscalculated a bit."

"Miscalculated?"

"I was thinking Sunday or Monday. Early next week."

I guess I was a bit dense but I had no idea what she was talking about.

"My period's started," she said.

This was one of those moments that I wished I had had long-term girlfriend or a sister. Even a close female friend. Because I was simply unaware of the impact of periods on individual women.

"I wanted to be perfect for you. I wanted to have a wild romantic weekend," she said. Her face was pale and anguished.

I wasn't sure what to say so I walked over to her and she sobbed in my arms for a few minutes. I stroked her mottled hair and as I held her I could smell a hint of the alcohol she must have consumed the night before. After a few moments, she pulled away, grabbing some tissues from a box on an end table.

"Do you have any tea?" she asked, dabbing her eyes and sitting on a kitchen chair.

"No," I said. "Well, not hot tea. I can make some iced

tea."

"No thanks."

I offered her a diet Pepsi but she shook her head. She sniffled a bit more in the tissues, then seemed to gather herself together and looked over at me.

"Paul, I have something to confess to you," she said.

"Confess?"

"That letter I wrote..."

I looked at her and remembered the letter that I had extinguished in my sink just five yards away.

"There *was* someone else. But that was mostly over with when I wrote you."

"You'd stopped seeing him?"

She hesitated.

"Not completely. But it was over in my own mind well before I went to Nantucket. When I got home I saw him a few times. He wanted to keep it going but I didn't."

"Then why didn't −"

"−I let you know?"

I nodded.

"I wasn't sure it would be right. There was nothing wrong with you, but you were a friend of Ryder Scott."

"Ryder? What does he have to do with anything?"

"I thought you might be like him. You know, a player. A user."

"I barely knew him."

"I just wasn't sure. We didn't know each other either. Don't you remember, it was only a week."

I nodded.

"The fact is I've been basically a social recluse for the past six months."

I looked at her still clad in a blanket.

"You don't believe that do you?"

At that moment I didn't know what to believe.

"I was falling in love with you," she said.

"You were?"

"Yes."

I smiled at the thought. But I couldn't help feeling a lingering sense of doubt.

Shelly thought a bath would help revive her for the evening dinner plans, so she ran her water and spent a good thirty minutes or so soaking. But when I looked in on her, she seemed to be falling asleep again.

"Are you all right?" I asked.

She looked up. "Better. I'm trying to rally."

She was able to finally rise from the water and I let her prepare herself for dinner while I watched the news on television. About seven, she emerged in an emerald green turtleneck and black pants.

"I'm afraid this is as good as I can get tonight."

"You look great," I said.

We strolled out into the crisp December air and clasped hands. The air and lights seemed to revive her a bit. She smiled at the sight of Santa Claus greeting children in his enclosed workshop; she chatted with his robotic talking reindeer. I pointed out the aged ship *Constellation* looming in the black water like a friendly ghost from the past.

We walked around the periphery of the harbor, the brick promenade, past a marina with ships lit up from bow to stern, from deck to mainsail with colored lights. The whole night glittered.

"Monet would have loved this," she said.

As in Nantucket we ate at a restaurant overlooking the water, the whole panorama of the Baltimore harbor spread out before us twinkling and still. Inside the restaurant was Christmassy as well, with brightly lit wreathes and a large Christmas tree glittering with white lights.

Shelly almost looked like summer in the candlelight,

the tendrils of hair loosened and her cheeks reddened from the walk, the candle flame darkening her eyes. I touched a wisp of her loose hair. She grabbed my hand.

A woman came around selling roses, and I bought one for Shelly. Passion pink. She sniffed it, held it under my nose, looked up at me.

"Let me ask you something," she said, leaning toward me. "I'm really curious. How many times have you been in love?"

"I'm not sure I've ever been in love before."

"Come on."

"I've had crushes, I guess. I thought I was in love when I was in college. I dated the girl for about two months. We even talked about naming our children." I felt embarrassed. She leaned forward, her face animated with interest. "Silly stuff really. I was hurt when she dumped me. But only for a day or two. Now I barely remember her. I think it was just ego."

"Did you tell her you loved her?"

"I don't remember. Possibly."

Our entrees arrived, crab imperial for me, a shrimp entrée for Shelly. I was glad she didn't discuss *her* experiences with love. I suspected they would be too numerous for one dinner.

After we ate, I had planned to take her on a walking tour of Fells Point, but her rally had ended and she said she wasn't up to it. So we went back to my apartment. We found an old Christmas movie she liked, something with Barbara Stanwyck, and we watched until she was about to fall asleep.

"Can you tuck me in?" she asked.

I undressed her and she put on a night gown she had brought, kissed me, and curled up into bed. I told her I'd join her soon and closed the door.

After she went to bed, I watched a CSPAN history

lecture I had recorded. Sometime after midnight I crawled into bed with her.

When I awoke the next morning, Shelly was gone, and for a moment I thought she might have left for the train station. I jumped out of bed and went looking.

In the living room, she was sitting on the sofa, legs crossed, dressed in blue jeans, her hair still wet from the shower.

"I forgot you don't drink coffee," she said. "I looked but I couldn't find any."

"I'm sorry."

"I really need some."

"Are you all right?"

"Fine. I just need some coffee."

"We could try the Harbor," I said.

I hurriedly dressed and we headed out for a coffee shop.

Just as we were about to walk out of my apartment, Shelly stopped by my bulletin board where my calendar and the Canton photos were.

"Who are they?"

"My nephew," I said. "And my cousin's wife."

"Where's your cousin's picture?"

Ethan's missing photo was certainly conspicuous by its absence, but I didn't want to get into their separation.

"I guess it must have been left out of the envelope."

"His wife's pretty."

I looked at Cindy's picture along with Shelly. I had to agree, she was pretty.

But I didn't say it.

We stopped at a bagel shop on the second floor at Harborplace and sat by the window. Shelly sipped her coffee and looked almost aloof.

"I have to leave at 3:15," she said.

"You can't stay another night?"

She frowned.

"There's this Christmas function in D.C." Meaning her friend.

"Is there anything special you'd like to do?" I asked.

She looked at me. No answer. I wondered what she was thinking.

"What's wrong, Shelly?"

"What do you mean?"

"You have the same look as Nantucket. The day you left."

"It's not the same."

"What is it then?"

She looked forlornly out to the horizon where smoke stacks of commerce loomed.

"I feel so unsure."

"About what?"

"I don't know. I just feel nothing will work out. I mean you're in Baltimore and I'm in Boston. It's so far."

"We can visit."

"How often?" It was almost an accusation. She shook her head. "Even then, I have so much work and a part-time job at the firm. You don't know how frazzled I get."

"What are you doing over Christmas?" I asked.

She didn't say anything at first.

"I'm going to see my parents."

"Maybe I can come up," I said. "My mother invited me to Florida. But – "

"No," she said. "My family are dreadful bores."

The idea sank like a piece of lead in the harbor. She looked up at me directly.

"Can I ask you something?"

"What?"

"Have you been with anyone since I saw you in the summer?"

"What do you mean?"

"You know what I mean."

I was startled by the implication of the question.

"Have I slept with anyone?"

"Yes."

"Why are you asking that?"

"You did didn't you?"

I was confused and I searched her eyes, but they were searching mine.

"You told me you were seeing someone," I said. "I wasn't aware we were monogamous. As far as I knew you weren't."

She looked away suddenly, lowered her head and nodded.

"I know," she said. Her eyes filled up. Some tears began to flow. "You see I *have* been in love before." She dabbed at her eye with a napkin from her coffee cup. "I thought it was real. Maybe my Catholic training. But it meant something. Down deep, I mean. But not to him. Then I meet you at a summer resort, have a fling ...."

She sobbed and looked up at me.

"I never thought I'd fall in love with you."

I reached for her, but she shook her head. "I suppose I was trying to protect myself. That's why I wrote the stupid letter."

Later we strolled through the harbor. We dropped in the Science Center and watched a movie on whales, then logically moved over to the National Aquarium and studied fish and the rain forest. It all had a desultory dreamlike quality. I couldn't help feeling she was hiding something or not being wholly honest. We stopped at the restaurant where I had had drinks with Dr. Ott, but neither of us could eat much; we both pushed the food around our plates.

After we arrived at the station, I hoped the train would be late so we could talk some more, find some sort of resolution, to tie up the emotional loose ends. But it was on time and soon we were standing by the cold tracks listening to the train grind closer. When it finally pulled up in front of us, she embraced me tightly, looked at me once with a pained expression and said goodbye.

For the next few days, I felt a gnawing emptiness and sense of futility. I was tempted to call her immediately after she left. After a week, I thought she might call me. She must be back at her parents' house in Connecticut. I tried to call her but got voice mail several times. I didn't leave a message; I had given her my cell number so she would certainly recognize my number and return my call. Or even text. But there was nothing. A day later I decided I would try her at her parents' home. I went through what seemed like a network of operators to find her parents' number. Finally, I found it. A woman's voice.

"This is Paul Simmons. May I speak to Shelly?"

"Shelly's not home," the voice said. "What did you say your name was?"

"Paul Simmons," I said.

"Are you one of Shelly's law school classmates?"

Had Shelly never mentioned my name?

"No, mam," I said. "We met in Nantucket. In the summer."

"Oh."

"Perhaps I should call back tomorrow?"

"Shelly won't be home," her mother said. "She went out west for Christmas. Skiing."

The news hit me like a sheet of ice.

"I'm sorry. But I'll tell her you called."

Afterwards I sat stunned. Not only had Shelly not told her mother about me, but she had escaped to a ski resort without mentioning it to me or calling me back.

The next several days were busy: last minute orders

to fill, gift buying for my mother, fighting the cold slush of winter. And still no call back from Shelly. I did call Stevenson and he told me about a lavish Christmas Party at the Hyatt coming up on December 22. He suggested we go, that we could discuss my romantic issues while we enjoyed the festivities.

On the night of the party, I left my apartment and walked through the cold mist for a half mile until I saw a sign blaring "World's Largest Office Christmas Party." I had just stepped into the hotel lobby when I got a call from Stevenson saying that he couldn't make it. A minor emergency he said; his sister needed him to take care of a repair of some sort.

I debated whether to go in by myself, but decided to pay the hefty cover charge and went into a cavernous ballroom. A band was playing at one end and bars were lined up around the periphery. Everything was glittering red, green, and gold, with the exception of an immense silver Christmas tree in the middle of the room. It was a robust crowd and everyone seemed to be having a festive time. I made a circuit of the ballroom, and to get in the Christmas spirit I stopped at a bar and ordered a scotch. I had had scotch maybe once before in my life, but it seemed like a nice sophisticated winter drink, and I finished three doubles in thirty minutes. The hell with Shelly, I thought.

I strolled around, watched the well-dressed dancers on the ballroom floor, saw some rather attractive women in a group drinking. Santa Claus was also making the rounds. I shook his hand, asked about Rudolph and Mrs. Claus, but he didn't seem interested in small talk and turned away. There were all sorts of wondrous Christmas creatures including a table of elves and a man dressed as a reindeer. I made a full circuit and came back to the first bar where I had started. I let the barmaid hand me my fourth scotch as I scanned the crowd.

I saw a woman glance at me and look away quickly. Attractive, about forty-five, she was standing alone. In my heightened sense of hopeful intoxication, I convinced myself she was interested, her glance an obvious signal for me. So I walked rather unsteadily over to her.

"Do you want to dance?" I asked.

"The band's stopped," she observed.

I hadn't noticed that and thought about saying something witty like "We could make our own music," but that struck me as a bit cheesy. Perhaps I needed a more sophisticated line, something from Dickens maybe, to fit the season. But I couldn't think of anything.

So I just asked her if she were with someone.

"Yes," she said.

"Your husband?"

"No."

"Your boyfriend?"

"No."

"Your significant other?"

She ignored that.

I contemplated her responses for a minute. Let the scotch clarify my perspective. Perhaps, I thought, she was a lesbian. But I didn't want to pursue that line of inquiry just yet. So I asked her if she wanted a drink.

"I have one," she said.

"Have another."

"Really, no."

"I noticed they have some specialty wines."

"No," she said rather firmly.

I smiled. I understood her ploy; she was playing hard to get. Ryder Scott would have this woman in a split second. Perhaps in the back seat of his Audi.

"Be right back," I said. I walked over to a bar and bought the woman a wine and myself another scotch. I even winked at the barmaid. I was ready to apply the masterful touch.

As I approached the woman again, I tripped on something and spilled some of my drink. Oh, well, I thought. No use crying over spilled scotch; her wine cup was still full.

"Here you go," I said, thrusting the plastic cup of wine in front of her. "It's a delightful pinot noir."

"No thanks. I told you I'm with someone."

"Where is he?"

"*She'll* be back in a minute."

Maybe she *was* a lesbian. I sipped my drink. Tasted hers.

"Good wine," I said.

I heard the band begin. "Great party. Sure you don't want to dance?"

"No," she said. "Why don't you find someone more your own age?"

I was about to tell her that age should not interfere with affairs of the heart. I thought that might be a good way to lure her in, but another woman walked over. Apparently her companion.

"Are you all right?" I heard the new woman ask. She was addressing her friend but I answered her myself. "Fine," I said. "Wonderful actually. Would you like a drink?"

They started whispering together, casting a few glances over at me. I smiled back, hopeful that they were determining which one had the privilege of going home with me. Or maybe they both would.

But they just walked off. My ménage à trois simply strolled away.

I stood sipping two drinks, the combination of scotch and wine not really working out too well on my palate.

A few minutes later, as I was wandering the periphery

looking for another lucky girl, I felt a tap on my shoulder. A security guard. Smiling brown face.

"Are you all right, Sir?"

"I'm just great," I said. "Care for a drink?" I offered him the wine cup.

"I think maybe you've had enough."

At first I thought he might be referring to Shelly.

"Take a walk in the cold," he said. "Clear you right up."

He took my elbow and started walking me out of the ballroom. I thought it wonderfully hospitable of him.

"Have a nice Christmas," he said at the door. Even waved.

I walked back to my apartment still feeling rather wonderful. I thought suddenly of the girl from the Dead Duck, the girl with long dark hair that I had spent a frenetic drunken night with. I wished she would turn up right about now in my hour of desperation. But I had no idea who or where she was.

Then I thought of an even better idea. Call the flight attendant from the Jungle Club, Sarah, the woman who owed her life to me. I actually had her card. And she was easier to get on the phone. Much easier than Shelly who was out west in the mountains, skiing and fornicating.

I heard the phone ring about six times before she answered.

"Who?" she asked when I told her my name.

"Your savior," I said. Reminded her of my heroic deed.

"Oh, hi." Barely awake.

"Listen, why don't we meet for a drink?" I said.

"What time is it?"

Seemed like a silly question. I looked at my watch. 11:50 exactly. Peak of the evening, I told her.

"Where are you?" she asked.

"Downtown Baltimore," I said. "Quite beautiful right now."

"You do remember I live in Hartford?"

That nugget of information I had indeed forgotten. I should have recognized the area code.

"I forgot," I said.

"Jesus, I've got to fly tomorrow morning."

"Me too," I said.

"Where?"

"Florida."

"Good for you. I'm going to Cleveland." She yawned audibly into the phone. "Listen, why don't you give me a call after Christmas."

"Sure."

I decided to call Shelly on her cell phone, but she didn't answer. So I took a deep breath and left my message.

"I am directing this call to Michelle Constance Moran, better known as Shelly. It is December 22nd at 12:17 in the a.m. Which makes it actually, to be perfectly precise, December 23rd. I just wanted to say that I hope you are enjoying your skiing trip. I myself am going to Florida very soon, in a matter of hours, to be exact. I am calling to officially announce my engagement to ... well, I can't remember her name ... but she's a flight attendant from Cleveland and I once saved her life."

15

My mother had moved to Naples, Florida three years before, when, at the age of sixty-four, she decided that she preferred tennis and golf and a warm climate to the machinations of laws, judges, and clients in the dreary cold of the Mid-Atlantic region. In those three years she had returned to Baltimore three times: once for business purposes, twice for funerals. She had invited me down on a number of occasions, including the two prior Christmases, but I had yet to make the trip.

My mother greeted me at the airport. She looked quite lovely and tropical – tan, lean, almost buoyant. Wearing a colorful skirt and sleeveless top. And driving a red sports car. A convertible. Most of her working life she had driven a somber black BMW.

"This is yours?" I said as soon as I saw the car and tossed my bag into the little trunk.

"Thought I'd spice up my image," she said. Smiling, she revved up and we left the parking lot for the sunny highway. "We'll have lunch on the way."

The weather and ride were delightful. The mild air and the palm trees and the fragrances of the tropical flora seemed to gush out of the richness of the soil.

"It's been rather warm down here," she said, "but quite a relief from Baltimore, I imagine."

She was right. Waking up with a hangover, I had to face a dreary intermittent rain on the drive to the airport. But I inhaled the Florida air, tried to expunge the bleary absurdity of the night before.

At lunch, Mother was drinking her usual chardonnay;

I had iced tea. We were sitting outside on a stone veranda surrounded by tropical plants.

"I wanted to tell you something before we got home," she said. "I wasn't sure how you'd take it."

The red sports car was one surprise; her tone was another. I could not remember my mother being unsure about anything or at least admitting it. She even seemed a trifle uncomfortable. She was actually fidgeting and looking tense.

"I'm sure I can handle it," I said.

She looked serious and I thought it might actually be serious. Perhaps a health issue.

"I'm living with someone," she said.

I immediately assumed she meant another woman, a friend, perhaps, who was helping her recapture her youth.

"He's a retired contractor from South Carolina."

She was living with a man! I was amazed. Despite my mother's attractiveness and her athletic grace, I still found it hard to imagine her having physical intimacies with anyone.

"Are you offended?" she asked.

"Offended? Why should I be offended?"

"One hears so much of this down here. Children objecting to their parents finding new ...." She struggled for the right word. I couldn't help but smile; she had always been in such command of language.

"Lovers," I offered.

She looked embarrassed.

"Paramours? Stud muffins?"

"Do you find this amusing?"

"I do actually."

"What exactly amuses you?"

I shrugged.

"I don't know. I guess the whole ... incongruity." I

said. "The ice woman melts."

She leaned forward, looking surprised.

"Is that how you see me? As an 'ice woman'?"

"In a way, sure. You know, cool, in control. It's a compliment really."

"And this new arrangement dispels that image?"

"Look at yourself," I said. "You're driving a red sports car, a convertible no less, and you're actually nervous and concerned about my reaction to something."

She took a sip of her wine, brushed her lips with a red cloth napkin, exhibiting the proper etiquette learned in the charm schools of the Old South.

"I suppose," she said, now deliberately weighing her words, "that we never really discussed such matters very much."

"What matters?"

She glared at me as if to say: You don't really expect me to indulge in a discussion of that sort. Unfortunately, she had started the conversation and now she was stuck with the topic.

"Matters relating to men and women," she said.

"If you are referring to sex," I said, "the answer is no. It was not a subject that was discussed."

"Your father –"

"Never said a word. You forget. He was absorbed in cowboy books. Besides, about the time I could have used a little fatherly advice, he decided to take a permanent ride into the sunset."

"You sound bitter."

"I didn't mean to be."

"I thought that you might be disturbed that there was another man in my life."

"Not at all," I said. "In fact, I think it's great. What's his name?"

She hesitated. Then said: "Buck."

"Buck?" I laughed out loud, almost expelling a morsel of shrimp across the table.

"I knew it would strike you as funny."

"You say he's a contractor?"

"Was. He's retired."

"What kind of contracting?"

"Concrete," she said.

I contemplated the reality of it: debutante, litigator, garden club president, patron of the fine arts, now living with a guy named Buck who poured cement for his life's work.

"Dear Lord," she said, smiling. "I guess it does seem odd. Me with a construction worker."

I formed an image of my mother dressed in a dainty nightgown handing a hardhat and steel lunch box to a brawny guy in a sleeveless t-shirt.

"Well, how did you meet him?"

"At a cocktail party. At the club."

"Is he good looking?"

She looked at me with impatience.

"I don't know how one can evaluate such things."

That from a woman who, as a chaperone on one of my middle school field trips, once corrected a guide at the Baltimore Museum of Art about Matisse's use of color.

"Is he?"

"I would suspect that the general consensus - "

"What do *you* think?"

"He has a rugged appeal."

"You *are* living with him, aren't you?"

"I stipulated that."

"You aren't roommates?"

"Not exactly."

"Then you're live-in lovers. You're shacked up with a dude."

I wanted her to admit it. She was sleeping with a man and they weren't married. She didn't have to elaborate on techniques or positions.

"That might be a vulgar way to express the situation."

"Good."

"Does this give you some special satisfaction?"

"It makes my day."

Their modest one-level house was situated on a canal with a dock, a small tidy lawn, delicately placed gardens, and shell paths meandering about multi-tiered wooden decks. My mother gave me a brief tour of the interior and I noticed I had my own room, with pictures of me on the walls and the chest of drawers. I was younger in most of them, in a little league uniform, in a swim suit at Nags Head, and jumping up after a victory in a youth tennis match. One picture was of me and my father. He was dressed in a suit and his hand rested awkwardly on my shoulder. I looked about ten, but I couldn't remember where and why it was taken.

I didn't meet Buck that night – he was in Orlando playing golf – but he was expected the next day.

"He'll take you for a boat ride," my mother said.

"There's no boat at the dock."

"It's being checked over at the marina."

"Is it a big boat?"

"Smaller than the Queen Elizabeth," she said drily.

We had dinner that night at another restaurant – something inexpensive. My mother was rather proud of her ability to hold onto money. Not that she didn't like quality, but she was never terribly self-indulgent. And she added up the bill.

We started talking about my experience with Ethan. My mother had never been fond of his family; I think she regarded them as common, without grace or style or a hundred other attributes of the shattered South. I didn't bring up his marital difficulties, but at the mention of the IRS problem that Ethan was supposedly experiencing, she perked up and transformed from mother to attorney. She questioned me about the specifics; I said it was simply a vague rumor; I could offer nothing concrete.

"Keep records of everything you're involved in," she said. "Maintain receipts for everything you purchase. Document all business conversations you have with clients and most of all anyone with Canton."

I had to admit to myself that she was probably right; I had been remiss in my record keeping.

My mother went to bed early that night – a long-standing habit of hers. She would probably be up about 6 a.m. to walk in her gardens no doubt and devour her two or three newspapers, if she still received that many. I was left alone on the deck, cooling now under the fluid Florida sky. I listened to the strange sounds from the night – birds cackling and palm fronds flapping in the gentle wind.

Standing in this tropical paradise, I couldn't help forming an image of Shelly somewhere in the majestic mountains, perhaps walking through a snowy sheet of wind, her whole body wrapped in layers of cotton and flannel underneath a heavy ski parka.

But thinking of her engendered too much romantic angst. So I took a deep breath and let the fresh Florida air displace the icy images of the West.

16

As I stepped outside the next morning I had to remind myself that it was actually Christmas Eve. The warm colors, the lazy palms, the soft fragrant air defied the reality of the date.

My mother was already outside, making the rounds of her garden, straw hat on her head. Lithe and tan, she was now the girlfriend of a man named Buck.

When I came out on the deck, she walked over to me.

"Did you sleep well?"

"Fine."

"I forgot to tell you, we're having a little holiday party tonight," she said. "So why don't you take a swim. The beach is up the street about a half a mile."

I found the beach and slipped into the water, still cool in December, but a balm for frayed northern nerves. I sat on a beach chair and read a new novel involving an attorney from the South.

Sometime around 3 p.m. I looked up to see a silver-haired man in shorts and an untucked polo shirt walking toward me. Squinting in the sunlight, he was weathered, like a deep sea fisherman.

"I'm Buck Ramsey," he said, extending his hand.

The voice was a deep southern rumble. Starting to rise, I shook his massive hand.

"Sit down," he said, pressing me back down in my chair. He sat on the sand next to me.

"Good to meet you, Mr. Ramsey."

"Buck," he corrected. "Call me Buck."

But it was hard to imagine that happening any time

soon.

"Did you have a good flight?" he asked.

"Fine. I've never flown first-class before. Thanks."

"You're most welcome."

He gazed out to the sea. "You like the water?" he asked.

"Sure."

"Do you like to fish?"

I confessed that I had little experience.

"Fishing is wonderful," he said. "But basically it's an excuse to drink."

We shared a little chuckle over that.

"You know, I taught your mother how to fish."

Another precedent established.

"She was a bit reluctant, I'll have to admit, but she handled herself tolerably."

"How did your golf match go?"

He winced. "Exasperating sport. You think you have it down and then it seizes you by the throat."

All the while he had been talking, he was squinting and smiling.

"Listen, I thought we'd take the boat out for a while before this Christmas bash. You up for it?"

I said certainly and we headed back to the house. As we walked, I realized how big a man he was. Linebacker big. Solid and strong – quite different from my father's tall gauntness.

The boat had been returned to their dock, and we boarded after I dropped off my beach gear.

"Just us two," he said. "Thought we'd get to know each other. Man to man."

The boat itself was impressive but not ostentatious. Primarily a fishing boat, it could also serve as a simple pleasure cruiser without need of a crew. It was named *Sweet Charlotte* in honor of his late wife.

"We were married for thirty-three years," he said. "We got married right out of college."

This surprised me. I had assumed he was simply a self-driven, self-made man, who had started working out of high school and succeeded because of practical instincts and simple determination. I hadn't envisioned a college graduate. I must have looked surprised because he laughed.

"Don't look like a college man, do I?"

I shrugged dishonestly. "I'm not sure what a college man should look like," I said.

"Majored in history," he said. "Like you. Had every intention of going to law school. But my father got sick and I started helping out with the business during summer vacations. He owned a small contracting firm, dry wall, but he wanted something better for me. Anyway I liked the work – the fact that you could see the product of your labor – and I just took over after college, when he really couldn't work at all. It was rough at first, being married at twenty-two, but it worked out."

"Mom said you were in the concrete business."

"That came later," he said. We had pulled away from the dock and were easing our way down the canal. "I took over the business at the right time. It expanded substantially over the years."

He drove the boat with powerful hands and forearms, knotted, heavily veined. As he stared across the sun, his eyes crinkled under the white South Carolina cap he wore. In a few minutes we had pulled out of the canal and were entering deeper water, the aqua and royal blues mingling, hinting at deeper blue beyond.

"Help yourself to the beer," he said.

I noticed the small cooler by his feet and yanked out two beers, pulled the tabs, and handed him one. He took a big swig and the can seemed miniscule in his grip.

"We never had children," he said. "We waited for about five years after we got married to get everything, you know, squared away financially. Then we started trying. But no go. A medical problem. Back then there wasn't much you could do. Now, of course, they have all these fertilization techniques." He paused, took a long swig of beer. "Didn't really consider adopting. I don't know why." His voice drifted off and he drove out toward the darker water away from the land.

"She became everything, my wife. When you don't have children, your spouse becomes everything."

I nodded.

"I loved Charlotte more than anything. I met women in my business travels – especially when the business was really getting going – they were pretty and pretty willing, if you know what I mean. But I loved my wife. Whenever I was out of town in some hotel bar with a bourbon in my hand and an itch in my pants, I thought of Charlotte. Could see her right in front of me. That's a pretty good way of avoiding trouble. Imagine your wife right there in front of you."

He paused and looked over at me. Then he boomed out a laugh.

"Lord, I must sound like a Puritan dinosaur."

"Not really," I said. Nothing like Jonathan Edwards.

"I just think you have a right to know something about me. My wife died nine years ago. Cancer. She suffered enormously and every day I felt like I was dying too. I just couldn't stand the thought of living without her. When she died, I cried so hard, was so full of grief I could barely move. But you know something? At the same time, I almost felt a sense of relief."

All the while he had been staring out to the sea. Then he turned to me. "I hope to God you never have to experience that."

He wasn't tearing up but the painful memory gripped his face. He gazed out at the spiritual solace of the sea.

"She must have been a wonderful person," I said.

"One hell of a woman."

He pointed to a school of dolphin and we followed them for a while. The sun was falling but Buck seemed content to point out spots for good fishing and diving. He had taken up scuba diving, he said, and had become something of an amateur treasure hunter.

Then he started talking about the time after his wife's death.

"For a while, a year or so, I kept the business alive, but with Charlotte gone, there didn't seem any purpose. I mean my whole everyday life was gone; going to work and coming home to her. I realized that the going to work meant nothing if I didn't have her to return to. We had friends, but when I became single, the social balance was out of whack. Besides, I realized they were mostly her friends. By myself, things just dropped off. Realized I was pretty lonely. That's when I sold the business. Took my cash and moved down here.

"After a while I decided to start a new life. I actually started thinking about other women. But I felt guilty as hell. The idea of going out with another woman still seemed like cheating to me. Then I told myself, Charlotte would want me to get on with my life. And so I did. In fact, after I started back onto the dating scene, I became sort of a ladies man."

He looked over me, almost embarrassed.

"I mean younger ladies especially. To be honest, I started acting like a fool. Showing up at restaurants with girls half my age – or younger. They were interested in my money, of course. I was pretty much aware of that though I'm not sure I liked to dwell on it. But at the time I didn't give a damn. Talked myself into thinking I was having a good time.

"That lasted about two years. Fooled myself for a while. Deep down I knew the truth. I might go out with Miss Sarasota Orange Peel for a night or two, but I was still Buck Ramsey, the cement mixer from Charleston, the guy who had been married to the sweetest woman in the world."

He glanced over at me.

"Bored to death yet?" he asked, smiling.

"No, sir."

"It's seldom I get a chance to talk to another man about this." He paused and drained his beer. "In all honesty, I never told anybody half of what I just told you, not even your mother." He wheeled the boat around. "About time to head in." He kicked up the boat's speed and we headed toward shore.

"What I'm trying to say, Paul, is that I love your mother. I never thought it would happen again. I used to look for someone just like Charlotte. But your mother," he grinned, "she's quite different. Real special. But I guess you already know that."

I nodded. Thought about it a little.

"I asked her to marry me," Buck said. "I don't know if she told you that. She wasn't ready for that, she said. So she suggested that we move in together. At first, I resisted it. But then I said what the hell."

He looked at me. "I hope you understand. I love your mother and I believe she loves me."

But it was still hard for me to imagine that my mother could love in that way.

"You don't object?"

"Not at all," I said.

"I mean your father –"

"Mr. Ramsay, I barely remember my father. I hardly knew him when he was alive. He was a good man in most ways, I guess. But we weren't that close."

When we were back at the house, Buck went off for a shower, and my mother, dressed in Christmas colors, asked me about the cruise.

"Very pleasant."

"What was your impression of Buck?"

"You're not seeking my approval, are you?"

"I was just asking a simple question."

"He seems very nice," I said. "Very different from Dad."

"My God yes," she said. "In so many ways."

"He said he loves you."

My mother actually blushed, then turned away to fiddle with a flower vase.

"Go," she said. "Change. The guests will be arriving soon."

As I walked away I could not help but look back at her and notice a girlish look of happiness.

17

When I had showered, dressed, and returned, guests had already arrived and more were flowing in. I had not expected a large party, but it seemed to be growing into exactly that. The dress was Florida formal, some sport coats, no ties, dresses for the women – mostly Christmas red, gold, green, or bright tropical colors.

My mother had hired a caterer who brought along a bartender, two or three servers, and a piano player whose jazzy Christmas melodies wafted through the living room and out to the deck, now lit by handsome red lanterns. My mother escorted me slowly through the crowd inside, most of whom were in the forty to seventy range. I listened to the people from "up north" or "out west" and commented that yes there were still ice and snow and frigid weather with school closings. After one such whirl about the living room, I noticed Buck lingering in the space between the living room and the open door leading to the deck. Standing alone, his plastic cup wrapped in a red paper napkin, he looked rather sheepish and lonely. I walked over to him; he grinned instantly in appreciation.

"This is more your mother's kind of thing," he said. A server walked by with a tray of canapés, shrimp wrapped in bacon. Buck shook his head. "No thanks, sweetheart." I took a sample.

I was about to speak but something caught my eye. At first it was merely a familiar look, a stance, really. Upon a second glance, the image clarified. I excused myself and stepped out onto the deck, into the dimming light. I listened to the voice, watched the movement of the back of his head; then he turned around and there dressed in a kelly-green polo shirt and navy blazer was Ryder Scott. Standing next to two women who looked to be in their early forties he was gesturing and regaling them about something when he happened to turn toward me, his eyes widening, the memorable smile forming. I moved toward him and the women.

He stepped forward and met me a few yards away from the group he was with. We shook hands.

"What a surprise!" he said.

"This is my mother's house."

His eyebrows arched impressively.

"Even more amazing. The world shrinks once more."

"How did you find your way here?" I asked.

He put his hand on my shoulder and whispered in my ear.

"Long story," he said. "Winter hiatus. I'm living with a woman."

I looked back at the two women he had left.

"No, that's not her. She's not here. Not in Florida. Not now anyway. Flew to Michigan to see her daughter."

"Who are –"

"Listen, it's a bit complicated. Let me introduce you to the woman I'm with tonight." Pause. "Oh, by the way, tonight I'm Derrick Walsh."

"Derrick who?"

Ryder put his finger on his lips and waved back to the more attractive of the two women he had left.

In a minute he introduced us. Renee something and Laurie something.

"Are you a tennis pro too?" one of them asked.

I looked at Ryder.

"No," I said. Told them I was the hostess's son.

A few minutes later Ryder was able to break away and

pulled me toward the dock.

"Who are you living with?" I asked.

"Widow of a successful industrialist. Met her on the island after you left. Wonderfully accommodating."

"What does that mean?"

Ryder smiled. Or was it Derrick?

"Well, after we had acquainted ourselves in August, she suggested we continue our arrangement down here. At that point, approaching Labor Day, I couldn't help but agree."

I stared at Ryder, astonished that he could continue to astonish me.

"You're a gigolo?" I asked.

" 'Gigolo'?" he said, as if the term were new to him.

"Does she pay you?"

"If you mean a salary, no. She *is* generous in many other ways." He smiled broadly.

"Who is this other woman?" I asked, meaning the woman at the party.

"Renee. Met her at a cocktail lounge. Highly sensual."

"Let me get this straight. Your live-in girlfriend –"

"Hardly a girl, she's 52."

"She's where?"

"Visiting her married daughter in Ann Arbor."

"And this woman Renee invited you to the party?"

"Fortuitous, wouldn't you say?"

We both looked at attractive Renee who at that moment was chatting with my mother.

"And you're sleeping with Renee?"

He grinned.

"Jesus, Ryder. How do you do it?"

"Derrick, remember."

"Derrick then. I mean how do you manage it?"

He shrugged, smiled boyishly.

"I'm a magician," he said. "Don't you remember?"

Renee came over and she and Ryder slipped off to have some of my mother's catered food, the woman holding onto Ryder as if he were a prized possession, albeit only for a few more nights, until Ryder's true meal ticket returned from Michigan. Or would he stay with Renee, who seemed much younger than fifty-two?

A few minutes later I was standing near my mother and Buck, the party having just peaked, the food on its way to annihilation.

"Renee says her escort knows you?"

She nodded toward where Ryder and lovely Renee were standing.

"Oh, yes," I said. "He's a gigolo."

That got Buck's attention; he leaned over my mother to hear more.

"He's a what?"

"A gigolo," I repeated.

My mother laughed. "I rather doubt it. He's the son of a Richmond debutante. Pure DAR *and* UDC."

We looked at the loving couple. Renee was placing a plump white shrimp in Ryder's mouth.

"He does seem a bit young for her," Buck offered.

"Ryder?" I said.

"His name is Derrick," my mother said. "I thought you knew him."

"Oh, I do," I said.

Ryder had certainly charmed my mother. He must have reminded her of the gentleman callers she had had in Richmond.

"Well," she said, "I have guests to attend to."

When my mother was gone, Buck and I watched Ryder and Renee some more.

"Is he really a tennis pro?" Buck asked.

After the party, I stayed up late that night reading. I heard the house phone ring three times and then stop. A few minutes later my mother rapped at my bedroom and appeared in a rather sheer nightgown, her hair down. She was carrying a cordless phone.

"I think you better take this," she said.

"Who is it?"

She just handed me the phone.

"Hello?" I said.

"Ryder?" An older female voice.

"No, he's not here," I said, trying to figure out who it was. I thought it might be Ryder's mother. But how was that possible?

"Do you know where he is?" The voice was troubled, trying to stay in control.

"I'm afraid not," I said. "He came here for a party and left a few hours ago."

"He should be back then," the voice said.

"Who is this?"

There was a hesitation.

"Amanda. Amanda Hartwell."

"Well –"

"Ryder's been staying – he's been my guest. I found a note on the counter about a party and this number. I just returned from Michigan to surprise him. For Christmas."

"Oh."

"May I ask you something?" She hesitated. "Did he leave alone?"

"I didn't see him leave," I said.

"And you're sure he's not there?"

"I'm sure."

"I'm very sorry to disturb you. Goodbye." The voice snapped off.

I felt a strange sensation when I hung up. I could almost picture the woman, distraught, face drained of color, hair disheveled. She had returned on a whim, abandoning her own family to surprise her younger lover on Christmas Eve. And where was Ryder, aka Derrick, the tennis pro?

My mother came in a bit later, took the phone.

"Any problems?" she asked.

"Not for me."

She looked a bit quizzical as she left.

Thinking about the mysteries of Ryder Scott, I drifted off to sleep.

The morning light was well into the room when I heard another knock on the door and saw my mother approaching me with the cordless phone once more.

Half asleep and groggy, I took the phone.

"Merry Christmas, Paul! This is Ryder."

Somehow his cheerfulness was grating.

"Sorry to call you so early, but I was wondering if you were interested in playing a little tennis."

"Where are you?"

"In bed," he said.

"Whose bed?" I asked. "That woman from last night?"

"Yes. Renee. She's gone out jogging."

"Amanda called," I said.

"Amanda? Amanda Hartwell?"

"You remember Amanda?"

"Certainly."

"She called last night."

"She called *you*?"

"Yes. She was wondering where you were. She came back to surprise you. She found my mother's number on the counter."

"She came back?" There was a pause. I could only imagine the neurons of prevarication operating in Ryder Scott's brain. "That was sweet of her. Does create a bit of a mess though."

"What do you mean?"

"Well, I sort of made plans with Renee. And there was

tennis with you."

"Ryder, it's Christmas! The woman's come back to be with you for Christmas."

"I understand. It's very thoughtful," he said. "But a bit awkward."

"Go see her. Be with her for Christmas."

I was almost speaking vicariously I think; I wanted so much to be with someone special, with Shelly I guess, that I projected my desires onto the soul of Ryder Scott – if he actually had a soul. We hung up, Ryder in a bit of a daze, caught between two older women with his penis as referee.

When I came out of my room carrying the phone, my mother and Buck were on the sofa sitting in robes, drinking coffee, and looking at the artificial Christmas tree still glittering as it had Christmas Eve.

"Any problem?" my mother asked.

"Probably not for Ryder," I said.

"You mean Derrick?"

"Him too," I said.

"What *is* his real name?" Buck asked.

"With that guy, who can tell."

Without pursuing the issue, we started exchanging gifts. Normally, my mother would have sent me a check, perhaps a few practical gifts – socks, underwear, a tie. This time my Christmas take was more lavish. Much more. There *was* a check, a stock certificate for a local Baltimore blue chip, a membership in an athletic club in Baltimore, and luggage.

"You're traveling a lot," my mother said. "Besides, Buck thought it would be a good inducement to have you visit us more."

Like a child, I sat on the floor with my pile of loot. There were also books on American history, tennis balls, shorts, a polo shirt, and a snorkel mask with matching flippers.

Later that morning I took my mask and flippers to the beach. The sea was like another present, a serene aqua mystery. I submerged myself in the cool water and began exploring the silent undersea world. I snorkeled up and down the beach for over an hour, and on one dive I even found a true treasure – a necklace made with coral shells.

After I came back, we took a cruise. Buck motored us out of the canal, and as we headed into the deeper blue water, he revved up the engine and we took off. We were all standing on the bridge when my mother cracked open a bottle of champagne. With the pop of the cork, the wine burst out in a spray that blew back into our faces. A bit damp, she poured us all a glass and made a brief Christmas toast. Buck finished his champagne in one swig and grabbed a beer from his cooler.

"This is more my speed," he said, laughing.

A while later I went down to the lower deck and sat in a canvas chair as Buck cut a swath through the blue water. When I glanced back up to the bridge, I saw something I had never seen before – my mother actually kissing a grown man on the lips.

Just before we returned to shore, she came down to join me. We were looking at the approaching marina.

"I'm really glad you came to visit," she said.

"So am I," I said. "Thanks for inviting me."

"You know you're always welcome here. Besides I think Buck needs a special connection to a younger man. He never had children, you know."

"Yes. He told me."

"What do you think?"

"About what?"

"About Buck," she said. "And our ... arrangement."

"He's a great guy. The arrangement is fine. It's your

business really."

She leaned over and kissed me on the cheek.

"Yes," she said. "But your opinion matters too."

After we docked about four, my mother disappeared into the kitchen to prepare dinner. When Buck offered to help, she shooed him away.

While my mother worked in the kitchen, Buck and I sat in the den and watched a football game. He had brought in beers and a basket of big hard pretzels, and as we watched we got a bit looped. I remember becoming incensed by a clipping call against a player and team that meant nothing to me.

"I can't believe he's not kicking," Buck said one time, his voice booming across the den.

"He doesn't trust him," I said.

"Doesn't trust his kicker?" Buck said incredulously.

"No, sir."

"Hell. He better buy himself another fucking kicker then."

For some reason, this struck me as hilarious.

Dinner was a fish entrée of some sort, along with a pasta and vegetable salad. With all the drinks in our systems, Buck and I ate ravenously, mountains of food.

"Heathens," my mother said.

About nine I went to bed. I was thinking about getting up early the next morning and going deep sea fishing. Buck had said he would take me out for my first lesson, and I think I was dreaming of the sea colors when my mother knocked on the door, the phone in her hand.

"You've received more phone calls in two days than we usually receive in a week," she said.

"Who is it?" For an instant I thought of Shelly.

"The gentleman with two names. Sounds urgent."

I took the phone.

"Rather a mess here, Paul," Ryder said.

"What do you mean?"

"Amanda. Seems she was somewhat distressed over my absence last night."

"Did you go over to see her?"

"Well, not immediately," he said. "A few hours ago."

"You were with Renee all day?

"Yes, actually."

"It's Christmas, Ryder!"

"I know. But Renee's Jewish."

"What about Amanda?"

"That's why I'm calling. When I got to Amanda's condo, the door was open and I could smell something burnt. When I walked out into the kitchen I found a turkey on the island that looked like it'd been through the Chicago fire. I started looking for Amanda. Found her asleep on a wicker chair in the bedroom. At least that's what I thought. I tried to wake her but she was out. I thought she had tanked up on some Jack Daniels – she has a taste for the heavy stuff, you know. Anyway I was about to leave when I noticed the medicine bottle on the carpet next to her."

"She tried to kill herself?"

"Well, that seems to be the –"

"Where are you now?"

"The hospital. I called 911. She's recovered. She'll be just fine. A day or so and she'll be good as new."

"What are you going to do?" I asked.

"Well, I was thinking about having a late dinner."

"I don't mean right now. About Amanda. The whole situation."

"That's obvious, isn't it?"

"What does 'obvious' mean to you?"

"I'll have to leave, of course."

"You'll have to leave? Now? What about Amanda?"

"The doctor said –"

"For God's sake, Ryder, don't you realize why she tried to kill herself?"

"I mean if she really wanted to kill herself – "

"You're missing the point."

"No, I think I see the essence of the situation. She's rather disturbed. I should have realized that."

"Because of you!"

"I don't know, Paul. That's rather simplistic, don't you think? I mean an individual's psychological state is complex."

At that point he started to drift into paradigms of logic that only he could comprehend. In the end he said something about sending Amanda flowers and moving in with Renee for a while. He even asked me if I wanted to play tennis the next day.

I never told my mother about Ryder's entanglement with Amanda. But two days later, on the day I left for Baltimore, she received a thank you note and flowers from him. She regarded his gesture as especially gallant for someone of his generation.

18

Soon after I returned to Baltimore, I received two voice mails: one message from Shelly and one from Vinnie, who, in a one minute tirade of drunken exuberance, announced that he was marrying the girl he had met the summer before, Clara, invitations forthcoming for a spring wedding, gala event, orgy of wine and food, etcetera. The message from Shelly I listened to a few times. The words slow and drawn out as if she were depressed or medicated: "I hope you had a lovely Christmas. I miss you. I got your message. I'm sorry. My plans changed. I hope you were kidding about the girl from Cleveland." There was a pause. Then: "I really need to talk to you. Please call me." Her voice was shaky.

When I called her, she surged into a monologue: on the train away from Baltimore, at her friend's house in D.C., on the way to her parents' house in Connecticut, she felt the "need," the "compulsion" to just get away. She knew some people from school who had lodging in Breckenridge; she got home, packed and was off. Just like that. She was sorry she hadn't told me, sorry she hadn't called me back, wanted to be off on her own, afraid of losing something, "needed some distance" and so on. In her rambling there was a tone of desperation.

"Can we spend New Year's Eve together?" she asked.

The sudden switch surprised me.

"Anything," she said. "Whatever you want."

I was teetering: one element of my brain, the clear and rational part, was telling me to say no, to let her fears and insecurities dissipate; the other irrational part was imagining her naked in front of a raging fire at a white clapboard inn.

"I think a romantic New Year's Eve is just what we need," she said. "What do you think?"

"Sure," I said, feeling the unsureness creep in.

She became animated again, offering all sorts of suggestions. We could meet in New York? Boston? How about Cape Cod somewhere, maybe even Nantucket again? That would be romantic, wouldn't it? She knew some nice winter inns there. But, on second thought, that was probably too much travel and too costly. She mentioned Newport, Block Island, and Mystic Seaport. But those were dismissed as well. Then she remembered the Poconos in Northeastern Pennsylvania. She had gone skiing there a few times. Maybe that might work. About the same drive for both of us. Yes, she said that was probably the best place overall. What did I think?

I told her it sounded okay.

She said she'd look into a place and get back to me.

"I can't wait," she said finally.

I should have been ecstatic. But I wasn't.

After the phone call, I went to the kitchen and got myself a beer. I sat down and mulled over the whole one-way conversation. Shelly had seemed so different from Nantucket, both during the Baltimore visit and on the phone. I couldn't figure it out but I felt that there was something mysterious still going on in her life and that I was some type of back-up plan. The more I thought about the New Year's Eve date the more doubtful I became.

As I started walking back to the kitchen for another beer, I noticed something on the floor beneath my bulletin board. It was one of the photos of Bryan Canton that had fallen, and as I pinned it back up I glanced at his mother's picture. There was a certain look on Cindy's face that I hadn't noticed before. Her face was tilted slightly, and she was smiling back toward the camera with a hint of impish independence.

The next day I called her. I had bought a few presents for Bryan in a shopping mall near my mother's place in Florida, and I told her I'd like to drop by and give them to him. I had one for her too but I didn't tell her that.

They'd be home all day, she said, Ethan was gone, moved out completely.

"Why don't you drive out for dinner," she said. "We'd love to see you!" Her voice sounded enthused; I could almost see the twinkle in her eyes.

That evening when I drove up, the Canton house presented a cheerful scene: the hedge rows sugarcoated with frost, smoke curling up from the chimney; white Christmas candles in every window; a vibrant wreath on the front door – a perfect rustic postcard. It looked so ideal that it was hard to imagine it was now the home of a couple on the cusp of divorce.

When the door opened, I was immediately stunned when I saw Cindy standing in the doorway. Dressed in a bright red turtleneck and black skirt, she looked so dazzling that I hesitated on the doorstep a second, just gazing at her. There was something different about her, but at that instant I wasn't sure what it was.

"Well, are you coming in?" she asked with that impish smile from the photograph.

I stepped in and she helped me off with my coat and tucked it away in the foyer closet.

"You look very handsome tonight," she said, smiling.

Her compliment surprised me, caught me off guard, and I felt my face redden.

When she hugged me, I realized what was different about her. On the other occasions I had seen her, she had worn a simple ponytail. Now her honey blond hair spread down her back in shimmering waves. Holding her in my arms, absorbing her warmth and familiar floral scent, I couldn't help touching her long loose hair, stroking the silky strands. We held onto each other, her breasts pressed against me firmly, and in that moment something happened that surprised me, that frightened me actually. I didn't want it to happen, I didn't expect it to happen, I didn't even want to admit it to myself, but as I held her and stroked her hair, I became aroused – and the suddenness of it, the intensity of it, made me almost dizzy with confusion.

We heard Bryan yell something in the next room, and we separated slightly, but I was still holding her hands, staring into her gorgeous aqua eyes, feeling something changing, something wonderful but not quite right at the same time.

When Bryan ran in, I noticed he seemed changed too. He was smiling and seemed quite happy.

"Did you have a good Christmas?" I asked.

"Yeah," he said.

"I did too," I said. "I went down to see my mom in Florida. Do you know where Florida is?"

"Where Mickey is," he said.

I looked at Cindy.

"Mickey Mouse," she said.

"Right. Well, I brought you a couple of things."

I pulled out a bag with the gifts.

His little fingers stripped the Christmas paper and the first present appeared – a realistic-looking foot-long plastic alligator.

Then he was on to the next present, a jigsaw puzzle of a Civil War battle scene.

He thanked me and he ran into the family room with the presents. When he was gone, I removed the gift I had for Cindy.

"I have something for you too," I said.

"A present for *me*?" She seemed very surprised.

"I'm sorry it's late."

She unwrapped the treasure I had found in the Florida waters. I hadn't thought of giving it to her when I had found it, but the more I had looked at the color of the tropical water, the more I had been reminded of the color of her eyes.

"A necklace!"

"Do you like it?"

"It's adorable!"

She seemed so happy that I didn't tell her I had found it on a snorkeling dive.

"I'm going to put it on right now," she said, stepping toward a wall mirror in the foyer. She slipped it over her head.

"Just right," she said, fondling the coral necklace that seemed to match the turtleneck.

She walked over to me and we hugged again.

"You're really a very sweet man," she whispered in my ear. The tender reverberation of her voice tantalized me.

As I held her, I felt myself aroused again, and for a second I thought she might kiss me. But we separated somewhat awkwardly, and she led me into the kitchen where she poured herself a glass of red wine and handed me a beer.

"I've been drinking more wine," she said, sipping. "Even joined a wine club."

She looked flushed in the kitchen light, and I noticed the bottle, a large Cabernet, was half empty.

I asked her how things were going and she beamed.

"Wonderful! Absolutely wonderful!"

She told me she had been rehearsing for her play at Fells Point; a woman from the neighborhood had been babysitting. Her job was fine. She had even gone on a few "nothing special" dates.

"How does Ethan take that?" I asked.

"Well, I don't make it a topic of conversation. I try to limit our discussions to concerns about Bryan. I let the lawyers handle the rest."

"Has it gone that far?"

"Oh, yes."

Then Bryan came into the kitchen.

"Wanta do the puzzle with me?" he asked.

"In a minute, honey," Cindy said. "We're having a grown-up conversation right now."

"Be with you in a few minutes," I said

"You do look really happy," I said after Bryan left. In the middle of the sentence I was about to say beautiful but caught myself.

"It's a sense of relief really. It's been very difficult these last few years. "

I could only imagine how incredibly difficult it was being married to a man like Ethan.

"Has Ethan seen Bryan?" I asked.

"Once. On Christmas. He brought us presents. It was embarrassing how much he spent."

She sipped her wine.

"He's called a lot. When he tries to pry into my social life, I say goodbye and hang-up. Mostly he tries to talk me into taking him back, how much he misses me, all that crap."

"He sounds desperate."

"He is." She smiled. "Even his girlfriend is giving him trouble. I'm not supposed to know about her. She called me a month or so ago. It hurt at first; then it all seemed rather trite and funny."

It must still hurt, I thought. She was putting on a very strong front. But I decided to change the subject.

"Have you ever heard about Ethan having trouble

with the IRS?"

"Not recently. Though he used to bitch about them a few years ago as I recall. Why? Is there anything I should know about?"

"I'm sure it's nothing."

"He did say something about losing a few customers."

"What customers?" I asked, surprised.

"I don't know but apparently they were pretty big."

"I didn't hear anything about it," I said.

"Well, he could have been making it up," she said. "To make me feel sorry for him."

I decided I would let the matter drop, but it was interesting that I hadn't heard anything about losing big customers. Ethan serviced those mega clients himself, so I wondered if he hadn't said anything because he was embarrassed. Or maybe Cindy was right; maybe he had made it up to solicit sympathy from her.

We finished our drinks and Cindy started dinner. I gazed at her as she turned her back to me near the stove, stared at her lovely hair. She looked so good it took a feat of restraint not to go over to her and plant a kiss on her head.

I went back to the living room. The television was on and Bryan was half watching and half working on the puzzle. I sat down on the floor next to him.

"Awesome," Bryan said suddenly.

I looked up at what he was watching and saw a lion chasing a snake. The lion grabbed the snake in its mouth and hurled it into the dry brush. We watched a few other African wildlife devour each other. In one scene a tiger was sitting peacefully on the dry grass, calmly munching the entrails of a gazelle.

A few minutes later, Cindy came in from the kitchen and watched the action on screen.

"Look, Mom," Bryan said.

"I see, sweetheart," she said. "I hope it makes you boys hungry."

She leaned over me, resting her hand on my shoulder. "Sort of reminds me of my marriage," she whispered.

We all watched the show for a few minutes more, and then Cindy's phone rang.

"Speaking of the devil," she said, glancing at her phone. "It's Ethan."

She ignored it, but a minute later it rang again. She smiled at me, shaking her head.

"He used to call in the morning. I guess to check on my whereabouts. Now he calls to disturb our dinner. I usually don't answer."

The phone rang for the third time.

"I guess I better get it. He might just keep calling all night." She picked up her phone and left for the kitchen.

"What happens to the animals when they die?"

I had been watching Cindy walk back into the kitchen and had forgotten the show for a moment. Bryan was now looking at me.

"I don't know," I said.

"I thought teachers knew everything."

I smiled. "Maybe that's why I don't teach anymore." That didn't impress him. "You know what I do now?"

"What?"

"I work for your daddy."

He thought for a moment.

"What does my daddy do?"

The question hung in the air long enough for Cindy to come back into the room and announce that Ethan wanted to talk with me. I was a little surprised, maybe a little guilty.

"Your mother will explain," I said to Bryan.

"Explain what?"

I let Bryan ask the question again and went back to

the kitchen to talk with my boss, whom I had not seen for about ten days.

"You're not fucking my wife are you, Paul?"

The question shocked me for a second. It was almost as if he were somehow aware of what I had been feeling.

"Just kidding," he said. "How's everything? How was Florida?"

I told him Florida was fine. He wasn't interested at all.

"What are you doing New Year's Eve?"

I told him I had plans.

"Shit. Shauna wants to have a party here. But I can't get anybody to come. Charlie's down in North Carolina. Sam's out of state."

"I thought Shauna wasn't in the picture anymore."

"Jesus, Paul. Cindy won't see me."

I thought of stating the obvious: that one reason Cindy didn't want to see him anymore was that he was frolicking with women like Shauna.

"So, what's Cindy been up to?"

"Making dinner," I said. "Looks like meatloaf."

"You know what I mean. Who's she been seeing?"

"You'll have to ask her that."

"I do. She tells me to fuck myself."

"Well."

"By the way, why *are* you there?"

"Didn't Cindy tell you?"

"She said you brought Bryan some presents."

"That's right."

I was glad she hadn't mentioned *her* present.

"I want her back, Paul."

"You don't seem lonely," I said.

He ignored me.

"Do you think there's any chance? I mean for her and me getting back together?"

It was none of my business, I said. That's something they would have to deal with together. He didn't like that answer better than the others, so he changed the subject.

"Listen," he said, "I want you to make an Eastern Shore run soon."

"That's Charlie's territory."

"He'll be busy with me in New York. It's convention time. I'd take you along but we need somebody to keep the customers happy. Anyway, you'll get to see Sam again. I told him you'd be coming down."

He spoke to Cindy once more while Bryan and I worked on the puzzle. I heard her voice rise a few times. "We've been through that, Ethan," she said more than once. Then she was back and dinner was served. Cindy drank a few glasses of wine with dinner; I had two beers; Bryan was sipping juice out of an Orioles mug.

After dinner, about eight or so, Bryan and I were in the living room finishing the puzzle when Cindy came in.

"Time for bed, young man."

"Not now, Mom."

"Brush your teeth," she said.

"I'll read you a story," I said.

Bryan looked at me, surprised. "You will?"

I nodded. "Go ahead. I'll meet you in your room."

"Nothing scary," Cindy whispered.

In Bryan's room, I tucked him in and asked what story he wanted to hear. He handed me a book about the Civil War.

"You like Civil War stuff, huh?"

"Yeah."

"Have you been to any battlefields? Gettysburg?"

He shook his head.

"It's really cool," I said. "There's this one place called Devil's Den."

"Really?" he asked. "Does it have devils?"

I laughed. "They say there may be some ghosts. But it's mostly a bunch of huge boulders – you know giant rocks – where the soldiers fought."

"Wow."

"Maybe I could take you sometime."

"Really? When? Tomorrow?"

I laughed. "Not tomorrow. When it gets warmer."

I thumbed through the well-worn book, found a piece on Jeb Stuart and started to read. After about ten minutes, I glanced over to Bryan who was now asleep.

When I came back to the living room, Cindy was seated on the sofa with her legs tucked under her. I sat down on the chair. She was sipping a fresh glass of wine.

"You want another beer?"

"I better not."

"Sure?"

"I've got to drive."

She sipped her drink, closed her eyes, reopened them.

"You know what Bryan said when you were on the phone with Ethan?"

"What?"

"He said, 'Mommy, can Paul be my next Daddy?' It almost broke my heart."

It almost broke mine.

"He really likes you," she said.

"He's a great kid," I said. "You know if you need a babysitter, I'd be glad to watch him."

"That's sweet. I can usually get one of my neighbors. Sometimes I take him up to my sister's in York. She has a boy a year older."

"Let me know. I mean it."

We sat there and looked at each other for a moment. I thought of telling her how great she looked in red. How great she looked period.

But I didn't. I couldn't.

Instead, I said that I probably should be going.

"Really?" she asked. "So early?"

Her voice and eyes were alluring and inviting, but I looked away, feeling aroused and confused.

I managed to stand up and headed for the closet for my coat. When I looked back at her, she hadn't moved. She was sipping her wine and gazing up at me.

"Are you sure you have to leave?" she asked.

She looked so lovely, so desirable.

"I think I should."

"Okay," she said. "I'll walk you out."

She got up slowly, helped me on with my coat, and we walked out together. We stopped by my car. The air was still and cold.

"Thanks for Bryan's presents," she said. "And mine."

We faced each other and she put her arms around my neck, let me look closely into her eyes, almost silver now in the dim light.

Then she took me into her arms, holding me tight, her body pressed against me. She stroked the back of my neck, ran her fingers through my hair, started kissing my neck, her lips firm and moist. She kissed my neck once, twice, three times. Maybe four or five more. I lost count, it felt so good. Holding her, stroking her hair, feeling her body pressed against me, I wanted to kiss her, I wanted her so much I could barely stand it.

Slowly she pulled away, grasping my hands, looking up at me.

"It was so nice seeing you," she said in a whisper.

At that instant, I was so turned on I couldn't speak.

"You need to visit more," she said.

"I really enjoyed the dinner," I managed to say but my voice was raspy.

"You're welcome," she said. "Anytime."

I looked in her eyes and I knew she wanted me to

stay, I knew I could walk her back inside and everything would change in a minute.

But I knew I couldn't, I knew I shouldn't. So I let her hands go gently and started to turn toward the car.

Then I thought of something.

"Let me know about your acting debut."

She laughed. "I almost forgot. Three weeks. I'll call you."

"Good," I said. "I look forward to it."

After I started the car, I looked back at her. She was standing by the porch light waving goodbye. I sat for a moment watching her until she put her hand down and walked inside. Full of longing and guilt, I turned the car around and drove away.

19

The drive north to see Shelly on New Year's Eve started with a leaden sky and snow beginning to fall heavily with evening traffic. After about an hour, an accident on 95 about ten miles south of the Pennsylvania line slowed traffic to a standstill. I sat in my car watching the snowflakes thicken outside, listening to the radio, my new suitcase thrown into the trunk, my nerves on edge.

Somewhere a 150 miles and hours ahead was Shelly Moran. She had called the night after I had come home from Cindy Canton's, breathlessly announcing that a last-minute cancellation had left a "sumptuous" room available in what was essentially a honeymoon lodge.

"They have a Jacuzzi in each room," she said. "A fireplace too." She told me she couldn't wait to see me.

When I didn't immediately respond, she asked if something was wrong. I told her I was fine, that I'd see her soon.

But the truth was my desires and emotions were in turmoil. My memory of Cindy Canton was too vivid.

I had left at five and soon the dark had come and before I knew it the hour was six, seven, and I was barely into Pennsylvania. Then eight, and the snow was falling more heavily, filling the windshield and highway. Shelly had expected me around seven, and I tried to make a call with the company cell phone, but the battery had died. I began to look for an exit to make a call. I was stopped again by another accident, the flashing blue lights of patrol cars and the red of brake lights, the only color in

209

the night.

My head pounded from the concentration it took to drive through the snow. The radio had turned into scratchy blather, so I put on a Frank Sinatra CD that Buck had given me, and I hummed along with Frank about the virtues of New York, Chicago, and approaching life my way. But I became increasingly aware that this trip was not going my way at all. I wasn't even sure what my way was.

I saw an exit sign, the possibility of a phone call, and I diverged from a steady path onto a blurry ramp exit and the dim lights of a service station. After I parked and stepped out, I slipped on an unseen layer of ice, felt a sudden turn of my ankle, a shot of pain, and my whole torso crashed awkwardly against the front of the car. I grabbed the hood, but my legs slid under the car, and I was lying on a blanket of fresh snow and ice. I'm not sure if I was afraid to test my ankle or if I simply didn't want to go any further. But after a sudden burst of icy wind, I pulled myself up. My ankle held my weight and I limped my way over to the office entrance. I slipped twice before banging my way through the door, hearing the ding of a bell ring as I entered.

The young attendant inside looked at me with some concern. He probably thought I was drunk.

"You all right?" he asked.

"I sprained my ankle outside."

"Yeah, it's really snowing."

He let me use his cell phone and I dialed Shelly's number. She answered immediately.

"Where *are* you?" Her voice was like a siren. "It's almost nine o'clock. I've been texting and calling you non-stop for two hours!"

"My phone died."

"You mean you didn't charge it for the trip?"

"I forgot."

"You don't have a charger?"

"It's in my bag in the trunk. I couldn't pull over until now."

"I can't believe it. You don't leave a charger in your bag, Paul."

"I should have thought of that."

"What time did you leave?"

"About four," I said, fudging an hour off the real time.

"Four? Where are you calling from?"

"A service station. I'm barely in Pennsylvania. It's snowing like hell here. I can't see two feet in front of me."

"It's snowing here too, for God's sake. Why didn't you leave earlier? Didn't you know it was going to snow?"

"I should have, I guess."

"When are you going to get here? The room is beautiful; I've got bottles of champagne ..."

"I don't know."

"What do you mean you don't know? I can't believe you left at four – what were you thinking?"

"That I had plenty of time."

I thought I heard her sob.

"Don't you want to see me?" she cried.

I don't know whether I hesitated, but I guess I did. My ankle was throbbing and who knows what thoughts were bouncing around my jangled brain.

"Sure, I do."

"You don't! I could tell by your voice the other night. God, I spent so much money ..."

"I'll pay you back."

"You mean you're *not* coming?" A scream now.

That was the real question, no doubt about it; outside I could see the snow growing against my wheels.

"I don't know. The roads are horrible."

"You don't want to see me. That's why you left so late ... that's why you didn't charge your phone."

I listened as she sobbed into the phone for several seconds, feeling more and more guilty and miserable with every sob.

"Shelly..." I started to speak but I wasn't even sure what I was going to say. I didn't understand it myself.

"What?"

"I don't think I can make it. I'm sorry."

I listened to more sobs, some breathing.

"I'm really sorry, Shelly."

She was still sobbing in the phone.

"Shelly?"

I heard a loud click and she was gone.

I looked over at the attendant. "Lover's spat," I said.

"Yeah," he said. "Hear it all the time."

He told me there was a hotel seven miles up the highway. After another half hour drive through the snow, I got lucky, they had two rooms left.

"You have a bar?" I asked the man behind the desk.

"We do. The band has already started."

He offered some help with my suitcase, but by then I was a storm trooper, accustomed to the pain, and I found my way to the first-level room that seemed about a half mile from the front office.

Inside the room, I pulled my charger out of the suitcase and left my phone charging on the nightstand. I turned up the heat, stripped off my wet clothes and examined my swollen ankle. Then I slipped on a pair of blue jeans and decided to hobble down the hallway for some ice. On my way, some people came flying out of a nearby room, almost knocking me against the wall.

"Whoa, man. Sorry."

I found the ice machine and dragged myself and the plastic ice bucket back to my room. I put the ice in a towel and pressed it gently against my swollen ankle. As I iced my ankle, I felt a growing sense of guilt. The trip had turned into a disaster. I had left too late to avoid the storm, I hadn't checked my phone battery, I had left the phone charger in the trunk. And I had lied to Shelly and myself. Now she was in a romantic inn, probably drinking her rage away. I thought of calling her, of texting her, but I knew I would feel compelled to lie again, and I felt I had done enough of that already.

I suddenly became restless. So I stood up, tested my ankle, and took a shower. When I was finished, I got dressed and headed for the bar. Maybe a few drinks would make the mess I had made seem better.

The bar was crowded, probably with the spill-over from travelers driven in from the snow. A band was perched on a little platform, playing too loud. I sat next to an older heavy-set couple in the middle of the bar and ordered a red wine, a cabernet. As I sipped my wine, I watched the group of people who had bumped into me in the hallway. They were sitting at a table, stuffing cocktail napkins in their ears. Perhaps it was because of the band.

I noticed the woman next to me leaning over and saying something. She appeared quite drunk.

"Excuse me?"

"Storm drive you in?" She had a big sloppy smile on her face.

"Afraid so," I said.

"We were going to a party," her husband chimed in, leaning around the back of his wife. "My brother-in-law throws a bash in the Poconos every year. First time we've missed in I don't know how many years."

"You by yourself?" his wife asked me.

I nodded.

"That's a shame."

"A shame? There's chicks all over the fucking place," the husband said.

He was clearly drunk too. In fact everybody in the place appeared drunk except me.

"You married?" his wife asked me.

I shook my head no.

"Wise choice. Stay that way. Sow the wild oats," the husband said.

They told me their names were Frank and Angie, but when I told them my name was Paul, Frank must have misheard me.

"Saul," he said. "That's a Jewish name."

"I think he said Paul," Angie said.

"He said Saul. Are you deaf?" Frank said to his wife. He turned to me. "It's Saul, right?"

They were so drunk I wasn't in the mood to correct them. Maybe I wasn't in the mood to be Paul Simmons.

"Yeah, Saul."

"See," he said to his wife, smiling. "You *are* deaf."

Frank turned back to me. "So, you're Jewish, right? I don't have anything against Jews, I was just curious."

What was I? My mother probably would have called me a lapsed Episcopalian.

"You don't look Jewish," Angie said.

I wondered if I looked like a lapsed Episcopalian. But I wasn't in the mood for that discussion either.

So I said, "I was but I'm not anymore."

Frank looked drunker and more confused.

"You know what I'd like to know," Angie said. "You being Jewish and all."

"He said he's not a Jew anymore."

"Well, he was."

"I'm a scientologist now," I said. I'd read an article about scientology so I thought I'd try it out for a night.

But Angie wasn't interested in my new faith.

"In Jewish weddings, why do they smash the glass with their feet?" she asked.

I had actually gone to a Jewish wedding a few years before and had asked someone that same question. But I couldn't remember the answer, so I decided to make something up.

"They break the glass to symbolize the breaking of the wife's hymen," I said.

"*Really*?" Angie asked.

"I used to teach history."

Frank laughed. "Sounds like bullshit to me."

"Don't insult the man's religion, Frank."

"I'm not," he said. "Besides he's not a Jew any more. He's a scientist."

With my religious affiliation settled, Frank and Angie waddled off to dance, joined by a mass of people.

As midnight approached, a cloud of multi-colored balloons appeared, the bartenders popped champagne, and there was a drumbeat from the band stand. The television mysteriously turned on to the big Times Square ball, the countdown rolling through the room like giggly thunder, until the final little orgasmic clash of horns and screams. There was a rush of smooching faces on the dance floor, people indiscriminately grabbing each other. I watched Frank and Angie press their flaccid faces together, and Frank looked about for other available lips. I lost sight of him attempting to slurp a tall blond ski queen. I lost sight because suddenly a barmaid had spun my head around and kissed me.

"Happy New Year," she said.

I was grabbed by another woman from the back and kissed. And then another. In a minute the earthquake was over, the tremors settled, and I was sitting with my plastic champagne glass alone as the rest of the crowd rediscovered lovers and husbands and wives and friends. The music resumed but I decided to leave. I limped down the brown-carpeted hallway into my room, took off my clothes, brushed my teeth, and lay down.

I noticed my phone still on the nightstand, and I could see it was lit up. When I picked it up, there were two text messages from Shelly.

> 10: 48:
> *your a complete asshole*
>
> 12:01:
> *happy fucking new year*

I texted her back and said I was very sorry. But she didn't respond. Maybe she was texting her friends about what a complete asshole I was. Maybe she was already in bed with somebody else. Maybe her Boston lover had come down to salvage the night.

I deserved it. I deserved it all.

I lay on the bed, staring at the phone and the nasty texts. It had been a long pointless night, and I deleted Shelly's messages as a way of relieving my guilt.

I tried to forget the travesty with Shelly and started wondering about Cindy Canton. What was she doing New Year's Eve? I wondered if she was with Bryan watching the ball fall, or if she was alone in her family room, watching the last embers of a dying fire. I wondered if she was thinking of calling me, of texting me. I hoped she was. I hoped she was thinking of a lot more than that. Lying naked under the hotel sheets, *I* certainly was.

I held my phone up and started to text her a message.

Happy New Year!
Was just thinking about you. Hoping

I stopped and deleted it. I couldn't text what I was really hoping for. Because what I was really hoping for couldn't happen.

So I turned on the television and immersed myself in an old *CSI* episode. It was actually comforting to watch the stellar forensics team dig up a pair of decomposed bodies in the Nevada desert.

20

A few weeks later, I was reunited with Cindy Canton through my voice mail. She called to tell me that her opening night was on Friday; she would leave two tickets for me at the ticket window. She hoped I could come. She hoped I was well. Her tone was sweet and suggestive, making me remember and imagine too much.

The next day, Ethan asked me to come to his office. Since he had left Cindy he had moved into an apartment in Columbia.

"Listen," Ethan said that day in his office after I had sat down. "I want to do something special for Cindy. She's really up for this play she's in. I want to give her an opening night party. I know she doesn't want to see me. That's where you come in. I want you tell her you're throwing the party."

"She won't believe it," I said.

"I thought of that. You'll have to make it sound sort of casual, you know, off hand, not planned. I was thinking it might be better to have it at your place. I'll pay for everything. Have it catered – everything she likes. Real special. The whole cast."

"If it's that lavish, she'll know you paid for it."

"Well, that's the whole idea, isn't it? That I cared enough to do something that big for her. I'd tell her eventually anyway."

"Don't you think it's a little deeper than that?"

"What did she say to you?"

"Nothing."

Ethan got up and played with his venetian blinds.

"Christ," he said. "It's a start." He turned toward me. "Can't you do that for me? Can't you help me out?"

It was a bad idea in so many ways I couldn't begin to count. But Ethan was standing above me, his face anguished. Perhaps a sense of guilt overcame me.

"All right, Ethan," I said and got up. He walked with me to the office door.

"Call Cindy. Ask her about the play, tell her about the party idea. I'll handle all the other details."

"Are you going to show up?"

"No. Definitely not. This has to be indirect." Then he paused. "Do you think I should come?"

"No."

"You're right. I'll stay out of it." He opened the door for me. Touched my shoulder. "You don't know how much I appreciate this, Paul. I mean it."

When I called Cindy that evening to arrange the party, I ostensibly called to check on the time of the event, something I could have easily gleaned from the internet, a phone call to the theatre, or a glance at the newspaper. She started talking excitedly about what a great bunch the cast members were. When she said she was really looking forward to seeing me, I felt a thrill and I almost forgot why I was calling. But I gathered my thoughts and dramatically declared I would throw her a party at my apartment.

"That's really sweet, Paul, but we all planned to go to this bar afterward; they have a back room. You can come of course."

I hadn't thought of that; neither had Ethan I suspect. I wasn't sure what to say. I couldn't exactly insist.

"Oh, well," I said.

"Are you bringing a date?" she asked suddenly.

I wasn't expecting that question.

"No," I said. "A friend of mine." I had already asked Stevenson to go.

"Good," she said.

When I hung up with her I called Ethan. A woman answered, I don't know if it was Shauna; then Ethan came on the line.

"Wait a minute," he said. There was a long pause before he returned. "Just wanted to be alone," he said.

I told Ethan what I had found out.

"Shit," he said. "Shit," he said again. "Okay, okay, I'll have to cancel the caterer. It'll cost me my deposit. Dammit." There was a pause. I could almost hear him thinking. "I got it," he said. "I'll just call the bar. I'll pick up their tab. Hell, that might even work out better. When the time comes to pay, the management will say it's been taken care of by Mr. Ethan Canton. A fucking white knight. Yes. That might work much better. Don't you think, Paul?"

"Sure. Whatever you say."

"It's perfect."

"Ethan, I wouldn't expect too much."

"It's a foot in the proverbial door, Paul."

The Thames Street Theatre is small, a renovated building on a quaint cobblestone street in the hubbub of Fells Point bars and waterfront antique shops. Inside, there is a homey kind of feeling, as if you had set up your spacious living room for a little show. About seventy-five seats, chairs really, the stage almost in your lap.

Stevenson and I were sitting in the second row; there was no curtain. I saw Cindy's name in the playbill and even a black and white photo; she was playing a woman named Colleen.

The play turned out to be a comedy basically, a sweetly sentimental piece set in what seemed to be a small Irish village. The lead actor was outrageously hammy. He started with a heavy Irish brogue, which became a slight brogue, then working class British, interspersed with a low dose of East Baltimore. He was a howl.

But mostly I remember Cindy. Her role was not as small as she had pretended; indeed it was pivotal. As the maid, she was given a number of pithy and witty lines. Her role, her portrayal, gave the play its heart. Her Irish accent, to my untrained ear and to Stevenson who had visited Ireland, sounded believable and natural. And her comic timing was deft. But even more remarkable was her stage presence. I have spoken of her luminous eyes before. Well, on the stage, enhanced with make-up and lighting, they animated her whole character. I could hardly keep my own eyes off her, even when she was in the background, setting the table, while other actors cavorted front and center.

At the end, when all the actors took their bows, when the audience's applause rose in intensity as she came back out on stage, she appeared elated. She even waved to me as she left the stage.

"Wonderful!" Stevenson said about Cindy. "And I believe she fancies you."

"Let's go," I said.

We were putting our coats on and heading outside toward the bar.

"Are you in love with her?" he asked.

"She's married," I said.

I didn't mention that she was on her way to a divorce. Nor did I mention my increasingly conflicted feelings about her.

The party for the cast was being held at an

establishment called Ed's (named for the illustrious Edgar Allan Poe), in a private room off the main bar. I had expected a small intimate crowd, the cast, a few others. But the event had escalated, and by the time the cast arrived, out of costume now, there was barely room to move.

Stevenson and I availed ourselves of the bar just before the major onslaught. When Cindy appeared, her dowdy maid persona had been shed. Her hair, which had been pinned back in a dull bun, and been released into a honey blond cascade. But the eyes remained the same, and when she saw me from across the room, she waved and hurried over.

"I'm so glad you came," she said, hugging me, her warmth and scent reminding me of the night in front of her house.

"You were great!"

I introduced her to Stevenson.

"You were brilliant," he said.

"Thanks. God I was nervous. Did you see me during that first scene? I almost dropped the stupid plate I was washing."

"You were the highlight of my week," Stevenson said.

She turned to me.

"Who is this guy, Paul?"

"Talent scout," I said.

"If I were a talent scout I'd acquire your talents immediately."

"What do you really do?"

I was about to say he was an engineer, but someone, a cast member or someone from the crew, suddenly came up to us, grabbed Cindy, and literally lifted her off her feet. And, laughing and waving, she was hauled away. As she left, I felt a twinge of anger.

"She seems very popular," Stevenson said. "Is that her husband?"

"No."

"Where's her husband?" he asked.

"I don't know."

We stood and drank for a few minutes, the crowd overwhelming us. It was a motley collection of guests and Stevenson commented that he should have a good number of opportunities tonight. The women were certainly plentiful, he said, and offered a "rich cultural buffet."

I was thinking of Cindy, however, remembering what had happened the last time I had seen her, wondering what would happen tonight. Unfortunately, my brief indulgence in fantasy was interrupted by Stevenson who was elbowing me.

"The phony Irishman seems to have taken a fancy to your girl," Stevenson said. "I guess that's the advantage of being the star of the show."

"What do you mean?"

"Look," he said. He pointed discreetly over to Cindy who now appeared to be with the cast members in the corner of the bar, clearly enjoying herself.

She was standing next to the tall hammy actor who had been so hilarious in his unintentional shifting accents. I watched as he put his arm around her, massaged her shoulders, and rubbed her lower back. Then, even more disgustingly, he let his fingers wander up to stroke her lovely honey hair. His caresses didn't last long, but they lasted too long for me. In my eyes, he was no longer a floundering comic figure, he was no longer hilarious at all. He was now an untalented and detestable prick. I turned away and ordered a double shot of bourbon.

In a matter of thirty minutes, the whole party had

become nauseating to me. Even the double shot failed to lift my spirits. Meanwhile, Stevenson had been scanning the crowd and soon began to wander about, sniffing out the lovely prey.

Dispirited, I retreated from the crowd, my back eventually pressing up against the exposed brick wall in the rear of the barroom. In the nineteenth century this room had probably been a filthy alley, frequented by thieves, drunks, and prostitutes. Perhaps even Mr. Poe himself had wandered here. I could almost imagine him intoxicated, staggering about in the darkness, and urinating on the very same exposed brick I was leaning against. Maybe, in a deep romantic despair, he might have tried to seduce a few local harbor tarts before passing out for the evening.

Through the raucous crowd in front of me, I caught sight of Cindy laughing and yakking it up with her other thespians and crew members, their whole assemblage exuding euphoria. I didn't see the hammy actor but I'm sure he was nearby ready to continue pawing her. It was all so disturbingly esoteric, so private I could not even vicariously enjoy their moment of comradery. Worst of all, Cindy did not seem to be aware of my presence. I was merely an insignificant spectator in her moment of glory.

After I finished my second shot, I walked over to Stevenson, who was chatting up a lovely petite black girl. He seemed captivated.

"I'm not feeling well," I said. "I think I'm going to take off."

"Sorry to hear that, my friend."

"I'll take a cab."

"Are you sure?"

I patted him on the back, wished him luck, and exited into the cold night. For a moment, I thought about reentering and saying goodbye to Cindy, but I kept walking away, not sure what I was really doing, or why. I walked up and down Fells Point, thought about joining the crowds in other bars, but I just kept trudging the streets, the cold air numbing my feet and ears. Eventually, I snared a cab, took the ten minute ride back to my apartment.

As I walked by my neighbor's door, I noticed that there was something caught in the door jamb, a leather strap or belt of some sort. For a second I just passed it by, but I suddenly felt like being neighborly; or maybe I just wanted to talk to someone. I hadn't seen him much, not since he had given me a ticket to a museum gala that I had failed to attend. So I rapped on the door.

I heard a shuffle from inside, then the door opened and there was Chad, his eyes bloodshot, as forlorn as a condemned man. I pointed to the strap.

"Oh, Christ," he said.

It was a strap from a raincoat, he said.

"Are you all right?"

He was crying. A rare sight really. A grown man standing in his doorway crying.

He invited me in, a beautiful place, the antithesis of mine, every piece of furniture, every plant and knick-knack tastefully arranged. We sat on a sofa. He dabbed his face with a tissue.

"What's wrong?" I asked.

"It's Davey," he said. "He broke up with me."

"I'm sorry."

I had no idea what to tell him. I felt much the same way. I felt abandoned too. I listened for a while as he talked about Davey, how kind and strong he was, even now that he was a worthless no good shit. The love-hate rant rambled on for about twenty minutes. When the story ended, I decided I had better leave. I told

Chad if he needed to talk, to drop by. It was all I could say. When I left, he was sitting on the sofa, ready, I knew, to resume sobbing.

I was exhausted when I got in my apartment. I dropped out of my clothes and fell into bed and fell asleep almost immediately.

Late the next morning I jogged to the athletic club and played a tennis match with Stevenson, who beat me for the first time in his life. He seemed buoyant.

"I'm in love," he said later over lunch at the club.

"Who?"

"Gorgeous creature! Such eyes!"

"Cindy?" I think I almost yelled because Stevenson looked at me surprised.

"No, my friend. Deborah. Deborah! You saw her. I was with her when you abandoned me."

I felt relieved.

"And you want to know something? I didn't have her last night. I was a perfect gentleman. In fact, I am actually reconsidering my whole approach to women."

He rambled on about dear Deborah, a graduate student at Hopkins, anthropology.

"And her father's an engineer, if you can imagine the coincidence."

I could barely eat anything, but he ate as if food had been spared him for a week.

"Oh, by the way, your friend Cindy was quite the hit of the party. Quite funny. Imitated the lead actor uproariously."

"Really?"

He nodded. "She asked where you were. Seemed heartbroken that you had left."

"What happened?"

"To her? Can't say. I was absorbed with Deborah."

I started to tell him about Shelly and Cindy, my mixed feelings, but I couldn't articulate it. Perhaps I didn't want to.

While eating, I received a call from Ethan but ignored it.

I checked the message later.

"Paul," the message said, "I tried to call Cindy at home but no one answered. Is she with you? How did the party go? Call me."

I had almost forgotten Ethan; it had been his party after all. And he was the last person I wanted to call. But I didn't have to. He called me again.

"Where's Cindy?" he blurted. "Is she with you?"

"With me? No."

"Then where the hell is she?"

"How should I know, Ethan?"

"I've been calling her all night and all this morning."

"So?"

"'*So*'!" he screamed back at me, horrified by the impertinence of the word.

"Well, maybe she spent the night with a friend?"

"What friend?"

"I don't know, Ethan. Calm down."

He paused but I could hear his breathing.

"How did my party go?"

"Fine."

"What do you mean 'fine'?"

"I didn't stay long. I got sick."

"What about Cindy?"

"She did a great job in the play."

"What about at the party?"

"She seemed happy."

"What do you mean 'happy'?"

"Come on, Ethan. These are simple words. She was a big hit."

"Who was she with?"

"The cast, the crew. I didn't know them."

"Anybody special?"

"Not that I noticed. I told you I left early."

"She fucked somebody."

"Ethan —"

"I know it."

I heard a voice in the background of the phone.

"It's Paul," I heard Ethan say. "Work shit."

"Who was that?" I asked.

He ignored me, but I assumed it was Shauna.

"I had a lot to drink last night, Paul."

"That isn't exactly news."

"Don't get moral with me. I've been desperate."

"Well, you have Shauna to comfort you."

"Christ." His voice was pure anguish. "Are you sure you didn't see Cindy with anyone special?"

I told him I was sure.

The next day I took a long run and a shower, and then blew out of town with an overnight bag. When I left, I had no idea where I was going, just that I had to get out.

At first I headed up 83 north, but the image of Cindy Canton loomed up, her house only a few miles away, and I took an exit and turned around, heading back to the beltway where I turned east, drove to 95 north, thought about going to Philadelphia, but I saw the turn off for the Delaware and Maryland shores. I had some deliveries and appointments on the Eastern Shore. I thought it might be a good idea to spend the weekend near the ocean. I could see Sam and the other customers Monday.

The day was bright and cold, the winter wind blowing the trees, swaying the bridges, and drying out the whole countryside. I didn't care; I was behind my tinted sunglasses behind my tinted windshield, trying to lose myself in a University of Maryland basketball game on the radio, a game that was veering in and out. Finally I flicked it off and popped in a jazz CD mix.

The truth was I was feeling the same despair as Ethan. I too was wondering where Cindy had slept, whom she had slept with. But I had no justification or right to feel anything – none at all. In fact, Ethan, the itinerant whore, had more right to his suspicions than I did.

21

A few hours into my escape from Baltimore, I stopped in the scenic town of St. Michael's for an early dinner. The restaurant overlooked a lovely blue inlet. There was a modest crowd of watermen, along with tourists absorbing the local color and scenery. Dressed in blue jeans and a ski jacket, I could pass for either. Nodding to a few locals, I found a seat at the bar and ordered a crab cake sandwich.

In a nearby booth off the bar sat a man about my age and his wife. With them was a girl about five. The girl was coloring and oblivious of her parents who seemed to be arguing while perusing menus. I cocked an ear to try to capture the nature of the argument but could only hear the wife's insistent repetition of "You always do this." What her husband always did made me curious. He was sipping a draft beer, he was remaining silent – what could it be? Perhaps it was his inability to make a menu selection. Perhaps she had planned to eat at a more polished and refined restaurant. She kept talking and his eyes remained buried in the menu, but I had the suspicion he was merely waiting out the storm, waiting for the barrage to stop.

I imagined him wondering if it were all worthwhile, the pretty wife, the lovely daughter, the whole sweet veneer of matrimony. Then he looked over to his wife and said something. She smiled; she reached out her hand.

I finished eating and left, stopping in the dusk light to take in the fragrance of the water, feeling suddenly sleepy.

I stayed two nights in St. Michael's, spending my days wandering about the water and shops, driving over to Easton and Oxford for a quick look-around. I even bought Bryan a t-shirt, a sailing scene.

After leaving St. Michaels Monday morning, my first stop was a major poultry conglomerate whose headquarters was a glass monstrosity. I arranged for a renewal of a contract for their annual report and other printing needs.

Next I stopped at an outlet mall just outside Ocean City. I met with a neurotic general manager who smoked, paced, and whined. With the neurotic was a pale graphic designer who looked as if he'd rather be smoking pot. They were working on a routine brochure and what should have taken a few minutes took about two hours.

In Ocean City I stopped at a small market and sandwich shop. When I walked in, the place looked deserted. Had I wanted, I could have stripped the cash register to the bone. I called out and after a few moments a girl appeared. She looked surprised to see someone. Her eyes were red and she looked stoned, but I couldn't be sure of that. I asked for Tony, since that was the name of the establishment.

"No Tony here," she said. "You a cop?"

"No," I said, surprised. "Well, is the owner here? I have a delivery for him."

"Manager's here. Upstairs."

She stood there, smiling in a rather odd way.

"Could you tell him I need to see him?"

She didn't react at first; I think she was still trying to grasp the fact that someone had entered the store.

"Yeah, I guess so."

In a few minutes a tall man who resembled John

Brown with a shorter beard tumbled down the stairs and presented himself. He wore stained overalls and a gray t-shirt. The girl stood behind him.

"Who are you?" he asked.

I told him I was with Canton.

"Where's Charlie? He usually makes deliveries."

"He's busy," I said.

He looked at me some more, his eyes searching me for signs of deception.

"You have a card?"

I showed him my business card.

He looked at it and said, "Okay. Where is it?"

I went back to my car to get the box, half afraid that I'd be facing a shotgun when I returned. It was not unusual to make small deliveries in person, especially if there had been a major account nearby, but I had expected a chain of restaurants, not a little battered shop almost hidden in Ocean City.

"Here, let me give you a receipt," I said, after he took the box and handed it ever reluctantly to the girl behind him. I started writing out a receipt for him, but he stopped me.

"Come here," he said. He led me to the restaurant section, away from the girl who stood with the box in her arms.

"Charlie don't give out receipts. "

"I have to give you one," I said. "It's policy. You can do anything you want with it."

I handed it to him. He crumpled it up.

"Is there –"

"No," he answered.

By this time I realized my presence at Tony's had exhausted its value. So I left. It had all been rather bizarre.

The next two stops were small shops, a fudge store

and a gift shop. Both managers accepted my deliveries and receipts suspiciously.

My last stop was at The Dead Duck, Sam Bannion's palace of sin, in Dewy Beach, just north of Ocean City. The exterior of the place looked the same as I pulled up, but a sign on the door said "Closed for the Season."

I had a pretty good memory of where Sam lived, having walked back and forth a few times during the Labor Day Weekend. I stopped at his house about three, knocked about eight times but there was no answer. So I walked to the beach side, the ocean appearing closer now in the winter; wilder, more truculent in the wind. Sand blew against my face as I stepped on the beach and watched the whitecaps.

I looked back at Sam's deck, now deserted and bare. Beige curtains were drawn tight inside the sliding glass doors. Except for the eddying swirl of sand on the deck there was no sign of life. For a moment, I thought Sam might have abandoned Dewey for other geographical playgrounds. Then I recalled that Ethan had said Sam would be expecting me.

I stopped at a restaurant that was open in Dewey Beach and drank a beer, sampled a special of fried shrimp. An hour later I arrived at Sam's to see lights on, the signs of habitation.

The door opened as I walked up, and Sam, in a beard and a fisherman's net sweater, greeted me like a long-lost sailor.

"Glad you could make it," he said. His smile was expansive, and I suddenly wondered if it was lonely here in the winter.

We shook hands and I handed him his Canton package which he quickly put in a hall closet.

We walked through the well-kept formal living room to the family room, somewhat sunken in a spread of thick tan carpet. A gas fireplace blazed. The curtains on the sliding glass doors were still drawn, the ocean's presence shut out from the homey quality of the room.

"Can I get you something to eat?" he asked.

"No, I just had something." He handed me a beer and we sat down. I told him about my earlier deliveries and the odd reaction from the John Brown manager. Sam laughed.

"Grover," he said. "He's a bird."

"You know him?"

"He works for me. I own his place as well as the others you delivered to. Sort of a sideline. Tax write-off. The Duck is closed in the winter. Thank God. Gives me a chance to breathe, do a little reading, travel. Private time."

We chatted a bit about nothing in particular, but when he mentioned that he had a bar-closing party in October, I remembered one of his guests from the Labor Day weekend.

"How's Mr. Pace?" I asked. The image of the older man who had ridden a motorcycle off the end of the dock came into my head.

"Not well," Sam said. "In fact, he's dead."

"Dead? How?"

"Killed in a car crash. Drove into a light pole on Route 50. Drunk as a loon."

"He seemed a very sad man."

Sam nodded. He had finished his beer in about three minutes and was now walking to the kitchen and fetching another. Looking around the room, I noticed something incongruous, something I didn't remember from the last time I had stopped by. Most of Sam's decor had a nautical theme, but there was a portrait now hanging above the mantel, a rather striking girl of about sixteen, long dark hair. When Sam came back he noticed me gazing at the portrait.

"A real beauty, isn't she?"

Her eyes were deep and dark; her smile dazzling.

"She is," I said. "Reminds me of some of my former students."

"She's a junior. She goes to school in California."

I began to form a sordid image of Sam Bannion humping the girl in the back office of The Dead Duck.

"She's my daughter," he said, staring at her.

Surprised, I simply looked at him.

He looked back at me and smiled.

"I just found out about her two months ago."

"That you had a daughter?"

"Hard to believe. I know. It was a woman I met when I was in California on a lark. Before I made any big money. Bumming my way around."

"Why didn't she tell you before?"

He shrugged.

"She's from California. Who knows how they think out there. She was in her thirties at the time, and I guess having a baby was just about the only thing she'd never tried."

"How do you know she's yours?"

"Christ, look at her," he said. She had his features all right. "Her mother is tall, blondish. Nothing like her. She's mine all right."

"There must be a lot of guys with those features though."

He sipped his beer and gazed at the painting.

"Maybe," he said. But I'm not sure he cared. "The mother doesn't want anything, she's got plenty of money. But she's also got cancer. She thought it might be good for Natalie to know her father. Took her a hell of long time to find me." He paused as if reflecting back to those California days.

"How does it feel?" I asked.

"Finding out I'm a father?" He thought for a minute. "You remember that walk we took last summer? That family we saw. I told you I thought that would have been me?"

I nodded.

"That's it. That's how I feel."

"Doesn't it bother you that the mother took so long to let you know?"

"Sometimes. But what the hell. Back then I was a fuck up. She was better off out there; and I was better off not knowing."

He took a deep gulp from his beer.

"Sure, it would've been nice seeing her grow up, pushing the stroller. But that's shit down the toilet now. I think it's best that it happened this way."

"Have you met her?" I asked.

"Not yet. We're going to try to get together spring break maybe. She might even spend the summer with me. Get her a job somewhere. Not the Duck, not yet anyway. But her mother's dying and she wants to stay close. So I'll probably go out there for a while."

The thought of fatherhood, perhaps the warmth of the gas fire and the sedation of the alcohol, made Sam Bannion seem calmer.

"Ethan and Charlie, they're really fucking up," he said.

He looked over at me, a disapproving shake of the head.

"Ethan calls quite a lot. Cries in his beer. He doesn't realize what he has. Or had. Even now as he's begging her to take him back. He doesn't see the whole picture. He wants a wife, a son, and a whore."

I saw the scene in the Canton house myself, feeling the pang in my gut.

"Charlie's a bit different. He just marries whores."

Sam went out and got some more beer.

"What about you?" he asked when he came back in. "Ethan told me about some true love in Boston."

"That's over," I said.

And just then, for the first time, I realized that it *was* over. Shelly, as a possibility for permanence in my romantic life, had been put in the moribund file.

22

A week after my trip to the shore, I walked through the creaking door of the Canton offices. It was about nine a.m. and I had arrived to put in a day of phone calls and paperwork. But as soon as I walked in, Grace grabbed my arm.

"He wants to see you," she said, gesturing toward Ethan's office.

"He's in already?"

Ethan was not known for arriving early, if at all.

She nodded. "And he's in a foul mood."

"Why?" I asked.

She looked reluctant to speak.

"You didn't hear it from me, but he lost another customer. A big one."

I thought of what Cindy had told me before about the loss of some big customers.

"Not one of yours," she said. "One of his!"

"Why does he want to see me then?"

"Don't know. But he's plenty pissed."

When I went in, Ethan was in shirt sleeves rolled up, tie loose, and he was standing nervously by his desk looking at some papers. When he saw me, he stopped and looked at me as if I were a speck of refuse blown in through an air vent.

"Sit down," he barked.

I did. He remained standing behind his desk; then he picked up a brown envelope and poured the contents out rather dramatically. I saw a few typed pages and what looked like photographs.

He looked at me with rage.

"I got this last night. You have anything to say for yourself?" he said.

"About what?"

"This!"

His voice rose and he pointed to the material from the envelope. Being about ten feet away, I had no idea what he was referring to.

"I can't believe it," he said. He looked pale and sick. "Don't you have any feeling, any loyalty?"

"Ethan, what are you talking about?"

He handed me some photos. One showed Cindy hugging Stevenson inside Ed's bar. One was of her and two or three men walking arm in arm down what looked like a Fells Point street. Another was very dark and blurred but appeared to be Cindy embracing a man in front of her house. It took me a moment to realize that I was that man.

"You hired a detective?" I asked.

"You got it," he said proudly. "I knew something was wrong. So I had her checked out."

"You're not serious," I said.

"What do you mean?"

"Did you talk to Cindy about this?"

"Not yet, but I will."

"I wouldn't if I were you."

He stared at me.

"Is that you in the picture?"

"Yes," I said.

"You're not fucking Cindy?"

"No. I was just saying goodbye."

That was one version of the truth. But when I spoke the words I felt guilty. I could remember Cindy's soft lips on my neck and the desire I had felt.

"Ethan, these photos prove nothing. She's not having

an affair with me or anyone else for that matter."

Of course, I had no proof about other men; I think I was indulging in a little wishful thinking.

"What about this guy? The black guy?" He pointed to the picture of Stevenson.

"He's a friend of mine. I guess he was saying goodbye after the cast party. He was with another woman that night."

"And the other guys?"

"What do you think I did, Ethan, set Cindy up with other men? So she could fuck them? Are you crazy? These guys were in the cast. They were just celebrating."

" 'Just celebrating,' " he repeated.

"Yes."

"But where was she all night?"

"Ask your detective," I said. "Wasn't he following her?"

"Yeah," he said. "He followed her home. Stayed about two hours. Then he left about 3 a.m."

"And she was alone?"

"That's what he said."

"What more do you need then?"

"But she didn't answer my calls."

"Come on, Ethan, she was tired," I said. "And she was probably tired of you too. Maybe she didn't want to talk to you. I mean you are separated."

He started to walk around the office, still holding an 8 x 10 photo. But he suddenly crumpled it up and hurled it against the wall.

"Do you know what that fucker charged me?"

"Who?"

"The detective."

"No idea," I said.

"$2,000."

"For nothing."

He looked at me.

"Yeah, for nothing."

He laughed bitterly and sat down, his hands on his head, the strands of hair falling loosely between his kneading fingers. There was a slight tremor; perhaps he was merely shaking his head, but his silence seemed agonizing to me and I guess to him. When he finally looked up, he had a strange sick smile on his face.

"I wanted to believe it," he said, his voice barely above a whisper.

"Why?"

He shrugged.

"I guess I didn't want to admit it was me who fucked up." He laughed in a bitter, self-deprecating manner. "It's a lot easier believing your wife's a slut." He paused. "Like Charlie's."

"What do you mean?" I asked. I had been in and out of the office and hadn't seen Charlie for quite some time.

"That's right, you haven't heard."

Ethan laughed again, more heartily. He relaxed in his chair and seemed in better spirits already now that his estranged wife was still presumably faithful to him.

"It's a classic," Ethan said. "Right up there with the Bannion stories."

I had my chance to hear the story a few weeks later when Charlie caught up with me after an afternoon sales meeting. We agreed to meet for dinner and drinks at a little place in Ellicott City. After his second Jack Daniels, Charlie told me the story.

"Ethan and I were supposed to run up to Philadelphia and spend a few days with this big client, and we were on the way up when the client called and cancelled. It was about 4 p.m., just about time for cocktails. We stopped at this mall restaurant on 95, we had a few, and I went looking for a Christmas present for Annette. We were a bit looped, you know, wandering through the mall and we came to this store that sold stuffed animals.

"Suddenly, Ethan yells, 'Hey Charlie, get her this.' It was an enormous ape, almost as big as me. 'It'll remind her of you when you're out of town,' he said. 'All it needs is a two-inch dick.' So I bought the damn ape."

Charlie paused and ordered another shot of Jack Daniels.

"So I get home that night," he continued. "Really wanted to surprise her, you know. Her thinking I'm out of town. Early Christmas present and all that shit. Great idea, huh?"

The bartender brought the shot, and in a second it disappeared. He ordered another.

Charlie went on, his eyes twinkling. "So I see the house looks dark and I sneak inside real quiet like and stop, just below the stairway. I hear the radio upstairs, pretty loud, which was typical of her. Anyway it's damn dark inside and remember I've got this giant ape in my arms." He laughed. "This is a pretty good story so far, isn't it Paul?"

I nodded, feeling a bit tense.

"So I slip off my shoes to keep myself as quiet as possible, and I creep up the stairwell, turn down the hall and burst into the bedroom, yelling 'Merry Christmas!' Then I tripped on something, a pair of shoes or something, and I flew across the bed.

"Christ, this is a good story," he said.

The drink came. "Down the hatch, old boy." And down it went. His eyes visibly teared. "Well, guess what I landed on, Paul? Oh, God, this is funny."

"It's all right, Charlie."

"No, this is funny, Paul. This is fucking hilarious. You see, I tripped and landed on this guy. A naked guy. The funny part was that the naked guy was fucking my wife. Isn't that funny? And here I am falling across the bed with a gigantic fucking ape."

He laughed and laughed and then the tears began to flow out of the laughter. After a while, he settled down a bit, but his face was red and so were his eyes.

"You have to admit, that's funny, Paul. A fucking comedy routine."

The guy with Annette had apparently scurried out after Charlie fell, grabbing his clothes and escaping before Charlie had a chance of recovering. What Charlie did to Annette he didn't say; and I didn't ask.

"The only thing funnier than the ape story was Ethan getting mugged."

"He didn't say anything about that."

"He wouldn't. But I heard it from Shauna. He was at her apartment. You know a little cozy dinner after he struck out with Cindy. Anyway they took to arguing and when Ethan goes out to his car for something, she locks him out, dead bolt and everything. So he started wandering around the street, trying to figure out what to do. That's when this black dude comes up from behind him, sticks a gun in his ear, and strips him clean. So Ethan, the law-and-order man, goes out and gets himself a piece."

"A gun?"

Charlie nodded. "Can you imagine that, Ethan with a gun? Christ, he can't even control his own dick. Anyway, Shauna let him back in after the police came."

The restaurant was getting crowded by this time, and Charlie's booze consumption was in full throttle, his predatory instincts awakening.

"Why don't I give you a ride home," I said.

"Hell no. Lot of leg coming in right now."

"It's a mirage," I told him.

"Just one beer."

I went to the men's room and when I came back, Charlie was sitting at a table next to two women. By the looks on their faces, they had no interest in his presence. I walked over to him.

"Hey, Paul. Want to meet my next wife?"

"Let's go, Charlie," I said.

"Your friend's drunk," one of the women said.

"Come on, Charlie."

He ignored me, looked at the women.

"You all like funny stories?"

They both looked embarrassed.

"Let me tell you a funny story," he said. "It's called 'Charlie and the Ape.' Or maybe I should call it 'Charlie and the Slut.' What do you think, Paul?"

"I think we have to go," I said, putting my hand on his arm.

"It's a real side splitter," Charlie said. "It'll bust your gut."

Just then a man from the restaurant came over. I assumed he was the manager.

"Is there any trouble?"

"We were just leaving," I said, yanking Charlie's arm.

"No trouble at all, sir," Charlie said, extending his massive hand to the manager, who took it reluctantly. "I was just about to tell a story. Fucking hilarious story right, Paul?"

"I think it might be best to tell the story another time, sir," the manager said.

Charlie turned toward the women.

"You want to hear my story, don't you?"

One of the women spoke up. "Go home."

"It's fucking hilarious," Charlie said.

"I'm afraid I must ask you to leave, sir."

"We are," I said. This time Charlie stood up and

glared at the shorter manager who, although looking a bit squeamish, held his ground. I stepped between them, and began drawing Charlie away, finally out the door. Then I went back in and paid the bill.

When I went back outside, I noticed Charlie slumped against a bench several yards down the street. He was holding his head in his hands and for a moment or two he looked just like Ethan.

23

Valentine's Day came and I thought of sending Cindy a simple card, perhaps a text, but it didn't feel right and I did nothing. I was actually hoping I would hear from her as well, but I didn't. I even thought I might hear from Shelly. But I guess she was long gone, probably back in the arms of her real boyfriend. The only woman who called was my mother who told me I'd always be in her heart.

A few days later, though, I did receive a phone call from Cindy Canton. I hadn't seen her since the night of her opening, and her voice was like a shot of adrenaline. She told me she was auditioning for a new part on Thursday night and needed someone to watch Bryan for a few hours, that I had once, many years ago it seemed, volunteered to babysit him any time.

"I'd love to," I said.

I remembered the t-shirt I had bought for Bryan; it was probably still in my overnight bag. "How is he?"

"I'll let you talk to him yourself."

His voice had that giggly nervousness that kids have on the phone when they can't seem to understand how you can talk to someone thirty miles away. We chatted a few minutes and Cindy was back on.

"Not much of a telephone conversationalist," she said. "He misses you." She paused. "It's been a while." The phrase lingered.

"I know," I said. "I do too."

"It'll be good to see you."

"I'm really looking forward to it," I said. I wondered if

she could tell how much.

I found myself anticipating Friday as much as I had anticipated the arrival of Shelly on the train more than two months before. I scoured the place, went to the grocery store and loaded up with everything I thought a five-year-old might like. I even stopped in a toy store and bought a new game.

When the bell rang that night, I discovered that Bryan was armed with a back pack filled with his own personal supply. I leaned over and shook his hand, the little man dressed in a neat pair of tan corduroy pants and navy crewneck.

"Make yourself at home, Bryan," I said. "You want something to eat?"

He smiled and nodded.

"Check out the kitchen table."

He ran off to look.

Meanwhile I looked at Cindy. She looked fresh and lovely.

"I really appreciate this," she said.

"Just get the part."

"Oh, God, that might be tough. It's the lead."

"So how are things?" I asked. I could hear Bryan tearing into some paper in the kitchen.

"Ethan's been calling. He's even using Bryan now."

Bryan returned with a cookie.

"How is it?" I asked him.

He mumbled, his mouth and lips smeared with chocolate.

"Turn on the television if you want," I told him.

Cindy and I watched him gradually make himself comfortable, finding a show with the remote, dumping his bag of toys. We walked out toward the kitchen.

"Dear Lord," she said seeing the stash of food. "He'll expire from sugar poisoning."

"What's Ethan been saying?" I asked. She snared a cookie herself, nibbled an edge.

"He's been telling Bryan that he'd like to come back so we can be a family again. But I'm preventing it."

"You are?"

"Of course. Anyway, I don't think it's had much effect on Bryan in the way Ethan wants. Bryan seems much happier now with Ethan away. It just confuses him."

She looked nervously at her watch.

"I've got to hurry," she said. She swallowed the cookie.

Before she left she gave me a big hug. "Wish me luck," she whispered in my ear.

When she pulled back from me, I held her hands and said. "You won't need it."

"I hope you're right," she said as she hurried out the door.

In thirty minutes my living room became a miniature Civil War battlefield. With a little string, a few pieces of tape, pillows, some recruited books from my book shelf, Bryan Canton, now wearing a St. Michael's t-shirt so big it fit over his sweater, had forged an attack strategy that would have enthralled military historians. I watched Bryan manage his soldiers, talking to them with the earnest voice of a general attempting to motivate his infantry for a massed assault on the sofa.

He let me watch a basketball game while he played, and I watched for an hour. He went through about ten cookies and was on a pile of peanut butter crackers before he tired of war. I asked him if he wanted to play Candyland, a game he had brought.

"If you want to play." He did not sound enthused.

I showed him the new game.

"Sure," he said.

Match Up was a memory game in which a player

turned over a pair of pictures on a square; the object was to remember each picture and match them up. Bryan proved quite adept; I didn't even have to let him win.

After we finished, Bryan pulled out a checkers game.

"You know how to play checkers?" he asked.

"Sure," I said, smiling.

We set the men up. As we were playing, I noticed Bryan occasionally looking up at me.

"Anything wrong?" I asked. "Something hanging out my nose?"

He smiled.

"What is it? My face turn purple?"

"Nothing."

"Okay," I said. He had a jump in front of him but he hadn't seen it yet. He seemed to be thinking about something else and he looked up at me again.

"Who's going to be my daddy now?"

"You already have a daddy," I said.

"He doesn't live with us," he said. "Daddies are supposed to live with you."

"Well," I said, thinking. "Sometimes they don't."

"Why?"

"It's hard to explain." Suddenly I wanted Cindy to come in fast.

"Does *your* daddy live with you?"

"No."

"Why not?"

Could he handle real death?

"When you grow up, you live on your own. Without your mommy or daddy," I said.

He thought about that. He was also working on licking the peanut butter between the crackers.

"I should have a daddy then. I'm not grown up."

"Well, Mommies and Daddies have arguments. And sometimes they just don't get along. Then it's better they live apart. So they won't argue."

I paused to catch his response; he seemed to be digesting my words as well as my crackers.

"Mommy and Daddy used to fight a lot," he said.

Suddenly, he saw the jump.

"Gotya!" he yelled happily.

"Good move," I told him.

The discussion of daddies seemed to cease at that point.

I suggested we watch a DVD on television, an old civil war movie called *The Horse Soldiers*. I set him on the couch with a glass of milk and some more crackers and sat next to him. In a few minutes, he leaned back against me, his head resting against my knees. I placed a small pillow under his head, and we watched the action for a while.

Maybe it was too out of date for him or there was too much of a love story, but I think he got bored. When I looked down at him I could see his eyelids fluttering; about 9:30 he was dead asleep, his face and fingers stained with chocolate, his little chest covered with crumbs. I switched off the television, picked him up, and carried him into my bedroom where I laid him right on top of the covers. From my closet I pulled out an extra blanket and spread it over him.

Back in the living room, I pulled out a book and read for about an hour. About eleven the doorbell rang and Cindy stood beaming.

"I think I got it!" She grabbed my hands in excitement. Then she looked around past me.

"He's asleep in the bedroom."

She tiptoed inside; I followed.

"Out like a light," she said looking in. She turned to me. "How was he?"

" Great."

"He's really very sweet," she said. "Thanks Paul." She squeezed my arm and I looked into her eyes and changed the subject.

"Tell me about the audition."

We walked back into the living room and sat down. She had slipped off her coat and I noticed she was wearing the coral shell necklace.

"Well, it's the play version of an old Ingrid Bergman movie called 'Gaslight.' "

"I haven't seen it."

"This woman is driven crazy by her husband. It's a mystery. Considering my situation with Ethan, I thought I'd be perfect for it."

"And you did well?"

"I think so. The director talked to me afterward. She couldn't believe I'd done so little. But she had seen me in the other production."

"Well, it looks like you've got a new career."

She laughed and leaned back.

"Hardly. I just like the magic of it all. Feeling yourself becoming someone else, the transformation."

"What about the audience?"

"Well, that's part of it. Instant approval. *If* you're good that is." She thought for a moment. "But I can't imagine a career in acting. Pretending too much would be just too unreal."

She had been looking down at Bryan's toys, perhaps reminding herself of that reality, when she suddenly glanced up at me. I wanted to reach out and take her in my arms and tell her that she could do anything, but I think she knew that; she smiled as if she knew what I was thinking.

"It's getting late," she said.

I helped her gather up the toys and I put Bryan's coat on and picked him up, still asleep. Cindy took the back pack and we headed to the elevator. We didn't speak; the silence broken only by the whir of the elevator on its descent and Bryan's breathing on my shoulder. She was parked two blocks away, and we walked through the cold air, the traffic buzzing about us. Bryan rustled a bit, then fell back asleep. At the car Cindy arranged Bryan in the back seat, adapting a seat belt to encompass him while he stretched out asleep.

"He'll be out until we get home," she said. She shut the door gently and turned toward me.

"Thanks again."

I was standing on the curb several feet away. I felt the urge to move toward her, to hold her in the cold, but I was half afraid of her. Of myself perhaps.

"You know," I said, "Ethan really wants you back."

"So bad he hired a detective," she said. "What a fool! He even sent me pictures." She laughed.

"He's desperate."

"It's over," she said.

She walked to the driver's side, unlocked her door, was about to get in, but stopped.

"Paul?"

"Yes?" I stepped forward, the car now between us.

"You can call me," she said. "If you want."

We stared at each other in the dark, each of us perhaps thinking the same unspoken thought.

"All right," I said. "I will."

She smiled, almost shyly, and got in the car. I listened to the engine roar, leaned down to look at her through the passenger's side window; she looked over and waved. The car eased off, blending into the traffic of Pratt Street.

On the way back up the elevator, I thought of Cindy driving back north. I imagined her driving up the highway, down the darker country roads a mile or two, pulling into the driveway with the lights on at the house.

I wondered if she was afraid so far out, so far away, so alone. I saw her waking Bryan up, walking him upstairs to bed, pulling off his clothes, tucking him in. Perhaps she would walk him into the bathroom, wash his food-stained face, watch him pee and brush his teeth, take him back to bed, kiss him softly on the forehead, tell him she loves him. Then she might think of having a cup of hot tea, perhaps an English muffin with honey. No. She's tired. She goes to the bedroom, *her* bedroom now. Sees her queen-sized bed.

She slips out of her clothes, dropping them straight to the floor, walks to the bathroom, staring first at her face, looking a bit more strained, checking her hair, growing longer now.

What else do women do, I wondered? What does she sleep in? What does she look like naked? Will she turn a bedside light on and read? Perhaps a long novel, a bestseller that she had claimed first from her library new fiction rack. I imagine her reading for about thirty minutes and then she is in the darkness, the light of her gorgeous eyes extinguished for the evening.

24

Vinnie's wedding was scheduled for March 22 in his bride's hometown near Harrisburg, Pennsylvania. I had received the invitation months before and had almost forgotten about it until one day I happened to glance at the clutter of items magnetized on my refrigerator and saw the white edge of the card stand out. I had wondered what to do about the RSVP card for about a week, hating the idea of going to a wedding alone, especially with Shelly seemingly long gone.

Two weeks before the wedding, Vinnie had called me to find out why I hadn't responded. He assumed I was disappointed that I hadn't been asked to be in the wedding party. He told me he had to use his brothers and his fiancé's brothers; it was all family, no outsiders in the wedding party at all. I didn't even tell him about Shelly; I doubt if he would have cared. By that time he was floating on air, chattering as fast as he could. Finally I told him that I'd be there.

Weeks had passed since my babysitting session with Bryan. Cindy had called, left a message to tell me she had gotten the part in the play she had auditioned for. She said she hoped to see me soon. The last time I had seen her she had put the ball in my court, and I thought of calling her back, wanted to really, but I didn't. It was hard enough seeing Ethan and thinking about her.

To avoid thinking about Cindy, I dropped by a few bars, went on a few dates, but there was no chemistry. One night I went home with a woman who was recently separated from her husband and wanted to have "wild sex" because he had been such a "complete loser." She seemed very grateful that I was going to help her cross back over to the single world. But when we got into her new single girl's apartment, the night turned maudlin. She began to talk incessantly about her estranged husband, his obnoxious habits, his breaches of fidelity. But those complaints eventually subsided and she finally confessed amid overflowing sobs and tears that she still loved him, that she would probably always love him. She apologized profusely for not being able to go through with the wild sex thing, but by that time I wasn't even interested.

Now two days away from the wedding, I felt a sense of dread. I would have to drive near Cindy's house on the way to the wedding to watch two deliriously happy people be married. The thought of witnessing that alone was depressing as hell.

Dressing on the day of the wedding, I tried to summon up all the faux cheerfulness I could. I studied myself in the mirror. I pretended I saw a magnificent reflection so utterly dazzling that women at the wedding would be devouring me like fire ants.

As I drove north, the air was fresh, almost balmy, a glorious Saturday. The trees on the edge of the highway oozing sweet green tendrils, a few bright flowers hugging the earth. The clouds almost reachable, so white and pure in the blue sky.

I saw the first sign for the exit to Cindy's house. I smiled, thought about possibly stopping to see her. But I was headed toward the sounds of music, the glitter of drinks, the allure of strange women. I didn't need anyone; I didn't need a Shelly Moran or even a Cindy Canton. I saw the next sign saying two miles to her exit, and I began thinking to myself, well, she had called me, it wouldn't hurt to stop by, just a little visit to say hello, nothing serious, I had plenty of time. So I took the exit for her house, and I was pulling down her street, down her driveway.

And there she was on the front lawn, near the porch, dressed in blue jeans, work boots, and down vest, her blond hair in a ponytail, some pruning shears in a green-gloved hand. She looked up surprised, almost startled, possibly thinking it was Ethan, but as I pulled up to the house, she recognized me and walked over. I got out and stood leaning against the driver's side of the car. A nonchalant imposter.

"Hello, stranger," she said.

"Hi."

"What brings you out?" She held her hand up to shield her eyes from the sun.

"Thought I'd drop in for a beer."

She looked pleasantly puzzled. "Okay. I have some inside. You look awfully spiffy. You getting married or something?"

"Close," I said. "I'm going to a wedding. An old classmate. Near Harrisburg."

"Sounds like fun."

"Want to come?"

The words just flew out.

She smiled; her eyes crinkled.

"Do you mean it?"

"Sure."

"Well ..."

"Where's Bryan?"

"He's with my sister. For the weekend."

It was a bright day and we were squinting at each other.

"I'm a mess," she said holding her arms out to display the utter horror of her loveliness.

"You look great."

She smirked. "I look like shit."

"Come on," I said. She was looking up at me now, and I think we were both contemplating the reality of the situation: I was asking my cousin's wife out on a date.

"Are you really serious?" she asked again. "About me going?"

Full of manufactured courage, I said, "Absolutely."

"Well, a girl normally likes to be called ahead of time, you know. I haven't heard from you in ages."

"I'm sorry."

She looked at me a moment, perhaps wondering what I was thinking, what my intentions were.

"It's okay," she said. "It just so happens that my rock star boyfriend canceled on me."

"Oh," I said. "Who?"

She smiled. "I'll never tell." She started walking toward the house. "Come on in. It'll take me a while to get ready," she said. "When's the wedding?"

"Wedding's at four. Reception right after."

She looked at her watch and shook her head.

She dropped the shears on the ledge of the window near a flower pot and we went inside.

When she went upstairs to get ready, I felt suddenly elated. The whole conversation had been fast and light. I went into the kitchen and found myself a beer. For a moment, I felt like a husband waiting for his wife to get ready, we had a babysitter, and ....

I stopped myself, walked back outside, inhaled the fresh air, about sixty degrees, the white clouds seeming to vibrate in the sky. Then I went back inside.

"Can you bring me a beer?" Cindy yelled from her room.

I went to the kitchen, grabbed the beer, headed up the stairs.

She was standing next to the bathroom door wearing

a green robe, a yellow towel wrapped around her hair. Still damp, she looked like a spring flower with drops of dew. I stood erotically transfixed by the pastel colors, the glow of her eyes, the steamy floral scent.

"Is that for me?" she asked.

I remembered the beer I was carrying and handed it to her.

"Thanks," she smiled. "By the way, how formal is this?"

"I don't know."

I was staring at her, still stirred by the intimacy of her robe.

"Hard to take without my mask, isn't it?"

"What?"

"Make-up."

"No," I said, looking at her eyes. "I mean yes."

She laughed. "Go back downstairs," she said. "Before I lose all my feminine mystery."

I followed her orders and ended up on the porch staring at the lovely spring day once more. About twenty minutes later she walked out.

"How do I look?"

I stared at her for several seconds. Her hair was down and seemed longer now, a shimmering honey-gold in the afternoon light. She was wearing a reddish-gold dress and around her neck the coral necklace.

"Terrific," I said finally.

"Took you long enough," she said.

"Nice necklace," I said.

"Yeah," she said, her smile playful. "This really cute guy gave it to me."

Then we were on the road, Cindy actually seated next to me, her scented presence filling the car and making me breathe a little faster.

"What kind of present did you get them?" she asked.

I looked over at her.

"You didn't get them a present!" Cindy seemed to enjoy that. "Well, I guess we'll have to pick up something on the way."

She directed me to a shop off the highway, an antique and gift shop. She knew the owner, spoke to her a few minutes.

"How much do you want to spend?" Cindy asked.

"I don't know."

Cindy turned to the manager.

"Don't you just love decisive men?"

After some discussion between the two of them, they chose a classic wooden mantel clock and the manager went into a back room. Cindy came over to me.

"I hope the bride will like it," she said.

"I'm sure she will," I said.

The manager brought out a box with a little card.

"Fill it out and sign it," Cindy said to me.

We were back on the road, heading out of Maryland into Pennsylvania. The whole trip seemed dreamlike to me; I could barely feel the tires touching the road.

We swept through the land of the Amish. As we drove, Cindy hummed along with the music on the radio. After a while I developed the courage to glance at her. I longed to run my fingertips along the rich fabric of her dress, to touch the silk of her hair. But I drove steadily ahead, allowing myself only peripheral glimpses.

Unfortunately, we pulled into the church parking lot just in time to see the first cars pulling out to go to the reception. I followed the departing cars to a banquet hall facility about three miles away.

When Cindy and I drifted into the main room where the reception was being held, the wedding party had not arrived, and the guests had begun filling lines for the two open bars. I dropped the present off with the card at a table set aside for that purpose and we picked up drinks from the bar. Not long after that the wedding party pulled up, or at least we assumed so, because many of the guests rushed toward the entrance to the hall. We followed like sheep. It was true; they had arrived. And in a hurried confused fashion, a makeshift reception line was formed by an anxious woman who I assume was handling the affair.

The phrase *monkey suit* must have been invented for Vinnie in formal attire. The seams of his tuxedo could barely contain his muscular torso. His bride, Clara – not wearing glasses now – positively glowed with happiness in her long white wedding gown.

"Great to see you, man!" Vinnie greeted me with a hug. When he looked at Cindy, he seemed overjoyed and gave her a hug too. "Glad to meet you," he said. "You got a great guy!"

The drinks began to flow through the hall, and the band assembled and started to play so badly that after a while it became amusing and a topic of conversation. The rumor was that Vinnie's father had actually hired them as a favor to an old army buddy. I hadn't seen Vinnie's father for about eight years, and when he came over later I barely recognized him; his grayish hair had turned completely white. But he had the same plump lips that always seemed to be on the verge of drooling.

"This your wife?" he said, referring to Cindy.

"No, sir."

"She should be. She's a looker." He stood directly in front of Cindy, almost her same height.

"I'm Cindy," she said.

"Great eyes, Doll. Are they contacts?"

"No, they're real."

Then he looked down at her chest.

"They're real, too," she said.

"I'll say. Your boyfriend here is a great guy. Got my boy through college, you know. Vinnie's not too bright. Best thing he did was marry this girl. Even if she is half colored." He took a healthy slug of what looked like bourbon. "God only knows how he got her."

"Are you with someone?" Cindy asked him. "Do you have a date?"

Vinnie's father raised his eyebrows, smiled.

"Sorry to break it to you, Sweets. You're about thirty-five years too late. I guess you're stuck with this guy." He elbowed me.

"He's pretty special," Cindy said, grabbing my hand and leaning her head against my shoulder. "But you do tempt a girl."

The old man laughed.

"I like her, Paul. She's a real tease."

When the old man had gone, Cindy laughed too.

"I wonder how his wife can stand it," she said.

"Being married to him?"

"Crawling into bed with him."

As we strolled about the room, Cindy held my hand, and I kept looking down at her slender fingers entwined in mine. I could hardly believe I was touching her as if she were my actual girlfriend. We sipped the plentiful wine and with each glass I slipped further into that alternative world where Cindy *was* my girlfriend.

There was no one there I knew but Vinnie, his new wife, Vinnie's parents and Cindy—no one else from Penn at all. But the crowd was friendly and it was a grand time.

Vinnie reemerged sometime later like a kid who had hit the lottery on Christmas. He stood next to Cindy and me, drinking beer, beaming, and bubbling over with words of lavish praise for his new wife – "a sweet angel" and "the greatest girl in the whole fucking universe."

He proposed an elaborate and incoherent toast in honor of his "dear bride" Clara, but he spilled half of his beer down his massive chest. He was really quite drunk.

Then he put his arm around me in a friendly fraternal manner.

"So why haven't you been dancing with this pretty young lady?" he asked me, nodding at Cindy.

"Yeah," Cindy said. "That's a good question."

They both looked at me.

"I'm not a very good dancer," I said.

The band had started a slow song.

"You can handle this. You can't be worse than the band," Cindy said, grasping my hand tighter and pulling me onto the dance floor.

"YOU THE MAN!" Vinnie yelled as we walked to the dance floor, and the last memory I have of him at his wedding was watching him chug down the rest of his beer and smile like a love-drunk lunatic.

Then Cindy's arms were around me and we started dancing to the tune of "My Girl."

At first it had all been rather a lark this wedding. We were just flirtatious friends, wife and husband's cousin, a simple excursion to Pennsylvania to alleviate our mutual boredom. But during the song, as we were experiencing "sunshine on a cloudy day," our bodies began to meld until finally we were fully embracing, our feet barely moving, our arms completely wrapped around each other. I brushed my lips against her neck and hair, inhaled her scent. She stroked the back of my neck, my hair. Entranced and aroused, I pressed against her and her body began to respond with subtle thrusts. By the time the song dissolved into its waning refrain "... my girl, my girl, my girl..." our life of romantic ambiguity had ended. We didn't say anything, but the change in our relations was palpable. There was no point in pretending this was a platonic frolic.

Holding hands, we walked out of the ballroom, past the half-drunken guests, the three-foot high wedding cake, and through the marble lobby. Behind a group of artificial palm trees, we found a secluded hallway, away from the crowd and the pathetic treacle of the band. Like star-struck teenagers at the prom, we walked about forty yards and stopped. For a second we just looked at each other, as if we knew what we were doing was somehow illicit.

But only for a second.

I took her head in my hands. I gazed into the aqua blue of her eyes. I leaned over and kissed her, softly at first, then deeper, tasting her lips and tongue. I ran my hands though her rich soft hair. I kissed her neck, her fragrant neck, letting my hands explore the swell of her breasts. When I slid my hand under her dress and caressed the inside of her thighs, she moaned softly. As I kissed her again and again, I inched my fingers up her thighs until they were touching the edge of her panties and then my hand was under the fabric, feeling her moistness. She moaned again, this time louder, and I stroked her more and more until finally she pulled her lips away from my mouth and bit my ear lightly.

"Let's go somewhere," she whispered.

Without saying goodbye, we walked to the parking lot and got into my car. There was a motel we had seen on the way in, about a mile off, and we drove straight there.

Inside the room, we stripped off our clothes and pulled each other onto the bed.

I remember the overwhelming wonder of her naked body, and I kissed her with a passion I couldn't control, kissed her whole tender body, felt a blind unrelenting desire to not miss an inch. When I entered her for the first time, I felt a rush of utter joy, and when I heard her moan, I drove into her harder and wilder, over and over again. I can remember thinking that I didn't want it to end. I never wanted it to end.

When I awoke the next morning, she was leaning over me, watching my eyes blink in the light that slanted in through a gap in the blinds.

"Good morning," she said, leaning further over and kissing my lips.

She popped out of bed, stretched out her arms, and shook her hair loose.

I watched her in the dim light of morning, her nakedness seeming strange now. It was hard to believe that I had spent the night with her, that I had actually made love to Cindy Canton.

She looked over at me. She was smiling, with a look of contentment.

"I'm hungover," she said, "but otherwise I feel great. How do you feel?"

I wasn't sure. My head hurt but that wasn't the main problem.

Cindy looked over at me closely. She must have seen something she didn't understand because her smile turned to a look of concern. She came over and sat near me.

"What's wrong?"

"Nothing," I said.

She looked into my eyes but I found it hard to face her.

"You feel guilty don't you?"

"I don't know."

She stood up and walked over to the curtains, opened them slightly, looked out for moment, and walked back to me. I looked at the goose pimples on her breasts; then up at her lovely face, her gorgeous eyes.

"Listen," she said clearly. "If you want to regard this as a one night stand, that's fine. In a way it was. It's been a long time for me. Quite frankly I'm not sure I would have lasted much longer. A woman has physical needs too. But I don't feel guilty. I don't feel guilty one bit."

She looked at me closely, her eyes tearing up, and in an instant she seemed to change.

"God, I didn't want this to happen. Not now." She turned away. "I just got through clearing out one man from my life. Hell, I'm still dealing with that."

"I understand," I said, sitting up now.

"No, Paul, you don't!" she said angrily. "You can't possibly know what I've been through dealing with that asshole."

"I'm sorry. I just ..."

"You're just feeling guilty because you fucked your cousin's wife!" she said, her face turning red. "Aren't you?"

I looked away, knowing she was right. And as I was staring at the carpet, she spoke again, softer but just as bitterly.

"Don't worry, Paul. I won't tell Ethan. You won't lose your job."

I looked up but Cindy had turned and headed into the bathroom. In a few moments I heard the shower run. We didn't say anything more. After my shower we put on our wedding attire and left.

We drove to Cindy's sister's house to pick up Bryan, and when he saw me, he jumped into my arms. For the rest of the drive, I made conversation with Bryan, but I felt as if I were simply miming responses; the distance between me and his mother had suddenly grown, even though we sat two feet away.

Approaching her house an hour later, I felt even more guilty; it was after all Ethan's house, it was after all

Ethan's wife and child. I was an interloper, a disturber of the peace, however illusory that peace was. When Cindy and I said goodbye, it was quick and perfunctory.

While he was walking up to their house, Bryan turned around and yelled out: "Can we go to Gettysburg soon?"

I looked at his hopeful happy face and conjured up a smile.

"Soon," I said.

But I felt guilty about that too.

25

A week passed. Then another. And more. I saw in the newspaper that Cindy's play had started its three week run, but she didn't invite me and I didn't go. I wanted to congratulate her on the wonderful reviews she got, but I didn't do that either.

The reality of the incident, the sweet blossom of love that had begun in Pennsylvania had dissipated, turning into a dim alcohol-induced hallucination. I felt I was floundering about in a cave. All I had was the blurred image of Cindy Canton, the sweet memory of her touch and taste.

For weeks after the wedding I drove around almost in a daze, avoiding the office and certainly avoiding Ethan as much as possible. I only saw him at a few brief sales meetings, and even then I could barely look him in the eyes. I was glad we were both traveling a lot.

Early one morning in May, after I had just returned from a two-day trip to Western Pennsylvania, I received a frantic call from Grace. I was still hazy from a bad night's sleep when I answered the phone.

"Paul, there's a fire!" she yelled. "The whole plant is on fire...."

I heard a siren in the background of the phone, and for a second Grace sounded as if she were crying, the tough office manager actually crying.

"What?"

Her voice seemed to dissolve in static. And I realized she must have been calling from a cell phone outside the plant office. I didn't wait to get her back on the line; her voice had been strained enough.

As I dressed, I formed an image of the Canton plant ablaze. I imagined burned dead bodies, perhaps Ethan a victim, his body melting in the flames.

My mind began to race as I rushed to the elevator. I remembered the detective he had hired. What if he had seen me and Cindy in the motel room, had reported to Ethan, and Ethan had wiped out his life and Canton in one pyro-maniacal act? But I realized that was ludicrous. Too much time had passed and after the last detective debacle it was highly doubtful Ethan was still employing him. Still, as I drove toward the office, the guilt about my affair with Cindy consumed me as much as my concern about the fire.

As soon as I got within two miles of the office, I saw black smoke pluming out across the horizon. I made two more turns and parked a quarter mile away. When I got out I saw fire engines and in the background the framework of the Canton plant engulfed in flames and smoke. It was spectacular from one perspective; the orange flames leaping out, the silvery fountains of water shooting upward to the smoky blue sky, the air pungent. The lights of the engines, the frantic cries of men in action. I even saw minivans with news reporters and photographers just outside the temporary barriers.

Bystanders had begun to form although it was early and in an isolated portion of the town. I moved around the barriers, working my way along soft spring turf on the side of the main access road, looking for some sign of Grace, or anyone. Then I saw her. She was standing almost rigid, looking at the fire, clutching a cell phone.

"What happened?" I asked.

"God knows," she said. I had been right. She *was* crying. "I got a call from a watchman from the mall nearby. I don't know how he got my number. There's probably an emergency listing somewhere."

"Where's Ethan?"

"He was in New Jersey yesterday. I didn't expect him back until today. I don't know if he got back last night or not. He went with Charlie."

"Does he know?"

"I called. He's on his way."

As the morning brightened, the firefighters eventually extinguished the flames, but it all seemed rather futile. The building appeared to be a charred wet shell now. The fire marshal and police questioned both me and Grace, but I had been unable to offer much help. I spent very little time there, I told them. Grace was better able to explain the layout of the plant, the location of products, power sources, the crucial elements of the operation. After a while, I sat on a fence rail, watching the smoke-stained firemen disengage.

About ten, I felt I had to escape, to glimpse something clear and clean and whole. But as I was walking toward my car, I saw Ethan and Charlie. Ethan just stood staring for a moment. Charlie stood behind him. They both looked completely stunned. I walked over to them.

"I'm sorry, Ethan," I said.

As soon as I said it, a quick flash of a naked Cindy went through my mind. Now her husband, my cousin, the man who had awarded me with employment and company benefits, was staring at the very corpse of his business life. I felt relieved that he was alive.

Both Ethan and Charlie were joined by Grace and the fire marshal, several other people who I assumed were attached to the investigation. A reporter from a local television station also rushed up. She was a pert blonde whom I had seen on screen a number of times. The mini-cam and microphone were thrust into Ethan's face, but he brushed them away, and the whole group shifted away from me and away from the camera.

There was nothing I could do but go home.

In my hurry to get to the fire scene, I had forgotten to take my phone so I wasn't able to check my messages until I got to my apartment. I saw that Cindy had called. She had seen the news report and had called Ethan and then me. She hoped no one was hurt. She wanted me to call her. But I couldn't summon the nerve; I could still see Ethan's face at the scene of the fire. The face of the man I had betrayed. That was the simple fact. Instead, I took a long walk, past the inner harbor, into Federal Hill and the Cross Street Market where the smell and faces of dead fish drove me back out to the fresh air.

I ate at Harborplace around two. When I left there, I went upstairs to Hooters, thinking I'd elevate my mood with beer which I ordered at a window table.

"You expecting friends?" the waitress asked.

She was wearing tight shorts and a top that revealed the ample promise of her breasts. In a different mood, I might have found it diverting. That day it sickened me. I told her no, I didn't have any friends. I didn't know what I meant by that, but it had a nice self-pitying ring. The beer tasted flat and I left half of it, but tipped the waitress well to offset my rudeness.

Nothing in the harbor area seemed to cure my restlessness, so I headed home. There I sat down and listened to the silence for about thirty minutes before my phone rang. It was Charlie.

"Ethan asked me to call," he said. "He said you can take a few days off."

He laughed feebly at the joke.

"What's going on?"

"They're trying to find out how it started," he said. "They think it might be wiring. Had some problems in the past. It's an old building, you know. Anyway, Ethan says he'll be in touch. He's not sure what's going to happen. They have to investigate, check out the origin, take some time."

"What do you mean he doesn't know what's going to happen?"

"He doesn't know, Paul. Not for sure anyway. Looks like we lost everything."

"I mean the business?"

"I don't know."

"Doesn't he have insurance?"

"Sure," Charlie said. "I guess."

"I can't believe it," I said. "Ethan must be a wreck."

"Yeah. He sure didn't need this. Especially with his other problems."

"You mean Cindy?"

"Yeah," he said. "Her too."

"Too? What else?"

I thought a moment.

"You mean losing those big accounts a while back?"

"You know about that?"

"I heard something."

"Big cash flow problem," he said. There was a pause and I heard him laugh. "Then there's Shauna of course."

"What about Shauna?"

Charlie laughed.

"Didn't you hear? She's pregnant again."

That was all I heard for the next three days, the phone call from Charlie. I perused the newspaper and internet for more information, but there was nothing new in the reports, and after a few days it was no longer a story.

I killed time walking, working out, reading. I called Stevenson; tried to make a time to play racquetball or tennis, but he was still in love, and we couldn't fit it in that week. I called my mother too, told her the news. She asked if it was arson. I told her it was probably an electrical problem. She asked if I needed an attorney. I didn't know why. She told me to be careful. I thought about Cindy a lot; I even drove out toward her house one evening, but I felt guilty and turned back.

On the third day Ethan called. He sounded tired but he wanted to see me. Could I drop by his place? I had never been to his new apartment, but I suppose he had nowhere else to meet now. When I arrived, he looked ragged; his hair tossed about, his face unshaven, his voice slurred.

"Do you want a drink?"

It was about 10 a.m.

"No."

I doubt if he was even listening to me; his mind seemed preoccupied. He poured us both gin on chunks of ice from a bag he had sitting on the top of a newspaper on the kitchen counter.

"I've begun to enjoy gin. Nice clear fluid. Never really drank it much before," he said.

We sat down in what appeared to be a half-furnished apartment. He wore business clothes, but his tie was loose and his pants were wrinkled and dusty. I couldn't remember if they were the same clothes I had seen him in at the fire or not. They could have been. He stretched out his legs, and his stockinged feet dangled over a hassock.

"Pretty fucked up, don't you think?"

I wasn't sure what specifically he was referring to, but I nodded anyway.

"My wife dumps me, my girlfriend's pregnant and driving me crazy, my business goes up in smoke. Now that's pretty fucked up." He appeared dazed. The drink in my hand felt like a cold grenade.

"What about the business?" I asked. "Can you rebuild and reopen?"

Ethan sipped his gin and looked at me as if I were pathetically dense.

"Possible, but not likely," he said. "Not for a long while anyway."

I was suddenly aware of what I had been dreading since my talk with Charlie days before: that my new sales career was probably over.

He laughed.

"Ought to keep the IRS off my ass for a while though."

"Why? What are they up to?"

"Not much now, I hope." He laughed again. "Can I get you another drink?" he asked.

"No," I said. "What did they want in the first place, the IRS?"

"Who knows. They're vultures. They've been after Sam and me for months."

"Sam? What does Sam have to do with it?"

Ethan looked up.

"Nothing. They hassle everybody."

"They've never hassled me," I said.

"Give them time," he said. "Give them time."

Then something clicked in my mind.

"Ethan, what did I deliver to those guys at the shore?"

"What?"

"The small restaurants and shops."

"I can't remember."

"One guy, Grover, didn't want a receipt?"

Ethan got up and walked to the ice. He filled his glass and grabbed the bottle.

"Sam owned three of those businesses," I said. "What does Sam have to do with your business?"

"Jesus, Paul!" Ethan shouted. His drink spilled. "Just shut up a minute."

I looked at him. I heard the click again.

"That's why the IRS was after you."

Ethan didn't say anything, and I wasn't sure what the truth was, but I think I had at least entered the playing field. Something illegal maybe?

"Listen, Paul, listen to me." He came back in the living room. "Don't say anything else. I called you over here to say I'm sorry."

"Sorry? For what?"

"That I got you involved. You're my cousin."

"Involved in what?"

"Christ, would you just listen. The less you know the better off you'll be."

"Know about what?"

He sat down.

"It doesn't matter now."

He reached over to a briefcase by his side. He pulled out an envelope and handed it to me.

Inside there was check written to me for $20,000.

"What's this for?" I asked.

I looked at Ethan. He looked devastated and drunk. I remembered my mother's question about arson. But why? To hide from the IRS? For the insurance? Because of the big accounts bailing out? Something else I didn't know about? All of the above. The check was Ethan's way of saying he was sorry for something he didn't want to explain.

But I couldn't take it. I felt that I had taken too much from him already.

"I'd appreciate it if you took the check."

"No," I said.

His eyes had reddened, welled up.

"Ethan –" I started to say something but whatever it was slipped my mind and I just stood looking at him. He was gazing toward a living room window, swigging his drink.

After a few moments of tense silence, I put my drink

on the kitchen counter.

"I better be going," I said.

He turned and watched me walk to the door.

"If you change your mind," he said, "let me know."

"I won't."

"Paul?" I had neared the door. "When all this mess clears up, I hope we can still be friends."

He offered me a thin smile.

I left feeling there was something else I should have said, but what did I really know? I had no evidence of anything illegal.

That night at home my phone rang and I answered it. I was sure it would be Ethan again, but it was Cindy.

"Paul, are you all right?"

"I'm fine," I said but I felt like a charred ember from the old Canton warehouse.

"What's going to happen?" she asked.

"I'm not sure. I just saw Ethan. He looks like hell," I said.

"I talked to him too. I actually felt sorry for him."

I thought of mentioning the insurance money to her, that if all went well Ethan should do fine. That she and Bryan should be okay too. But all that was muddled by the taint of illegality that I'm sure Cindy knew nothing about.

"Paul, about what happened in March. I want you to know that it meant something. It meant a lot."

I suddenly ached to hold her.

"It meant a lot to me too," I said.

For the next few weeks, I led a strange dislocated life. Like a Kafka or Beckett character, I wandered the streets of Baltimore, following the scent of history or art. I lingered in front of the splashy color of Matisse at the Baltimore Museum of Art, walked past the sculptured lions in front and crossed the street for a one-way communion with the grim statues of generals Lee and Jackson, true sons of Virginia. Occasionally I would drop in at the Enoch Pratt library and bury myself in historical journals, sometimes wandering about touching volumes and tomes, the vast sepulchers of truth and life. I had no central train of thought; I suppose I was merely trying to recapture the spirit of my previous academic life.

26

The new Orioles season had started so I became a fan again. I made a few trips to Camden Yards. My sleep was deep, but did not commence until three or four in the morning after I had watched a few old movies and dozed off amid pizza crust and crushed beer cans.

Then one day Ethan called. He sounded sober this time, and he told me that the fire investigation was ongoing, that they had yet to determine the fire's cause.

"What about the insurance?"

"They won't do anything until the investigation's done. Could take a few weeks, a few months, who knows. Maybe a year. They're all weasels too."

I assumed he was talking about the fire department and the insurance company in addition to the IRS.

"Listen, Paul, I'll be sending out a letter to all the employees soon. There's a lot of internal issues to clear up. I know everybody's been left hanging out to dry.

"But until then I thought I'd have a little bash, sort of a 'Thank You' dinner next week. Want to get everybody from Canton together."

He gave me the name of the restaurant and the time. We hung up and I was back to my life of indolence. Right then I wished I had taken Ethan's check; it would certainly have eased my newly developed career anxiety and financed my life as street vagabond. But when I thought about the offer, really thought about it, I felt it was tainted in some way.

The evening before Ethan's event, Stevenson and I met for a drink at his place. He wanted me to stay for dinner; he was preparing Jamaican jerk chicken that smelled marvelous. Sitting in his living room, I told him about the unraveling of my life, the fire, the loss of a job, finally the events with Cindy.

"And you haven't seen her?" he shouted from the kitchen, even carrying in a pot of what appeared to be steamed rice. "Are you crazy, Mon?"

I tried to explain the moral dilemma I felt.

"Bullshit! Her husband was a philandering ass and a possible arsonist. What devotion do you owe him?"

Put that starkly, all I could think of to say was that he was family.

Ethan's dinner was scheduled for seven at an Italian restaurant downtown. My reluctance to go intensified as the day and hour approached. Even dressing for it, the first time I had worn a sports coat and tie in weeks, was difficult. Looking in the mirror, I saw a tired face, a few more lines, perhaps, a little more strain.

There were a dozen Canton employees already in the private dining room of the restaurant when I arrived late. Grace, in a much more cheerful incarnation than when I last saw her at the fire; Calvin, the accountant; Herb, the plant foreman; several others. I wondered if all the employees had been offered plump checks. Surely Grace must have had her suspicions that something was sorely wrong. But they were all chatting amiably; as were Charlie and Ethan. In fact, if you had not been aware of the actual circumstances, you might have thought Canton had just landed a global account. It was so weird to me that I thought I would ask Ethan right there, from a purely utilitarian point of view, just how one goes about hiring a firebug. Of course, he hadn't admitted it; I knew that I could be wrong, but I didn't think so.

Charlie came over and shook my hand. I wondered if

he had known of the plan. *If* there had been a plan at all. He informed me he was getting a divorce, moving back home to North Carolina to take a job with his brother-in-law.

I saw Ethan standing next to us.

"I might try to lure him back," Ethan said. "You too."

"What do you mean?" I asked.

"There's a promising opportunity I've been looking at in Atlanta. I'm thinking of reviving Canton down there. Once the insurance money comes through. Cindy and I are definitely history."

"What about Bryan?"

Ethan blinked as if the name had some glimmer of significance to him. Then he frowned. "That's the hardest part. I'll really miss him. But the lawyers will work it out. I'll probably end up seeing him more when I've moved away."

I couldn't add anything to that logic. Ethan smiled and patted me on the back before drifting off to talk to a pretty secretary who had worked at Canton all of three weeks.

The cocktail hour fortunately broke up when the manager informed us that dinner was to be served shortly. I sat next to a fork lift operator and delivery man rather than Ethan or Charlie, and we discussed baseball. At one time, Justin had been a minor league player who had suffered a career-ending knee injury a few years into his pro career.

We had finished our salads and I was in the middle of a veal parmesan when I noticed there was a conspicuous silence suddenly at Ethan's end of the long table. Ethan was looking over to the door leading to the main body of the restaurant, and there was a young woman standing there. Her hair was pulled back into a long ponytail, her face seemed paler, but even so she was clearly the beautiful Shauna I had met at Colin's bar a year before.

Ethan stood up, his face flushed, moved toward her, reaching for her arm as she stood in the doorway.

"What the hell are you doing here?" he asked.

"Goddam you!" Shauna screeched, but Ethan had moved her through the door and the rest of her speech was cut off as the door was closed.

The table grew silent as we all stared at the door, half expecting something to happen there. I couldn't help feeling a smug satisfaction at Ethan's embarrassment.

A moment later, the manager stepped in and spoke to Charlie who was closest to the door. Apparently the argument had continued in the main part of the restaurant. Could he help? Charlie got up, looked back at me and headed for the door. Almost compelled by curiosity as much as anything, I followed him out.

As soon as I walked through the door, I heard the shrill sound of Shauna yelling, "You fucking son of a bitch!" Ethan was trying to lift her up, but she squatted down and had latched on to a post in the main restaurant dining room and was refusing to move.

"You fucking bastard, you goddam prick. You can't leave me, you can't leave me *now*."

So Ethan had told her of his southern business plans, and apparently they didn't include her or the unborn child. Charlie had begun to lend his muscle to dislodging Shauna from her position, and while they struggled with her, she continued her litany of epithets. I watched the other patrons staring in shock.

They finally managed to pick her up and drag her down the steps through the door the manager held open. I hesitated a moment, then decided to watch the show some more, the vicarious stink of it providing a feeling of poetic justice. Chickens coming home to roost perhaps.

When I got outside, I noticed Charlie standing on the

sidewalk. Ethan and Shauna were standing about fifteen feet away near a parked car. A small crowd had stopped and was watching the scene.

"Who are you fucking now?" she asked loudly.

"You're acting crazy," Ethan said. "Come on." He started dragging her down the street, and I found myself following behind. Charlie moved next to me.

"Get the fuck off me," Shauna yelled.

"You're going home."

"No!"

Charlie and I had moved to within ten feet now. A few of the bystanders around us had pulled out their phones and were taking picture and videos.

Ethan whispered something to Shauna that I couldn't hear.

She laughed. A crazy hysterical laugh.

"MONEY!" she yelled. "That's all you ever think about, Ethan. MONEY, MONEY, MONEY!"

"Calm down, Shauna. Calm down."

"You calm down, you fucking prick."

"Let's get in my car and talk about it," Ethan said.

"*IT*!" she screamed. "*IT* IS A BABY, YOU SON OF A BITCH! *IT* IS YOUR GODDAM FUCKING BABY!"

"Shauna!"

"YOU WANT ME TO KILL THIS ONE TOO?"

Her voice had reached multi-decibels, and the narrow street had a growing audience. But I suppose it was the screaming about killing the baby that enraged Ethan because he suddenly pushed her away hard and she fell back against a car. Then, as he stood there, she reached inside her purse and pulled something out. Something shiny that I suddenly realized was a gun.

"I hate you!" she screamed, amidst tears.

Ethan started walking toward her. I noticed the gun was pointed down and shaking as she yelled at him. I also heard someone nearby say something about calling the police.

"Give me the gun, Shauna," Ethan said.

"Fuck you, Ethan!"

Ethan suddenly lunged at her, reaching with his right hand. I saw the gun rise up in her hand as if she were instinctively trying to defend herself. There was a blur of activity as he grabbed for her, wrestling, and there was a shot. As I turned reflexively to my left to move away, there was another shot, and I felt something strike my right side; then I was falling to the ground, stunned, a sensation of pain in my side, everything growing lighter and fainter.

27

I don't remember a whole lot after that, just sounds and images. Screaming, movement, voices ... the wailing of an ambulance. I was short of breath and blurry and there were people all around, grabbing me, and I was lifted and thrust into the back of an ambulance. I heard questions being asked and then movement.

I found out later that Ethan and I were both transported to Shock Trauma, where I was immediately operated on. But the first shot had struck Ethan in the heart and he died on arrival. The bullet that struck me had apparently ricocheted off something and hit me in the side, nicking a bit of lung and ribs, but nothing mortal. My surgery was successful but I would need about ten or more days in the hospital and maybe a few months of recovery after that.

Several days after my surgery, after I was mentally alert and my doctor had told me I might live forever, I learned that my mother and Buck had flown up from Florida. They told me that Ethan had died, that his body had been taken back to Federton, the town he despised, where he was buried next to his parents and uncle in a family plot that apparently had been arranged for him all along. That was his ultimate destiny, an irony that almost made me laugh, though laughter was still very painful.

During my recovery, the police interviewed me, and my mother found legal representation for Shauna who had been hospitalized in the psych unit of a different hospital. In her third night she suffered a miscarriage, an event that further exacerbated her mental distress. Although she had killed Ethan and wounded me, I couldn't help but feel sympathy for her. She seemed as much of a victim as I was.

One day, after the investigation, my mother came in alone. She walked over to me, looked at the tubes and the medical equipment maintaining me. She took my hands and looked into my eyes. I might have been a bit woozy but I actually thought her eyes were welling up. She looked at me sadly.

"I'm so sorry, Paul," she said.

I looked up at her, not sure what she meant.

"You remember how you heard about the job with Ethan?"

A little more than a year ago.

"That's not your fault," I managed to say. "None of this is your fault."

"I feel responsible. I feel I pressured you into it. And I almost lost you."

I remembered the discussion. She wanted me to have experience in the real world.

"Well," I said, "now I know what the real world's like."

She leaned over and kissed me. Then she stood back up and looked down at me.

"There's something else," she said, her voice turning more professional, lawyerly. "You remember telling me about some problems Ethan had with the IRS?" she asked. "Well, I looked into it."

My mother's legal connections went back forty years.

"It was connected to some unspecified and alleged illegal activities. Did you know a man named Bannion?"

"Sam? Yes."

"How about a Colin Doyle?"

"Yes." Colin too?

"There was a guy at the plant too," she said. "Jason something, I think."

"Justin? Justin Schmidt?"

"Yes."

I couldn't believe it. Justin was a fork lift driver and part-time deliveryman, the guy I was sitting next to at Ethan's dinner.

"They might have been part of it apparently. Maybe a few others."

I thought of Grace and Herb. Could they have been involved as well? It was hard to imagine.

"What illegal activities?"

"I couldn't find that out. It was in the early stages of investigation. Some sort of money laundering maybe. Perhaps smuggling. I thought it might be drugs."

I thought of the deliveries I had made to the Eastern Shore and the odd customer reactions.

"I'm not certain," my mother went on. "Anyway, with Ethan dead, it's all moot. At least for him."

She moved closer to me now, leaning down.

"Paul, I want to ask you a question. It's important. Do you know how Ethan's building caught fire?"

I shook my head. But I knew what she was driving at.

"Do you think it was arson?" I asked.

"I don't know," she said. "They're still investigating. Given the fragile financial condition of the company, it's very suspicious. That's why it's important that you be straight with me."

"I never knew anything," I said.

"Ethan never admitted anything?"

"No."

She nodded and thought for a moment, probably running through her mind my possible liability.

"I've contacted a good criminal attorney if you need one. Buck and I are going back to Florida for a wedding.

We want you to come to Florida to recuperate."

I nodded.

Then she squeezed my hand and kissed me goodbye.

Stevenson La Plante heard about my plight through the news reports, and he came to visit me twice. Once to show me a YouTube video of the incident that had not yet gone viral, thank God – possibly because the quality was so poor. But I declined to watch; the memory of the real event was too painful.

The second time he came was to bring me my mail, mostly junk, but tucked in the junk was a letter from Ryder Scott. I guess he got my address from Vinnie. He apologized for his "total breach of ethics" in his dealings with his women in Florida. He said he was in Boston, ready to start a new "business opportunity" although he didn't specify what kind of opportunity that was. Perhaps another rich middle-aged widow. He also said he had bumped into Shelly Moran, that she was just about finished law school and had scheduled interviews at a number of firms in the New England area. She had, Ryder said, recently become engaged.

In my wakeful moments I remind myself that Ethan is dead. The cold horror of the fact still hasn't fully set in. Sometimes I think there was something I could have done that night. But I also remember that I had been enjoying the measure of his embarrassment just moments before he was killed. The psychologist who dropped in wanted to talk about this, my feelings of guilt, but I wasn't ready. I'm still not.

One day I had another visitor. I was glancing at a magazine Stevenson had brought me when I looked up. And there in the doorway was Cindy Canton.

She walked over and smiled.

And then she cried.

We held hands as she told me about the funeral, about telling Bryan that his father was dead, the whole trip out to Western Maryland. Bryan, she thought, didn't truly understand. And he hadn't gone to the funeral. But the whole situation had been so sordid and sudden that she had been overwhelmed.

She was talking to lawyers, Ethan's lawyer and her own, even my mother. The truth was Ethan didn't really have that much; he had debts and some creditors were already chomping at his financial remains. The house mortgage had gone unpaid for a few months. He didn't have a will. And with the insurance investigation into the Canton plant fire still incomplete, everything was up in the air. Who knew what would come from that.

I told her not to worry; it would all work out.

She leaned over and kissed me.

Now as I am resting alone, with only a few days left before my release from the hospital, I think of the warm Florida sunshine and the blue water darkening in the sunset, the tropical sights and scents that will serve as healing balm to my wounded body. I think about returning to graduate school, of once again submerging myself in the past. I have even contemplated applying to law school.

I daydream too. In one dream the day is hot, almost dusk. It is early July and there is the heavy fragrance of honeysuckle wafting from a clump of woods on the Gettysburg battlefield. I'm with Cindy and Bryan Canton, climbing the massive boulders of Devil's Den where long ago soldiers had battled back and forth for possession of this very ground. Now, in July's lambent light it has become a wondrous playground.

"Are there ghosts here?" Bryan asks.

I think first of the dead soldiers from the battle; then of the image of his father, also dead.

"Maybe," I say. "If you look real hard."

Bryan scrambles over the boulders, looking into crevices and cracks. I chase after him and we end up at the top of Devil's Den. I tap his shoulder and point to Little Round Top across the Valley of Death.

When I glance back at Cindy, she is standing on one of the smooth gray boulders. She turns toward us and smiles, her aqua eyes glittering, a sweet thrill of summer, as natural as the air.

44058674R00175

Made in the USA
Middletown, DE
26 May 2017